Haskell Free Library
Bibliothèque Haskell
P O Box 337 Derby Line VT 05830
1 Church Stanstead Que. J0B 3E2
(802) 873-3022 or (819) 876-2471
www.haskellopera.com

Library members may borrow materials, free of
charge, for 21 days. Charges will be made for
damaged or lost volumes.

GAYLORD

ALSO BY BRET LOTT

Novels

The Man Who Owned Vermont

A Stranger's House

Jewel

Reed's Beach

The Hunt Club

A Song I Knew by Heart

Ancient Highway

Story Collections

A Dream of Old Leaves

How to Get Home

The Difference Between Women and Men

Nonfiction

Fathers, Sons, and Brothers

Before We Get Started

DEAD LOW TIDE

DEAD LOW TIDE

A Novel

BRET LOTT

Random House New York

Published in the United States by Random House, an imprint of The Random House Publishing Group, a division of Random House, Inc., New York.

RANDOM HOUSE and colophon are registered trademarks of Random House, Inc.

Library of Congress Cataloging-in-Publication Data

Lott, Bret.
Dead low tide: a novel / Bret Lott.
p. cm.
ISBN 978-1-4000-6375-8
eBook ISBN 978-0-679-64425-5
I. Title
PS3562.O784D43 2012
813'.54—dc22   2011006154

Printed in the United States of America on acid-free paper

www.atrandom.com

9 8 7 6 5 4 3 2 1

First Edition

Book design by Liz Cosgrove

Woe to those who deeply hide their plans from the Lord,
and whose deeds are done in a dark place,
and they say, "Who sees us?" or "Who knows us?"

—Isaiah 29:15

DEAD LOW TIDE

1

"Hold on," Unc whispered, warning me.

I turned, saw him standing there at the stern and poling the jon boat in. He was only a silhouette in this dark, thin stars around him for the half-moon we had out here.

"*You* hold on, old man," I whispered, and turned, looked ahead.

None of this was my idea.

He knew we were almost there for how shallow he had to set that pole and give it the push. But it was me here in the bow about to toss the cinder-block anchor far as I could into the marsh, hoping I'd make it onto the dry ground past it. It was me could reach out and touch pluff mud and cordgrass on either side of us, the two of us at the head of this finger creek at dead low tide.

Like always, it was me looking out for the two of us, because Unc is blind.

Two-thirty in the morning, and we were where we shouldn't be.

Though a higher tide would have helped us get in a little farther, this was when Unc wanted to be here, for no other reason than two o'clock was too early, three too late.

The cordgrass and spartina and salt-marsh hay stood silver in the moonlight, all of it crowding up on us the closer we got in, the thick rim of black pluff mud a couple feet wide beneath it. To the left and above and past the marsh I could see a house a good twenty yards in, another one to the right, back through trees and maybe fifty yards away. All I could see of that one was an outside light, a coach lamp looked like, and the dime-sized halo it cast on the brick wall it was mounted to.

What worried me was the house to the left, the closer one. Like all the houses out here—they call them cottages, only thirty-three of them on this whole parcel of land—it was big, this one white stucco and two stories, two chimneys, a circular gravel drive out front.

But I only knew that from when I'd seen the place in daylight. At two-thirty in the morning, and creeping in through the marsh at the back of the place, all I could make out was the white of that stucco, and the waist-high brick fence that ran alongside the whole thing almost down to this creek.

And the light in an upstairs window somebody'd cut on a couple minutes ago. A light still on, right now.

"Let's go back," I whispered. "That light's still on."

We were almost there now, me already up on my knees and leaning a little farther out over the bow. I had the cinder block in both hands, the ratty nylon rope it was tied to trailing back to where I'd cleated it off, because I knew we wouldn't be turning back. I'd been out with Unc on these efforts enough times to know once we were this close there was no going back, and now here of a sudden and yet no surprise at all was the cold stink of the pluff mud thick around me.

"That light probably means ol' Dupont's nurse is up to change his diaper," Unc whispered. "He's got to be a hundred if he's a day."

"And what if his nurse takes a look out the window, sees—"

"*Oh*," Unc let out then, the word more a solid chunk of sound than a word at all, nowhere on it a whisper, and at the same time I felt a hard shiver through the boat.

For a second I thought we'd hit bottom, the creek shoaled in here at the head. But I knew this spot. I'd been here before, knew the bottom didn't come up until the very end. I quick turned back at Unc, saw he was looking down and to the left, the bill of the Braves ball cap he always wore part of that silhouette now, him in profile to me.

He'd touched something down there, had the pole up out of the water, held it with both hands like he was ready to gig a frog. And then I could feel that the jolt hadn't meant the bottom at all, and that we were still floating free, still inching closer to that pluff mud and where I'd have to heave the block to anchor us in.

Something'd scared him, made him flinch hard enough to shake the whole boat. That's what it was, and even though he couldn't see a thing he was still turned to it, ready.

"What?" I whispered.

"Don't know," he said, too fast. He lowered the tip of the pole to the water, eased it down slowly, like he was testing for something. "Thought it was a gator," he whispered. "But I don't think it was." He let it down all the way, until the top of the pole was even with his chest, let it set there a second. "Something," he whispered.

He turned to me, said again, "Hold on."

And then we hit ground for certain, and here I was, shoved forward out over the bow for the pitiful bit of momentum we had going in. I let go the cinder block, tried hard to get both hands on the gunwales or on the bow itself or just somewhere, anywhere, to keep me from tipping over and into that mud.

But it was too late, and I heard the huge aluminum *donk!* of the block hit the hull in the same instant I fell forward and into pluff mud to my elbows.

We were both silent for how loud that sound was, and the way it caromed like a billiard ball one end of the world to the other out here on the water. I already had words lined up in me, pissed-off ones it was everything I had to hold back for the cold of this mud, and the stink of it, and the stupidity of falling in like this when I'd been out on jon boats my whole life. I had words for Unc, and this mission, and how none of this was my idea. I had words. But all I could do was swallow them down.

And watch that window up there, past the marsh grass. Somebody had to have heard us. Somebody had to.

Nothing happened. Nothing: no face at the window of that Guatemalan nurse Judge Dupont had taking care of him, or no old Dupont himself, holding close a shotgun. No turning off of the light, or turning on an outside one so's to scare off whatever dangerous intruders these were out here. Nothing.

And so I leaned back as best I could, pulled my arms out of the mud, and whispered "Shit!" through teeth clenched tight for holding off every other word I had.

I held my hands out in front of me a second, looked at the pure black of them in this dark, whatever moonlight there was soaked right up in that black so that it seemed I had stubs for arms. "Shit," I whispered again, though this time there was nothing for it. Just me, pissed off.

"Nope," Unc whispered from behind me. "Pluff mud's only detritus. Organic material breaking down. Maybe you'd know this if you hadn't quit college."

"Not funny," I whispered. I turned toward him, made to move farther back in the boat to where I could lean over one side or the other, wash my hands off in the water, the bow set tight in that mud. "And one more time: I quit for good reason."

"I'm sure you did," he whispered.

I looked up at him, ready to spit words at him. Ready for it.

But he was looking off to his left again, and a little behind him now. Back, I could tell, to where whatever he'd touched had been. As though he could see anything at all.

"If it's a gator, he's long gone," he whispered, "but you might ought to wait a sec before you put your arms down in that water."

He turned, looked down at me: that silhouette again, behind him those thin stars.

"Thought I told you to hold on," he whispered.

My name is Huger Dillard. You say it YOU-gee, not like it's spelled. When I was a kid and people would ask about it, I'd tell them I heard it was French. That's all.

But then I went off to college, started after what my friends used to call an *edumacation*. By friends I mean the ones I used to have, before my mom and I moved out of the old neighborhood and into the new one. It's a different set I run with now, if you'd even call them a set, or if you'd call what I have to do with them running. I'm twenty-seven now, and still living at home though, like every one of us still hanging out with Mom and Pop at the ranch, I've got my reasons.

And Unc isn't my uncle. He's my father.

It's complicated.

But to my *edumacation*: Huger, I learned in a course called History of the South, taught by a tweedy and mildewed old professor who never once lifted his eyes from his notes to look at the class, is short for Huguenot, a fierce people who came here to Charleston from France once they'd had enough of being burned at the stake and forced to be galley slaves and whatnot because they wouldn't lick the silk slippers of Louis XIV, Mr. Sun King himself. Back in the day, the word *Huguenot* meant a kind of curse on who you were and what you believed. But then it became a good thing, and meant you were a durable son of a bitch who wouldn't put up with anything.

Huger. It was a good name before I went off and had my go at getting schooled, and it still is.

But it's come to me in the six years since I've been back that it's a name I don't think I deserve anymore. Because it was this kid named Huger who chose to quit said college after two and a half years, though the word *quit* is a lie: my grades kicked my ass all the way from Chapel Hill to here.

Some kid named Huger quit because he was lost up there. He wasn't as smart as he'd led himself to believe, even with an SAT of 1510.

And I don't think I can live up to being an endurable son of a bitch anymore because, if you were to ask me point-blank, I'd have to tell you I actually *like* being twenty-seven and living at home. I like watching after Unc, taking him to whatever appointments he might have with his financial adviser, or to the bank, or out to what's left of Hungry Neck Hunt Club on those Friday nights when we have a hunt on a Saturday. I don't even mind hauling him out to his Thursday night poker parties at that huge orange monstrosity of a house in Mount Pleasant, though I won't set foot in the manse for the bit of history I have between the host's son and myself.

It's a big event for Unc, even though it happens every Thursday night ten to two, Thanksgiving included. A weekly opportunity for Unc and thirty or forty of his closest chums to win and/or lose up to five grand a night, if they so desire. It's also an evening in which, because I don't want to leave Unc alone in case he taps out early but generally because I don't want to be at home alone with Mom, I end up sitting in the Range Rover out on the street with the other thirty or forty cars and playing solitaire on my iPhone, or feeding locations into the Maps app to see how I'd get from here to Fargo or Los Alamos or Palo Alto. Or I'll end up just sitting there and thinking about how empty the all of this life is, and how much I am queasily enjoying it.

Oh. And I'll ponder, some of the time, on a girl involved with this whole maudlin malaise thing I have working. Her name's Tabitha. She's on a postdoc at Stanford.

I don't think I deserve this Huger moniker, finally, because ever since I gave up, it's seemed a good life to do nothing other than fart my way through a day. Or a night.

Case in point: this excursion.

Because the truth of the whole thing, the absolute and pathetic and sorry stupid reason we were out here at the head of a finger creek backed up to a cottage in the first place, the reason for all this intrigue and mystery and worries over an old man at a window toting a shotgun or a Guatemalan nurse hot on the phone to Hanahan's finest for the dumb metal *donk!* of a cinder block dropped—the truth of the whole dense and gratuitous and embarrassing thing is that we were here because Unc wanted to golf.

Golf.

And as I leaned over the gunwale, made to put these pluff mud stubs into the water to wash them off, I couldn't help but think on my name—Huger Dillard—and how, for the life of me, I ought not to care how the hell anybody'd pronounce it.

Here was yet another moment in the crowded long line of them— a line more crowded and longer every day—when the me I am sneaks up on me, taps me on the shoulder, then sucker punches me when I turn around, and I realize I am, at the ripe old age of twenty-seven, smack in the middle of wasting my life, living the way I do.

This was what I had come to: sneaking Unc out to golf at two-thirty in the morning because he was too damned proud to be caught doing so in daylight.

None of this was my idea. But here I was.

I looked down at that water, and in the last instant before I put my hands in to start at washing off this detritus, this organic material breaking down—this shit that might as well have been me—I caught Unc's reflection in the water.

He stood behind me and to my left, his silhouette showing up clear and sharp for this still water at dead low tide. I could see that pole off to the side and in the water, and the bill on his ball cap, him turned from me again and looking back. I could even make out the thin wash of stars behind him. All of this in the water, and in an instant.

I heard him take in a small breath, then whisper low, "Now what in the hell was that?" the words no louder than a breath back out, meant for nobody but himself.

I put my hands into the water, troubled it big for how hard it was to get off this mud.

2

Unc swung the club, and here came the quick whip through air, then the strike, two separate sounds that seemed even louder out here than that block on the hull. The ball made a sharp slice, the bright green dot through the night-vision goggles I had on a kind of missile peeling off to the right into the trees. No way would I be going after that one. No way.

Night-vision goggles: AN/PVS-7D Generation 4 with an infrared illuminator. You couldn't get these unless you were military or law. Unc knew people in both.

"Sliced it," I whispered. "Big." I took in a breath, let it out in a hard sigh. "That one's gone."

I sat on the fold-up camp chair we always brought with us, Unc in the tee box ten feet to my left, me facing straight ahead down the fairway so I could watch where the ball went. Like always, I felt like some Borged-up cyclops with these things on, the gear strapped onto an old yellow hard hat I picked up a year or so ago from the work site out to Hungry Neck after they'd halted building.

It'd only taken a couple minutes to get out here once I'd gotten my hands cleaned up enough: first I'd tossed that idiot block out into the marsh grass, then'd pulled from the bottom of the jon boat the eight-foot plank we keep in there, slid it out over the bow onto solid ground. I'd picked up the camp chair in its long skinny nylon bag, and my old book bag stuffed with the paraphernalia we needed—six or seven balls and a few tees, the night goggles and hard hat, an old thermos of instant coffee, two beat-up travel mugs we'd bought one night years ago at the Hess station on our way out to Hungry Neck.

Usually when we were out on the jon boat—in fact, wherever we went, boat or truck—there'd be Unc's walking stick to bring along, too. The one I'd found for him when I was seven out on the land at Hungry Neck, Unc in bed in the single-wide we lived in back then and healing after what happened to make him blind. A stick so straight it seemed the old hickory it was off of had dropped it just for him, and that he'd used every day since. But right now it was in the kitchen back home, in the corner where the breakfast table sits, precisely where he leaves it and where he knows it'll be when we make to head out.

Tonight it was a golf club to grab instead, the Callaway three wood with its grip resting on the center seat. The only club Unc ever brought with us, though he had a whole set out in the garage at home, a bag of clubs cost him three grand, but this was the only one he ever used. Further evidence of the stupidity of his pride.

Because there's plenty of blind golfers out there. Really. There's even a United States Blind Golf Association, and an annual world tournament—last year's was in Dublin, Ireland, next year's in Palm Springs. The whole thing involves a coach who's there with you to help set up the shot, tell you where you are and distance to the hole and all else. You take the swing, wait to hear from that coach how you'd done, where it went.

So a blind golfer's no joke. The joke, though, is that in order to accommodate Unc and his fear of someone seeing him take crappy shots—the same crappy shots every golfer makes at every course in the world, blind or not—well, this fear of his has called for these special-ops escapades.

The camp chair under one arm, the book bag over my shoulder, I'd leaned over, picked up the club from where it lay, stood back up. I thought to say something to him—*Here we go,* or *Be careful,* or some such rot—but I only looked at him standing at the transom.

And now that I was standing, I'd been able to see behind him the whole of the marsh, the uneven spread of blacks and grays and silvers out here. Across it all, a good half mile away, lay a low jagged tree line, what always looked to me no matter what marsh I was on like a long line of men on horseback, watching and waiting. That was Naval Weapons Station land over there, the giant tract of woods that buffered the world against the dozens of ammo dumps they keep bunkered in there, a tract no one even dared think to sneak in on. To the left and a couple hundred yards off stood the trestle across the marsh and Goose Creek, a hulking structure that since I was a kid seemed the black backbone of some monster ready to rise up out of the water and tear us all to bits. I loved this place, loved being out here on water whether night or day, loved sometimes even the smell of that pluff mud.

But Unc could golf in daylight if he wanted. He could man up and get himself a coach, and quit this cat burglar crap, if he really wanted to.

I didn't say a word to him, only turned, stepped out onto that plank, and crossed on over.

Two steps onto hard ground, and here he'd been behind me, his moves as quick and easy as—maybe even easier than—mine along the length of the boat, then onto and across that plank. He'd taken hold of my belt, cinched onto it for me to lead, and given the smallest push to go.

I'd glanced at that light in the window at the Dupont house and whatever it might or might not mean, and started the hundred yards or so along the brick fence up from the creek along the property, then out onto the gravel drive. A few strides later we'd been into the grass, before us the wide spread of what in the dark always looked like only a meadow bordered by trees. But there, twenty yards in front of us, lay a little raised flat of grass: the tee box.

Now here we were, me in my camp chair, Unc swinging away. Though the night-vision goggles gave only a forty-degree line of sight, I could see everything in this dark: the live oak and pine along the fairway on the right, the bright white kidney of a bunker in front of the green 280 yards away—this was the thirteenth, a short par four—and to the left the two cottages on this hole. All of it green, corralled inside a round porthole of sight. One big rifle scope.

The farther house was red brick and slate-roofed, an outdoor fireplace and stone flower boxes beneath a white-columned pergola trying too hard to look like the Parthenon. Closer in, maybe halfway down the fairway, sat a huge Spanish-style thing, U-shaped with the courtyard facing the fairway. Red-tile roof, stucco, a rim of painted tiles beneath the eaves I could make out even from here.

Patio furniture sat out at both houses, nice stuff that cost more than the furniture Mom and I used to have inside our house over on Marie Street, back before we moved out of the old neighborhood. Over there, if you put a piece of furniture out in the yard or on a porch, even one of those thin white plastic chairs you can pick up at Wal-Mart for five bucks, you'd better chain it to the ground or it'd be gone the next day. But here they were safe and sound, all this fancy furniture sitting in the dark and smug for it, too: testimony to how secure people figured they were, given their money and how long they'd all had it. And our old neighborhood not even a mile from here.

I let myself look at that Spanish one a second longer than I should, a mistake I made every time we came out here: the umbrella and wrought-iron table and chairs, two sofas and a chaise lounge parked there in the courtyard. The low brick fire ring built out closer to the fairway, the row of five palmettos spaced evenly along this back line of the property. All that painted tile, and the arched windows, and that stucco.

I looked at it every time, of course, because the Spanish of it, that stucco and red tile, made it feel too much like what you'll see in Palo Alto. Specifically, on the campus at Stanford.

I'd been there once.

Unc whacked the next ball, and my eyes caught the bright green streak of it blast out even sharper to the right, even deeper into the trees.

"Jeez, Unc," I whispered, "what you been drinking?" and turned in the camp chair to face him full-on. "You never slice it," I whispered.

Here he was: big and green and filling that porthole of sight. He stood centered at the tee, already had the next ball teed up, the club head down and settled at it, him about to swing back for hit number three.

He had on his old windbreaker for the cool out here, on the right breast the bright block letters *MtPPD,* the jacket a prized possession from back when he was on the Mount Pleasant Police Department. He had on his same old khakis, and that Braves cap, the scripty white *A* sharp above the bill. And there was his face, the sunglasses he always wore, all of him green. He dipped his chin, leaned his head to the left a little, geared up to swing.

But he stopped, took in a small breath, and looked at me.

I saw my reflection in his sunglasses then, two white shocks of light the size of marbles: the IR illuminator on my goggles. Infrared light, reflected right back at me.

For a second it scared me, like it did every time since we'd gotten this new set. It looked like he could see me, like he was just wearing a pair of regular glasses, but his eyes behind them these white fires trying to burn into me something I didn't know and couldn't yet figure out.

The first set of goggles we'd gotten didn't have the IR illuminator built in. Those were the old Gen 1 things somewhere in the garage right now, buried under the pile of military and security gadgets Unc loves getting hold of for whatever reason he has. He'd won this new set one poker night a couple months ago off a Navy commander pal who'd tapped out early and'd been so convinced of his luck—no matter he'd lost what he'd brought with him—that he'd scrambled outside and gotten the goggles from his truck, then promptly lost the hand. Unc took him with three tens to his two pair.

"You should have seen him," Unc'd told me on the way home from poker the night he won them. "I could hear in the way he was breathing when it come to his bet how much he was sweating, all his money gone and him thinking about getting these Gen 4s out of his truck. The dimwit commander says, 'You want a set of night-vision goggles you can't get anywhere on any market? Guaranteed nobody anywhere's going to have these for another three years,' and I says, 'Like I could see with them.' I could still hear him sweating, and I let him twist there for a minute or so more before I nodded I'd take them, and he was gone. Ninety seconds later he plops them on the table, lets out a breath I can hear is some kind of smile for him thinking he's won the hand. And all he's got is his piddly two pair." He'd let out a laugh then, though I remember it wasn't for any kind of happiness. He shook his head, then'd whispered like it was some punch line only he knew the joke for, "I just wanted to beat the son of a bitch is all."

Maybe all this gear and dark-ops night stuff was his way of trying to hold tight to his life, I sometimes thought. Maybe it was all longing for the badass days when he was on the force. Way back when, in that time when he could see and work. Back before his wife, my aunt Sarah, killed herself by burning down their house over to Mount Pleasant.

Back before he'd been blinded in that fire when the window he'd been looking in had exploded, his wife, my aunt, inside and herself on fire. Hence those sunglasses, because they cover up the gnarled and shiny skin from where his eyebrows had been on down to his cheeks, the white marbles he has for eyes held in by eyelids just as gnarled.

I said it was complicated.

And that's why it scared me when I saw the IR reflected back at me like this: here were those marble eyes of his, taking me in and sizing me up. Me every time, I knew, coming up short.

"What?" I whispered.

He looked at me a second longer, then another. He let out a breath, and I saw him swallow, his mouth a straight line. He seemed about to say something, but then he looked down, those white marbles gone. He cocked his chin again, gripped and regripped the club handle, inched the club head along the ground until it just touched the ball: how he knows where to hit.

I turned, watched for where the next ball would go.

But instead of another one of those missiles taking off, I saw to the left, past that red-brick house with its Parthenon pergola, a growing glow through the trees, a moving green swell of light that grew brighter green, bigger and bigger in just that much time. Then here came around the edge of the house twin explosions of light that swung right through my line of sight, for an instant that porthole gone to pure bright white.

Headlights on a golf cart, speeding along the cart path on the far side of the fairway. Headed for us.

I flipped up the goggles, took off the hard hat. "Time to go, Unc. The muscle's here," I said. Here was Security, us about to get caught one more time.

I tried for a second to figure out who was driving—most likely, this being early Wednesday A.M., it'd be either Tyrone or Segundo. If we were lucky it'd be Jessup. But without the goggles on, the world was back to its plain old darkness, me stuffing the hat and goggles back in the book bag. Unc didn't want anyone knowing we had them, because it was illegal as hell to be marching around and watching the world, much less golf balls, with those things on. Golfing after hours was one thing, but possessing Gen 4s was another. And so I couldn't yet tell from here who it was hauling ass along the path past the red-brick cottage, now the Spanish one, and I turned back to Unc.

He was gone.

The club lay on the ground, I could make out in the dark, the ball still teed up too, and I quick looked to my left, saw him already ten yards away, headed fast toward the Dupont house.

"Unc," I called, and heard my voice way too loud out here. But I didn't care, because there he was, walking away. Without me.

Usually by this time we were picking up, pretending we were finished and headed out anyway. Of course the guard, whoever it was, would pull up and park the cart, then dutifully walk us, Unc holding on to my belt, back along that brick fence and to the boat, the guard all the while reciting the rules: No golf without signing in at the pro shop; no golf except during regular business hours; no golf in the middle of the night.

Even if you were members. Like us.

Because we live here—Unc, Mom, and me—at Landgrave Hall Golf and Country Club. In a 4200-square-foot cottage that sits on the green of the seventh hole. We've even got a dock off the back of the place, right out into Goose Creek, where we keep the jon boat cradled up in the rafters of the boathouse at the end. A dock where we shove off in the middle of the night and snake our way back along Goose Creek, only to put in at the head of a finger creek and sneak back in to golf.

As it turns out, we've ended up rich. And discovered we are members of the blue bloods too.

We live here, and act like perps on our own property. We take the jon boat over when we could very well walk because Unc doesn't want to chance being seen by any of his neighbors with a golf club in hand. He doesn't want to be caught, as it were, attempting something he might not be very good at. Something that might make him look like—dare I say it?—a fool.

But Unc'd never taken off like this, him without even the club to help him tap out what was in front of him. It was always with me. Always.

Now here was the golf cart beside me, the sharp crunch of gravel on the cart path as it pulled to a stop off to my right, and I turned, saw it was Jessup driving.

Good. At least he wouldn't be putting on any airs, talk tough like Segundo and Tyrone did, as though we'd be the ones reporting back to the Homeowners' Association on what a fine job Security did every time they kicked us off the course.

But even though it was Jessup, and I really *was* glad it was him, there was always this awkward thing between us here at Landgrave Hall, because Jessup and I had gone to grade school and middle school and high school together. He was one of the set I used to run with, those friends who used to make fun of getting an *edumacation*, back when we'd sneak out of our houses at night and sit on the railroad tracks at the end of Marie, and make fun of people who lived in places like this. Now here we were: the landed gentry, and the hired hand.

"What's he doing?" Jessup said as he climbed out, him in his black windbreaker and pants, that black ball cap they all wore.

"I think he's pissed off about something," I said, and started after Unc, the book bag over my shoulder.

Something was wrong, easy enough to see, and I thought of him looking at me as he'd set up for that last shot he didn't take. I thought of his eyes, those white marbles, and him gripping and regripping the club, saw now the nervous of it all, and those ugly slices the balls had taken. He never hit like that, sometimes only hooked it a little, but usually just hit it straight and high.

There was something. Had to be. And I thought of that light in the window at the Dupont house turning on as Unc'd poled us in, and then me dropping that block on the hull, giving us away even before we'd gotten out here.

Maybe that was it: me. Unc finally tired enough of me and the nothing of my life to decide he could just take off back to the boat all by himself, and that I, this deadweight in his life and mine both, could just take care of myself from now on.

He was across the gravel drive when I got to him, Jessup a little behind me, the two of us walking fast to catch up. I said, "Unc, hey, let's just relax. It's Jessup," and touched his shoulder, made to pull him to a stop. "I'm sorry," I said.

But he shook off my hand, walked even faster.

"Mr. Dillard," Jessup said, "no use trying to evade the law like this," and he let out a small laugh. "Suspect fleeing the premises," he said, and tried at the laugh again.

"You got you a flashlight, Jessup?" Unc said, and just kept on walking.

We were at the head of the brick fence that led back to the boat now, the white stucco of the Dupont house to our right on the other side, and as though he could see everything, Unc put out his hand, touched the brick just as he came even with it, let his hand pop along the top of it as he moved.

"No sir," Jessup said, and I could hear a kind of embarrassment for it. Of course Unc would make a remark on that, Jessup and I both knew, something along the lines *And you call yourself Security.*

But Unc said nothing, just kept going.

I glanced to my left over at Jessup, made out in the dark him slowly shaking his head.

"That light still on, Huger?" Unc said, and it hit me, his question to Jessup and me both: he was talking full-voiced, like it was daylight and maybe we were all out on a stroll outside our own cottage, just walking in the yard.

We were even with the back of the house just as he'd said it, and the timing of it—his knowing right when I'd be able to see that upstairs window at the back of the house—didn't surprise me a bit. I looked up to my right, saw the window up there. Dark.

"Nope," I said, just as loud. "Unc, it's Jessup, so ease off," I said, then tried one more time at what I figured had to be the real problem: "I'm sorry," I said. "For dropping the block."

"What light?" Jessup said, then, "Mr. Dillard, I'm just here to tell you you and Huger can't be out here and—"

"What time is it?" Unc cut in, his hand still popping along the fence.

"Unc," I said, "can't we just—"

"Time?" he said. He was slowing down now, his steps the smallest way more tentative. The end of the brick fence was only a few feet ahead of us, and I could see beyond him now the low spread of the marsh, the tree line across it, and here was the narrow gray slab of the plank out to the jon boat, still shoved up into the cordgrass.

I knew then why he was asking for the time: he wanted to know how far off dead low tide we were, so he'd know where the waterline might be for the tide coming in. He didn't want to get his feet wet before he stepped onto that plank.

"Quarter to three in the morning," I said, and stopped walking. "But I'm betting you knew that."

He stopped, turned to me. It was a sudden move, and though I'd been ready, it caught Jessup, who nearly flinched for it. He stopped, too, and we three stood looking at each other there at the end of a waist-high brick fence in the middle of the night, the tide creeping in.

"Maybe two feet in by now," I said. "No more than that. Plank's still on dry ground. I bet you knew that, too."

Unc looked away then, and out to the marsh. He reached up, touched the back of his neck again.

"You may think this is all about you, Huger," he said, "but the sooner you figure out it ain't, the better."

"I said I'm sorry," I said. "You just tell me what more you want and we can—"

"We got to get to this now," he said, and turned, took a few more steps toward the marsh before he stopped again, touched the toe of his boot ahead of him, looking for the plank. "You want to give me a hand here, either of you, I'd be obliged."

"Mr. Dillard," Jessup said, "it's just the rules out here. I'm just doing my job."

"We're going," I said to Jessup. In the dark I could see him look at me a long second, then nod once.

"I'll get that camp chair you left out there," he said, "have it up to the guardhouse tomorrow."

"You at least got your radio on you, Jessup?" Unc said, and I turned. He was already across the plank and out in the boat, back at the transom. He had the pole out already, too, and was standing there, waiting. "And I need one or the other of you two lug nuts to give me a hand, and I mean now."

"Just stop being a jerk, Unc," I said, and stepped to the plank, balanced my way across it, my arms out to either side, the book bag in my left hand, and heard Jessup say behind me, "I got my two-way up to Segundo at the gate, sir. But I'm not calling this in."

I stepped in, felt the bow of the boat still stuck hard on the pluff mud, even though I could see the waterline had come in a foot or so, and I said, "What the hell is your problem?"

"Just pull in the plank," he said, and here he was poling us out, digging in hard to warp us off the mud. Then we were free, and I squatted, set down the book bag and dragged at the plank, heaved it in and under the center seat.

"Get that radio out," he called to Jessup, his words way too loud. Something was up in him, a rush, I could see with the solid jab he made at the mud beneath us, and the hard lean into the pole, the pull to get us off and out as fast as he could do it.

But then we stopped hard, a sudden cold halt of the boat, and I looked behind me, back to the few feet of water between us and land. There, taut all the way in, shot a thin ratty line of nylon rope: the cinder block, still back there, still cleated off here.

I turned, ready for whatever shit Unc'd be laying on me now for this next sin against him.

"Don't matter," he nearly whispered, still working the pole, but not to move us anywhere now. He held it just like I'd seen when we got here, up like he was gigging a frog, and now I knew what the all of this was about: whatever it was he'd poked and that'd scared him when we were on our way in. "This way we won't be moving all over," he said.

"If this is about a gator," I said, "then you need to get out more often. They're a dime a dozen around here. You said yourself he's long gone."

He said nothing, and now the pole went deep, almost to Unc's knees, and he pushed down on it, the gunwale of the boat a kind of fulcrum he was working the pole over. He pushed, gave out a grunt, and pushed again, the boat heeling over for it, but still Unc pushed down and down.

"Unc," I whispered, and sat, leaned out over the gunwale on the opposite side to give him a little more depth.

Because there was something he was after, and he was getting it.

Now a sudden pitch of the boat away from his side toward mine, him nearly falling down for whatever it was being freed of the mud, and here was the sound of water against that side, a push of it against the boat, and the thick stink of pluff mud for all of it roiling up.

"Tell me what it is, Huger," he said, out of breath. He stood up straight, waggled a moment to get back his balance for the boat righting itself beneath him. The pole was still down in the water, at an angle beneath the thing.

I stood, looked over the edge into the black water there. "Nothing," I said, and swallowed. "Maybe lift it up a little more, to the surface."

He grunted again, lifted and lifted, and Jessup called out, "You all right?"

We didn't answer. Unc pushed down, and still I saw nothing in the water, the black of it so deep. That half-moon we'd had coming in was hidden now behind trees somewhere, and at the same instant the idea came to me, Unc whispered, "Get the goggles."

I sat, reached to the book bag up in the bow and zipped it open, pulled out the hard hat, the goggles still strapped on.

"What if Jessup sees them?" I said, though I was already putting them on.

Unc said nothing: answer enough.

I was on my knees now, and leaned over the gunwale again, flipped down the goggles. Green water was all I could see, the bottom edge of the porthole the gunwale, the top edge the line where pluff mud started. Between them water, green and green and green.

"Nothing," I said again, but then here it bulged up, something wet and thick and glistening, water streaming away off what looked like a log at first but smooth, and then, Unc still working to lift it, I saw a cleft halfway down its length, where it split in two on the right, and I knew of course it was a body: two legs, above them the torso, and now I saw two small mounds of a sort—breasts—then wider and higher above that two sharp points that were shoulders, all mired over in a thin cast of pluff mud, and I turned my head to the left, moved my line of sight to the head.

Mud over it, no features at all.

Then it disappeared, washed over by green water, Unc letting it back down.

"Unc," I breathed out, "it's—"

"I know," he whispered, and I felt him push down to bring it up again.

And then, like it'd forgotten itself altogether and started up just now, I felt the surprise shock of my pulse, and the roar of blood in my ears, and I heard too the odd and cold whir of cicadas I hadn't noticed out here yet tonight, and Unc's breathing loud beside me.

It was a body. I'd just seen a body, and in a moment I'd have to look at it again, and now I heard inside that whir of cicadas and the rush of blood through me water lapping against the boat, and heard too water everywhere on the creek, from the top of it where a cinder block lay holding us in place right on down to the Cooper River miles away. I heard all this, all this, and I took in a shallow breath, because there was nothing other my own body knew to do than to breathe.

Still I looked over the edge, and here came rising up through this green water not a body in mud but a bright green body only streaked with it, mud washed free for Unc's letting it back down and bringing it up again. A woman: that blank cleft of her legs, a thin snarl of mud-died hair there, her breasts. The pole was beneath the middle of her back so that she was arched as she rose, and I turned my head to the left again so that this time I might see her face, though I didn't want this. I didn't want this.

It wasn't a face I saw, but first teeth, a green and bright grimace inside a ragged pull of flesh away from them, the nose and chin the same ragged matter, and next her eyes, or what was left of them: a burl of loose flesh down to the cheekbones, the bones two green shards beneath where eyes should have been.

"God," I whispered.

"Huger," Unc whispered. "We need to get help in here."

"It's a woman," I whispered, then whispered again, "God."

I eased back slow until I was on my butt in the bottom of the hull. I felt my stomach going, felt it almost in my throat, and I swallowed, swallowed again.

"Jessup," Unc called out, the word the loudest thing I'd ever heard. "Call up to Segundo, get the Hanahan PD in here. Sheriff too."

I still had on the goggles, and I swallowed again, then one more time, and slowly turned my head to look at Unc, because he knew what to do. He always knew.

There he stood, looking back toward Jessup, the pole at an angle to hold the body up, him pressing down with both hands. He was fully lit and breathing hard for the work he was after, and I could see the stars above him weren't a thin wash but a green galaxy spread thick.

"Yessir," Jessup called back after a second.

I made myself stand, still with the scope on Unc, and looked at him, hoping in just these few seconds he'd have figured out some way to help me, and that with the goggles on I could see the words out of his mouth so that I could get them all the more quickly into me.

But all I saw was the reflection of the IR illuminator in his sunglasses: those two marbles of fire.

"Can't get it any higher than this," he said, his breaths still heavy, him nearly winded. "Not totally free. Anchored on two ends, feels like." He leaned down hard yet again on the pole, and disappeared from my field of vision, those white fires gone.

But here they still were, smaller but sharper, closer together and a long way off.

I blinked quick, squinted a second.

Two lights, pinpoints far off but certain and sharp as lasers pointed this way. They bobbed a second, and I could see now they were inside the tree line all the way across the marsh. A good half mile away, there in the Naval Weapons Station tract.

Infrared illuminators. Had to be. Looking right here.

Then they disappeared, first one, the other an instant later.

"Unc," I started.

"Can you spell me, Huger?" Unc said, and stood, filled my line of sight: those marbles again. "Just hold the pole right here until they—"

"There's somebody out there," I said. "On the other side of the marsh."

"What?" he said, and turned, still holding on to the pole.

I looked past him, to those trees, and the nothing of them now. Only trees.

"On their way!" Jessup called from behind us, and then, quieter, he said, "Huger, what you got out there?"

"A body," I said, and slowly flipped up the goggles, took off the hard hat. It didn't matter how quickly I put them away now, I knew, the whole idea of taking them off what felt already a year too late.

Because if I'd seen them all the way across the marsh, two somebodies a half mile away on the Naval Weapons Station tract, both of them wearing night-vision goggles at least as good as mine, then they'd seen my IR looking right back.

Somebody over there had been watching us without our even knowing.

"It's a body," I said, and I turned, looked back at Jessup: a man dressed in black in the plain old dark of the world, standing at the head of a finger creek into Landgrave Hall.

And then, like what I'd said was a cue, that light in the upstairs window turned on.

"Here we go," Unc whispered behind me.

3

I took over for Unc, just like he'd asked, traded places with him so it was me stood there at the transom pushing down on the pole. Though I couldn't quite figure why, given there might very well be a gator out here and us now dangling a body in the water like it was bait.

A body. A woman.

I wouldn't look down there. Not that I could have seen anything, or seen it as sharp and clear as I had with the goggles on. But I wouldn't let my eyes go down to the water.

Unc sat on the center seat getting back his breath, head down, elbows on his knees, and now an outside light on the back of the Dupont house came on behind him, flooded the yard and its patio furniture and French doors. Jessup, still back there on dry ground, turned to it, his radio up to his mouth.

Next, at that house with the coach lamp I'd seen when we first put in, the one back about fifty yards through the trees, an even bigger outside light smashed on, the woods between here and there filled just like that with the black silhouettes of trees.

"Here comes the neighborhood," I said, and looked down at Unc.

"Of course." He took in a breath, shook his head at the ugly fact of what always happened next when we were busted for golfing: one or another of the neighbors would show up as we were being escorted off the premises, there to give us intruders a kind of self-satisfied send-off. But this time it'd be different. This time whoever it was would find something more than they'd bargained for after calling us in for whacking at golf balls in the middle of the night.

And now it began: one of the French doors on the Dupont house opened up, a small black-haired woman—had to be the nurse—standing there in a pale robe.

"Everything here is under control, ma'am," Jessup called up to her.

"Judge Dupont wants to know what's going on out here," she nearly shouted, her voice high-pitched and thin.

"It's under control, ma'am," Jessup said.

She stood there in the door, and it occurred to me she didn't sound Guatemalan at all. It'd been Jessup who'd told me once where she came from, and she looked like she was from somewhere down there, but she'd had no accent at all, and I watched as she took a step out the door onto the patio, held herself in the cool out here.

"What you saw could have been just a couple boys out patrolling for whatever reason," Unc breathed out. "Over to the Weapons Station." I glanced down at him, saw he still had his elbows on his knees, but now he was looking past me across the marsh.

I turned, looked out there. The light from off the back of the house let me see only about twenty yards out into that cordgrass and spartina, this narrow lane of black water snaking away. The stars were gone for that light, too, the jagged line of trees across it all now only a dull rim on the horizon, black and far away.

But I could still feel the hot of my blood up in me, my chest pressed down on and at the same time pushing from inside for those pinprick lasers of light looking right at us. And I could feel my blood up in me because of this body.

I said, "What does it mean? I mean, soldiers watching us. Even if they were on patrol." I swallowed, felt how heavy this pole was for the weight at the other end, thought of those teeth bright and green, her face like it was melted away somehow. I turned from the marsh back to the house, careful not to look down at the water.

Jessup was at the porch off the French doors now, talking to the woman, who still held herself. His back was to us, and I could see her looking up at him, listening.

"Sailors," Unc said. "Not soldiers. And it don't mean anything." He sat up, his palms on his knees. "Means we might have to turn in those goggles is all. So we got caught with them, we turn them in. Won them fair and square off Commander Prendergast, and if anyone wants to charge us with anything, a little reminder to him of how he lost government property in a hand of poker'll make sure the matter's dropped."

He looked up at me, his face dark altogether for the light behind him. He said, "How you doing?"

"Fine," I said, too quick. "Seen them before."

"Sorry," he said, and looked down again.

Now out from the shadows along that fence we'd just walked and into the light from off the back of the Dupont house came the next guests at this little gathering: first Mr. and Mrs. Cuthbert, the real estate couple owned the place back through the trees, him in a pair of sweat shorts and a T-shirt, her in a running suit, the both of them with hair matted and snarled for sleep; next, shriveled and old and with her helmet of white hair done up perfect, came Mrs. Quillie Izerd Grimball, the widow lived in the Spanish place back on the fairway, a woman had to be even older than Judge Dupont. She stopped a couple feet to the right of the Cuthberts, and had on a dark skirt and white blouse, a sweater draped over her shoulders like it was a cape. Of course she'd show up dressed for the event, her so old school.

And of course the first residents to see Unc and me tending to a dead body on the property would be these three: the realtors who'd sold us our place over on the seventh green, and the lead dog in the fight to keep us trailer trash from moving in here in the first place.

"The Cuthberts and old lady Q are here," I said low to Unc, and because of this pushing down and pressing out in my chest, and because here was the first posse of these old-money folks we were surrounded with by living out here to Landgrave Hall, and because I didn't know what else to do with any of it but to fill in the dark with words, I tried to make a joke: "Guess Mrs. Q was right when she said we'd bring the wrong element into the neighborhood."

"Ain't us brought a dead body in here, that's for damn sure," Unc said right back. "And like I said a hundred thousand times: I got just as much right to live here as that battle-ax'll ever have."

Slowly he rubbed his palms on his knees now, what he'll do when his own blood is up. "When are those boys going to get here?" he whispered, and already I was sorry for trying even to make him laugh. It was an old fight, the one about the element we were bringing into Landgrave Hall, and whether or not we could even buy a place here. It was an old fight. I should have known better.

Unc stopped rubbing his knees, sat up straight. He took in a breath, held it a moment. He half turned in his seat, called out toward the house, "Jessup, you call in DNR?"

Jessup, still talking to the nurse, spun quick to the words. He was quiet a moment, then said, "Who?"

"Department of Natural Resources," Unc called out. "The warden'll have to be in on this too."

"Leland?" Mr. Cuthbert called out, "you got you a gator?" and I saw him put a hand to his forehead to block out the light from the house. He took a step forward, said, "Must be a good one to have to call in DNR." He took his hand down, put his hands on his hips. "Don't suppose you could just clobber that bad boy with that three wood you're always out here with."

"Just let the local fauna alone," Mrs. Q said in her high-pitched and wobbly old lady voice. She gave out a solid *tsk*, said, "Wrestling alligators won't prove anything of your worth out here, Mr. Dillard. Neither you nor the boy both."

"Quillie," Mrs. Cuthbert said, her arms crossed, and I could see her shake her head, that hair of hers at odd angles. "That's enough."

"I've already called your momma, Huger," Mrs. Q said. "She's on her way as we speak."

"Perfect," Unc whispered. He let out a hard breath, called out, "Jessup, just get the DNR boys on down here too."

"Yessir," Jessup said.

"You bag that son of a bitch," Mr. Cuthbert called, "and we'll cook us up some steaks tonight, you want to, Leland. We'll barbecue us some fauna, I tell you what."

He let out a laugh, a loud one that seemed more forced than anything else. And even though it was a kind of innocent laugh, meant only to poke both at that old bag Mrs. Q and at the fact he knew Unc was out here golfing in the middle of the night again, still that laugh echoed cold and easy across the marsh, and very very wrong.

There was a dead body right here with us. A dead woman right here at the end of this pole I was pushing down on to hold it up. A laugh out of Mr. Cuthbert was the wrong thing to happen out here, just as an idiot joke about the trailer trash element we'd brought here was wrong too.

There was no joke to any of this.

But there was still in me this pressure in my chest I knew wasn't going to leave any time soon. Still in me, too, that rifle-scope view of the body, my line of sight filled with those teeth, that flesh, and whatever had happened—whatever had been done to—her face, and the glow and glisten of water runneling off a body, and I had no choice in that second of Mr. Cuthbert's laugh echoing back across the marsh but to bark out sharp, "It's a body."

I said it loud, and heard my own echo come back to me, same as that laugh.

Nothing happened for a moment, everyone in the Dupont backyard just standing there, frozen. The only thing alive seemed that echo back at us, hanging right here in the air around us.

Mr. Cuthbert, hands still on his hips, took another step forward, said, "What you mean, 'a body'?"

"He means a body, Grange," Unc said, the words quiet. "A woman's body. Now we need to just wait until the authorities get here before we can—"

Right then Mrs. Quillie Izcrd Grimball took in a breath that tangled up and warbled in her throat, a hard intake of air that made her shoulders seize up to her ears, and she fainted, dropped backward into the shadows like a deer shot through the neck.

Right then the Guatemalan nurse let out a screech pure and true, a long, high scrape of animal sound.

Right then Unc flinched there in the seat in front of me, put both hands to the gunwales, and jerked toward the sound; Jessup flinched too, dropped his radio and turned back to the nurse, his arm up to the sound as though it were a fist coming down and him ready to block it.

The nurse put her hands to her ears, backed away and into the house, then turned and disappeared, still screaming.

Everything broken, just like that.

The Cuthberts knelt in the shadows where Mrs. Q had fallen. Jessup bent over and picked up his radio, spoke into it again. The nurse's scream broke into ragged shards somewhere inside the house, and Jessup went on in after her to try, I figured, to calm her down.

I let go the pole then, felt the lever of it lift in my hands like a slow seesaw until it stopped in the mud. I didn't care that Unc wanted me to hold the body up. Let it settle into pluff mud again, where somebody'd stashed it thinking it was gone forever, and where soon enough cops and the sheriff and even the game warden'd be out here to fish it right back up.

"Knew what it was when I touched it," Unc whispered. "Damn."

I'd seen bodies before. In fact, if you wanted to trace the picture that way, you could say it was the bodies I'd seen that got us here to this one.

I don't know how to get into it without getting into it, but some things happened back when I was fifteen and a sophomore in high school, things that involved Hungry Neck Hunt Club, 2200 acres of land down past Jacksonboro, a good forty miles down 17 from Charleston. The clientele for the club was and is and will evermore be the South of Broad lawyers and doctors you see on TV and read about in the paper for all their professional opinions and do-good parades. Most all of them fancy themselves hunters, too, part of the whole Bubba persona they cultivate, never mind they went to Duke and Yale and Harvard. Early Saturday mornings of deer season it's still me and Unc driving around in my Toyota Tundra—the Range Rover we drive in town and to poker night is Unc's—dropping them off in the woods at deer stands along the road. That's where they'll wait in their crisp clean camo outfits, guns at the ready, for some real men we hire—Doug Watkins and Oscar Porcher—to ride through on horseback, their dogs off in the woods and scaring up the deer from where they're sleeping, so that the good doctors and lawyers can blast away in hopes of landing a buck.

Unc owns the club, just a tract of land the family's had in its hands for going on a hundred years. Some of it trashland, good for nothing, some of it pretty, set on the Ashepoo. Live oak and pine, dogwood and palmetto and poison ivy and wild grapes and all else. Marsh grass down to the Ashepoo. That was about it.

Until somebody found, and tried to keep a secret, what amounted to a diamond mine down there: a tiny little island on the property that turned out to be a significant—and very illegally lucrative—historical treasure. I know this sounds like some NatGeo special or the History Channel or whatnot, but it's true. And that's when people started turning up dead on the property, Unc the one framed for it.

Long story short: this wasn't the first body I'd seen. Longer story even shorter: I killed one of the sons of bitches tried to make it seem Unc was a murderer. Shot the fucker dead the same second he shot me.

I've seen bodies.

But the problem with seeing them, and especially with the way I have, is that people want you to go to therapy for it, when all I'd wanted was to talk with Tabitha, my then-girlfriend and now Stanford postdoc. She'd been there with me when I shot that bastard. As had Unc, and Mom, and even Miss Dinah Galliard, Tabitha's mom. They all went on to deal with what'd happened in the predictable way, even Unc showing up for his shrink sessions twice a week the first few months.

But I wouldn't do it. I had my own way to handle what I'd done, and knew it would work. Even with that whole herd urging me to carry on to a paid stranger in some carpeted office about how killing a man made me *feel*, I wouldn't do it.

Instead, all I did the rest of high school was to spend every Saturday and Sunday I could out to Hungry Neck sitting in the cab of my beat-up '72 Chevy LUV pickup, alone or with Tabitha out on that land I'd loved so much my whole life. The land I'd grown up on before my parents split and my mom moved us to Marie Street in North Charleston and into the shadow of the Mark Clark Expressway.

Mom wanted me home. She loved me, longed for me to show up whole soon as I could, and tried to make it happen by cooking for me what I wanted, mowing for me what little lawn we had out back, letting me stay up late to play video games out in the front room of the house, where she'd look at me with long stares she thought I couldn't see out the corner of my eye. She made sure I knew when my appointments were with the shrink, left little Post-it notes on the bathroom mirror and on the fridge and on the steering wheel of the Chevy LUV. And when I blew them all off, she'd bitch at me for a minute or so, and I'd see her with her teeth clenched at me, her head shaking slow. And then she'd cry, and I knew what harm I was doing to her. I knew, because she loved me.

But Hungry Neck was where I did my therapy, me sitting in my truck and looking out onto the wide cold blue of the Ashepoo, and the spartina and cordgrass and salt-marsh hay, the all of it a green I couldn't name, mixed down in it reds and browns and a color like bone.

I got through it. I'm not going to lie: I could have done a better, maybe quicker job of it if I'd listened to everyone who had an opinion about how I was supposed to deal with killing someone. Eventually I stopped sitting bolt upright in my bed four and five nights a week to see the ceiling fan turning above me, me screaming about how it was a shovel coming down hard for my throat. I got over it.

But here it was again, all of it coming right back at me: another body. Me barking at people and angry for it, and this pressure in my chest and on it at the same time—what I had no choice but to understand was flat-out plain old cold and ugly fear. Fear here one more time, like a piece of shit I thought I'd scraped off the heel of my shoe, only to climb in the cab of my truck and still smell it, find the heel of the other covered with even more, and ground into the floorboard.

We waited. The nurse's shrieks had died down now, Jessup in there with her and probably talking to her. There was still no sign of ol' Dupont anywhere, and the thought occurred to me he might've gone on and had a heart attack and died himself, what with all that screaming going on inside his house.

And still no sign of Mom.

Mrs. Q had come out of her faint only a few seconds after she'd fallen, sat up with the help of both Cuthberts, her looking quick from one to the other like she'd never seen them before. Then she shivered, looked straight out at me standing here in the boat, and struggled up, stood. She didn't say a word as the Cuthberts touched her, talked to her, tried to coax her to let Priscilla walk her on back home—Grange wouldn't be leaving this adventure, no way—but it was obvious she wasn't budging, this violation of the sacred ground of Landgrave Hall so egregious, and Unc and me the agents of its debasement. She wasn't going anywhere.

And still we waited, no one talking at all out here, not Unc to me, or the Cuthberts to Mrs. Q or each other. The only sound was the creep of the tide on its way, filling in the marsh inch by inch with its quiet wet clicks and pops, the calm of it a kind of empty reverence suddenly upon us: here was a dead body, and here was the natural world without a pause over it.

Maybe Mom wouldn't even come out here, I was thinking. Maybe—lucky for her—this would be the night she'd finally given us up to ourselves, and the stupidity of Unc's big idea to learn how to golf.

Then, slowly, Unc took hold of the gunwales with both hands, sat up straight, and stood, all of it before I'd even heard the pop of a single pebble under the tires of whatever vehicle it was pulling up out front of the Dupont house. And now, even from here on the water, pushed off the edge of the world and out onto this finger creek, I could hear the crunch of gravel from the drive that Unc'd already taken in, the sound sudden and quiet, followed by the slam shut of one door, then another.

Unc turned from me to face the house, as though he'd be able to make out who it was coming up out of the dark, and I caught the jittered-up shards of a flashlight beam in the trees and on the ground, closer now and closer, until finally the Cuthberts turned and Mrs. Q too, stepped aside like a curtain parting, as though whatever first responders it was coming up on this all—Hanahan Police, County Sheriff, maybe even those Department of Natural Resources boys already—were the stars of some screwed-up game show.

But just before that flashlight beam made it around the corner of the house and blew full bore into my eyes—because that's what happened—Unc whispered, "I don't know who this is," the words astonished at themselves, pinned down by the surprise of what he didn't know, and whoever it was coming in.

Because he always knew what was going on. He knew. He'd know from the crunch of the gravel the sort of cruiser it was out there, whether it was one of those Dodge Chargers the Hanahan police drove or the heavy Crown Vics the sheriff's office still used or the big Chevy Silverado pickups the DNR tooled around in. And if not from the sound of the tires on gravel, then he'd know from the slam shut of those doors exactly who it was.

But not this time.

The flashlight beam busted into my eyes, and I put a hand up. I should've known better than to be looking right where they'd have to be.

"Command Master Chief Petty Officer Stanhope" boomed out deep from behind the light. "Master-at-arms, U.S. Navy."

"You got to be kidding me," Unc let out hard. He didn't move there in the front of the boat, the flashlight beam no challenge to him. "The Shore Patrol?"

"Master-at-arms, sir," the voice boomed out again, the last word a broad and flat *ahhhms:* he wasn't from around here. "I am placing you under arrest. Do not move."

I took my hand down, squinted toward the voice, and the flashlight beam fell away.

There were two of them, moving toward us: the one with the flashlight, his other hand at the holster on his hip; beside him a man holding what looked from here for all the world like an M4, the short barrel pointed down, the butt against his biceps. The one with the flashlight—Stanhope—was white, the other one black, and they were both big, over six foot, both in digital camo BDUs and billed caps. But the fatigues weren't that desert brown and beige, I could see in the porch light. From here they looked almost blue and black and gray.

They stopped, the flashlight down, Stanhope's hand still at his hip, the M4 down but ready. They'd passed the Cuthberts and Mrs. Q, the three of them backed away and against the low brick fence, their eyes open wide. Mrs. Q had a hand at her throat holding tight the neck of her sweater, Grange Cuthbert with his hands at his sides, Priscilla leaning into him.

What the hell was a *master-at-arms*?

"On what charge?" Unc said, and I could hear the steel in his jaw, the set of his teeth and bright tough edge of his voice that signaled this was a load of shit he wasn't about to be putting up with, and who ever was shoveling it was about to get his ass kicked. It was a sound I'd heard only a few times—one of which was when we were about to be killed out on an island at Hungry Neck, just before it was me who'd done the killing—and I wondered for an instant if either of these two sailors had a clue what they were up against.

But they had the guns, and they were the Navy. And of course I knew what this was about: two infrared illuminators on us from across the marsh. At the Naval Weapons Station.

"Leland Osborne Dillard and Huger Simpson Dillard, you were observed trespassing on property owned by the United States Navy. You have the right to remain silent. Anything you say can and—"

"What in the hell!" Unc roared out. "We got the body of a dead girl here in this godforsaken muck and you come over here and treat us like we're a couple terrorists just busted out the Navy brig—"

"Trespassing?" I said out loud, me too stunned at the all of this—how'd they know who we were, us a half mile away across marsh when they'd seen us, and us in the backyard of someone else's house?—to even understand what he was talking about. All I'd done was see them over there in the tract, me with my own night-vision goggles on. How was that trespassing?

"If you want these—" I started, and bent down, reached for the book bag at my feet. If it was the goggles they were after—these things some commander had sweated over losing at poker, and that nobody anywhere was supposed to have, goggles valuable enough and unlawful enough to dispatch sailors with guns to get them back—then they could have them, because there was a body here, a dead woman who needed to get out of here and be taken wherever she was going to be taken.

It was the woman I was thinking of. Just give them the goggles and maybe they'd let go this stupid idea that even looking over there was trespassing.

I bent to the bag, but before I'd even touched it or started in to finish my sentence—*then take the damned things!*—I heard "Freeze!" boom out even deeper.

I looked up, saw Stanhope with his gun out of the holster and on me, that M4 barrel staring right at me, the second sailor's head cocked to the sight on it.

"Ahms up, hands behind your head," Stanhope said. "Both of you. You have the right to remain silent. Anything you say can and will be held against you. You have the right to an attorney—"

And heard from behind me, out on the creek and just a few yards off, a voice: "Major Tyler, Department of Natural Resources here. Y'all need to calm down a little bit."

The words were even and solid, a deep surprise inside all this surprise of trespassing and guns drawn, and before I could turn around two things happened at once: first came a sudden and huge sweep of bright light—the searchlight this Major Tyler must've had on his boat—across the back of a white stucco cottage, and across camo BDUs of sailors with their guns up, and across Grange and Priscilla Cuthbert kneeling now to the once-more-fainted Mrs. Q, the whole crew squinting for that light; and next came the cold hard ratchet of a shotgun pumped: Major Tyler geared up and ready to go.

"Let's all of us," the major said, his words somehow even calmer now, "just put our toys away and square up what's going on here."

"Snuck up on me, Alton," Unc said, him turned back toward me but still standing, Tyler's flood full on his face and those sunglasses. "You DNR boys going to have fun with this one."

"What's this I heard about a body?" the major said, and I made to turn and see who this man was Unc seemed to know, and how he'd pulled in so quiet even Unc hadn't caught it. Of course he'd have switched to an electric outboard before he ever entered the creek for how shallow it was, but he had to be crowded in for how narrow it was back here.

But before I even made it around to him, I saw her.

She was right here next to our boat, a pale gray sheen just beneath the surface, like some ghost moored beside us. The pluff mud we'd roiled up had settled for how long we'd been waiting, the water between her and the surface clear, the mud on her washed away even more, her lit like all the rest of us with the floodlight from this DNR boat behind us.

I could see the cleft between her legs, and her breasts. I could see those two points of her shoulders, her arms and legs anchored, fading off beneath her.

And I could see now her face, unaided by the goggles: a grimace of teeth, raw pink flesh, the smeared place where her eyes should have been. All of it only a couple inches beneath the surface.

From somewhere off to my left and a thousand miles away, Stanhope called out "Stand down!" like he was on the bow of a battleship, the whole U.S. Navy waiting for word only from him. Somewhere to my right and just as far away I heard Major Alton Tyler break open the shotgun, then the smallest scratch of sound: him drawing out the two shells in the barrel.

Then, like a further curse on whoever this woman had been, here came up her shoulder and onto her neck a big blue crab, right there under the water. It paused a moment just below her chin before it reached a tentative claw up, delicately snipped at the ragged flesh of her jaw, and snipped again.

"Well now," the major said off to my left, the words quiet. "Well, well, well."

I closed my eyes, sat down on the seat here at the transom of the jon boat. Then the push pole, still leaned against the gunwale, gave way, and I heard it slide slowly down the length of the boat, drop into the water.

And for a moment I wished somehow I could be just like Unc: blind, disburdened of the visible world.

4

Major Tyler got on his radio, and I heard that solid voice call in an officer in boat, another in vehicle. He paused, then told the dispatcher to get hold of the dive team.

The single word "Rescue?" cracked out of the speaker.

He was quiet a second, said, "No. Recovery."

I still had my eyes closed.

"We're here on a trespassing charge," Stanhope called out. "If there's a body involved, we need to get my commanding officer to—"

"Your jurisdiction as regards civilians not on U.S. Navy property don't even exist, comrade," Tyler said. I heard him step forward on his boat, move toward us, felt the smallest rock of the jon boat for that movement in his own.

"Well put, Alton!" Unc said loud, on the words a kind of tight glee. "And we wasn't over on the base. Period."

"You were observed," Stanhope started up, and Unc cut in, "We never set foot—"

And in the midst of the bitchfest the two of them started up, I heard suddenly down closer than I'd imagined he might be, me still here at the transom and still with my eyes closed, Tyler's voice yet again, quiet and calm: "Huger, you going to be all right. But you need to move so I can help."

I'd never met him before. I'd seen these Department of Natural Resources men out on the water most all my life, one time got written up out on the Combahee, the river edge of Hungry Neck, for having no life jacket in the old jon boat I used to mess around in down there, another time stopped in the channel back behind Capers Island by some overweight geezer in a nineteen-foot Action Craft flats boat complete with a ten-foot tower rigged with all the radar you could want, only to check my fishing license.

I didn't know this Major Alton Tyler. And Unc'd never mentioned him.

Yet I believed him, right then, enough to open my eyes, to see what next I had to do here, and I turned, looked up at him.

He was squatted there at the bow of his Boston Whaler, the boats most all the DNR drove, its hull almost overhanging the stern of the jon boat. He'd worked some kind of magic getting it in here, the hull pressed into the cordgrass all around, and Unc not hearing or feeling a thing. The searchlight, mounted back at the steering console, made him a silhouette to me, and I could see he had on the ball cap they all wore, and the holster at his hip, the pistol there. He had his elbows on his knees, but beyond that I couldn't see his face for the light behind him, and for a second I thought of Unc against the night sky before all this had come down, the stars scattered behind him, before us nothing but the dumb idea of golf.

"Let's go," Tyler said, and reached down, touched my shoulder.

And as though I had no choice but to believe him, I stood up and moved past Unc in the boat, knelt at the bow, pulled on that ratty nylon rope tied to the cinder block onshore until the boat hit bottom. Unc'd stood tall the whole time, still carrying on with Stanhope— "You come on out to private civilian property," Unc was yelling, "and try and pass it off like it's military business, so let's just see what the courts have to say," while Stanhope seethed out, "If you continue to disregard our authority, I will have no choice but to further charge you with resisting arrest"—and I hauled out that plank yet again, dropped it and walked back on across, then moved right past Stanhope and his silent partner.

Stanhope turned from Unc then, said to me as I passed, "You will not leave the premises, Mr. Dillard, until my commanding officer notifies me of the status of our situation."

But I just moved on up the lawn at the back of the Dupont house and onto their patio. I pulled one of the wrought-iron chairs from the wrought-iron table, scraped it across the brick pavers out here loud as I could, and sat down, my back to the house so I could watch it all.

Unc and Stanhope kept on over who was where when, never a word out of either about any night-vision goggles anybody'd seen, nor about this body. Eventually Unc strode on across the plank without so much as a wobble, came in close to Stanhope, the bills of their caps almost touching while they still yelled, and I knew Stanhope had no idea Unc was blind for how the two kept right on. Still nothing came out of the black sailor with Stanhope, the M4 down, trigger hand flat against the stock, his head turning now and again to scan the grounds.

Once in a while he looked at me, held his eyes on me long enough to let me know he was watching.

Mrs. Q came around again, and once she'd made clear to the Cuthberts she wasn't going home, they ushered her over to the table, sat her in one of the chairs. Priscilla in her jogging suit and snarled hair hovered around her as though she might take the old lady's pulse any second to see if she was still alive, while Mrs. Q sat stone still, hands locked in her lap, eyes out to the creek and the logjam of a jon boat and a Boston Whaler.

"The idea," the old bag whispered right there next to me, unable even to look at me for how close I was and the mange she must've figured she'd get if she were even to glimpse my way. "The idea," she whispered, "the idea."

Grange Cuthbert took a seat across from me at the table, flipped the chair around so his back was to me, him just watching and shaking his head now and again. "A body," he said once. "What in the hell is a body doing out here?"

It was then Jessup stepped into my line of sight on my right, his back to me too as he made his way across the patio and the ten yards or so down the lawn to Stanhope and Unc and the other sailor.

I'd forgotten about him for the big stinky pile of all this going down out here, forgotten for these few minutes about him going into Judge Dupont's house to get that screaming nurse to quiet down, and I glanced behind me to the French doors to see if she was back out here, maybe cooled enough now to watch.

But just as I turned, I saw over my shoulder the door close from inside, heard the slide of a dead bolt into place.

Didn't matter if she thought she could lock herself away from a dead body, I thought, and turned back to face the melee. The authorities'd get hold of her soon enough. She'd end up questioned, just like the rest of us.

Jessup stopped next to the sailor with the M4. They looked at each other, nodded. Jessup put his hands on his hips, then crossed his arms, like he was waiting his turn. The sailor didn't say anything to him, didn't ask for his name or what he wanted. He only gave him that nod, then went back to scanning, hand still flat on the stock of his gun.

And though he had to be able to see Jessup maybe a couple feet away from him, Stanhope, still toe to toe with Unc, didn't move his eyes from Unc for a second. It was like Jessup wasn't even there, this man dressed in a black windbreaker and cap and pants who'd come from inside the house everything was all happening at.

Maybe they knew him, I thought. Or maybe they'd spotted him for being security: he still had his two-way in one hand.

And beyond them, still a silhouette for the searchlight, was Tyler, tending to the only thing really mattered out here: the body. He was kneeling way up on the hull and leaning over the edge, a big Maglite LED in his hand and pointed down to the water, its beam sharp as a Star Wars lightsaber. Slowly he moved it back and forth, looking at the woman. Now and again he put his radio up to his mouth, said something I couldn't hear.

Then here was the Hanahan police, two dudes who looked no older than me coming like the rest of the world around the side of the house and into the light from that flood on Tyler's boat. They had on their black wool sweaters, badges on their chests, hands on their holsters, and sort of nodded at us here at the table as they made their way down to Unc and Stanhope and the sailor, Jessup still without a word.

"Mr. Dillard," they both said at the same time, the words solemn and quick. Unc turned his head to them, let out "Boys," and nodded, then went on again with Stanhope, and maybe a few seconds later here came around the side of the house a deputy from the sheriff's office, brown windbreaker and Smokey Bear hat on. "Leland," he called out, then, quieter, said, "Poston, Danford," to the two cops, and stepped up to the congregation.

That was when Stanhope broke, let his head drop so that he was looking at Unc's chest. But even in the shadows and light out here I could see the way his jaw was working, the set of it. He wasn't done.

"Harmon," he said, and the black sailor shot out "Sir" and turned to him, the word and move so quick it seemed like bad acting, a bit player jumping his lines.

Unc hadn't moved, his face still to where Stanhope's had been, and I could see the smallest smile on him: he'd won this round.

Stanhope looked up at Harmon beside him, nodded hard to his left and away from the crowd, and the two moved a couple yards away toward the woods.

Unc looked over here at the house. He moved his head a little side to side, like he was scanning the place same as Harmon had, then called out loud, "Huger?"

I let him look for me a couple seconds more before I said, "Here."

He lasered in on exactly where I sat, those sunglasses right on me. He looked at me a long moment while the cops and deputy and Jessup—everyone down there but the sailors—turned to me.

"You get us your thermos out that book bag of yours and pour us each a cup of that glorious instant coffee. This is going to take a while." He nodded, held his look on me.

But I hadn't brought the bag with me from the jon boat, had left it there when I'd stood and walked away. "Left it on the boat," I called out.

He pursed his lips, turned to the creek, then looked right back at me. "Sure would like a cup," he said.

And it came to me, what Unc was trying to tell me: he wanted me to have hold of those goggles, no matter what.

I sat there a few seconds, the all of them—even Mrs. Q had turned to me by then—looking at me, waiting, like a cup of coffee out of a thermos was the only next thing could happen on the face of the earth. But Unc and I knew this wasn't anything at all about coffee. It was about those stupid goggles, and nothing else. Unc'd found a body, but it sure seemed he was only worked up about being spotted with the goggles. All we had to do was to name Commander Prendergast, the fellow poker night chump Unc'd won them off of, hand them off to Stanhope, and the whole thing'd be over.

But Unc wasn't going there. And the problem was I couldn't tell why.

"Huger?" he said, and I could see now, over at the tree line past

Unc and his brood of lawmen, Stanhope and the black sailor, Harmon, looking at me too.

I wanted to let Unc twist out there on his own right now, for whatever reason it was I had of my own. Maybe it was because I didn't want to get up and walk all the way back down there and back across that plank again, and risk seeing one more time that body. Or maybe it was because I'd wanted to just give the damned goggles up when they'd first got here, because of what they'd made me see for Unc, me as always his eyes: the woman's face torn up, the pale green of her flesh buoyed by the pole beneath her.

Maybe I wanted to have my own life, to live on my own and not have to ferry Unc through his days, me his chauffeur and caddy and coffee bearer and eyes every day I was alive.

Or maybe—and I knew this was it, finally—maybe it was because it didn't seem like Unc gave a shit about this body, some woman who'd been killed and left in the marsh. Maybe what made me sit there a few seconds without answering him was because of that glee he seemed to be deriving at having beat Stanhope this round. While behind him down in the water was a body.

"Here you go" came from behind him, and I sat up quick, saw making his way across the plank from the jon boat Major Tyler, holding out in front of him my book bag, and already I was up and around the wrought-iron table and jogging the few yards down the lawn toward him, and then I stood among them all, these Hanahan police and the deputy and Unc, and Tyler.

He was taller than I'd thought, maybe six four or five, and I could see his face now for Dupont's back porch light: he was a little jowly, had heavy eyebrows and a thick neck. Football, was the first thing came to me. He'd had to play somewhere when he was in college.

He nodded, gave a smile that was all business, my bag held out in his hand like some kid's toy for how big he was.

I took the book bag, slung it quick over a shoulder. I nodded, said,

"Thank you," and wondered for a second why I'd never heard from Unc any mention of an Alton Tyler with the DNR.

Here was Unc with a hand at my elbow, leading me off and back toward the patio. "Thank you so much, Alton," he said over his shoulder, then, a little too loud and meant, I could hear, for nothing more than show, "This coffee's sure gonna do me good."

And off to our right, at the edge of the woods, stood Stanhope and Harmon. I looked straight at them, too, saw their eyes were right on me, their mouths thin lines.

Harmon, his hand still flat on the stock of his M4, looked right at the book bag, and back up to me. He nodded.

I set the bag on the table once we'd gotten to the porch, opened it, careful not to let Grange or Mrs. Q or Priscilla see inside. There lay the goggles, and that construction helmet, at the bottom the old thermos and the travel mugs, and I pulled one out and the thermos, poured off a full cup for Unc, set the bag at my feet.

Unc made a big show of sipping at it, all for those two sailors watching every move over there. He wouldn't sit down, though Grange had stood up when we'd gotten here and offered his seat. I'd offered him mine, too, but he'd have none of it, while Mrs. Q sat beside us whispering loud "The idea, the idea."

By this time Priscilla'd given up trying to monitor the old lady, and stood beside Grange, all of us facing the creek while here came more neighbors: first the Bennetts, then the Moores, the Michauxs, the Balls, the Legares. The usual suspects, all of them anchored to Landgrave Hall for as long as the place had been here, each with portraits aplenty of dead ancestors inside the hallowed halls of their cottages, each with their own dedicated tables at the clubhouse. I knew already the front of the Dupont house was clogged with the golf carts they'd all driven over here, all of them talking low to each other now, shaking their heads, arms crossed, now and again nodding toward us here at the table, watching.

Tyler took first the deputy out onto the plank and across our boat onto his, shone that Maglite down into the water, the two of them talking, the beam darting back and forth. Then the deputy left, the two Hanahan cops moving out next to have their own peep show.

A minute or so later the EMTs came bumping up amidst all the neighbors, a gurney pushed and pulled and lifted and prodded by a man and a woman in white shirts and dark pants and latex gloves already on. The two of them labored to get the gurney close as they could to the water, no way for the truck itself to back in here. On the gurney was stacked their equipment, what looked all the world like a pile of tackle boxes.

Another shuffle and twist of the neighbors, and here now were two men and a woman coming out into this all, the three of them in wet suits and with a black duffel bag each, scuba tanks on their backs. They headed right down to the water, stepped across the plank one at a time—the Hanahan cops'd come back on ground when the EMTs showed up—and then were out there with Tyler.

That was when I left.

I leaned over, picked up the book bag with one hand, and sort of took a side step away from Unc and Grange and the table. I looked one last time at the whole circus going on out here, at the dozen or so people standing in their bathrobes and whatnot all watching, and at these lawmen with their hands on their hips, and at Stanhope and Harmon too, who'd been caught up like the rest of everyone else by the ghoul-work coming up next, and at the boats jammed in here, and at Tyler back on the bow of his, the only man out here, it seemed, who'd had the kind of bearing and calm the finding of a dead body called for.

I meant to go around the house on the other side. I meant to keep from having to say word one to anybody. Pretty soon SLED would show up and the whole South Carolina Law Enforcement Division investigation would start in earnest, not just the retrieval of a crab-picked body out of pluff mud. They'd find me. They'd come over to the house, knock on the door, and start asking away the predictable questions—Why were you out here? How did you find it?—with a bonus question thrown in for good measure: Why did you leave the scene?

And none of this—none of it—would be over for who knew how long.

I sure didn't know, because, I understood as I looked at them all, I still wasn't over the last bodies I'd seen. Though I'd told myself I was, managed enough times to convince myself that the all of that was over, I knew, with this girl coming up from the dark into that green porthole of sight, that here it all was again. My life and what I'd seen and done only as far away as the thin skim of muddy water that'd kept her hidden until Unc levered her up.

I turned then, safe, I figured, and already on my way home, though Mom was probably up and sitting with a cup of coffee, fuming at why her son and his father couldn't just play golf in daylight like the rest of the whole stupid world.

And there, inside the French door window, was that Guatemalan nurse. She had a handful of curtain pulled back, her face nearly pressed to the glass, her black hair tight into a ponytail or bun, I couldn't tell which.

Our eyes met a second, just long enough for me to pause, to take in the fact she was there and looking at me, before she let go the curtain, disappeared.

But the moment between us lasted just long enough for my momentum to shift for that pause, my feet already moving, and I bumped the smallest way into the wrought-iron table.

Not a second later here was a hand on my shoulder: Unc.

I turned to him, had no choice. But he only looked at me, those sunglasses lasered in yet again.

"Go on," he whispered. "Hide the goggles. Tell your momma we'll all be all right."

I took a breath, nodded, though he had no way to see.

But he knew.

5

The strobe on the orange and white EMS truck shredded the front of the Dupont house into bright red pieces, the clot of golf carts and the cops' Charger and deputy's Crown Vic all quivering in the pulse. Up closest to the house was a black Suburban, no doubt what the sailors had arrived first on the scene in; behind the EMS was parked another truck, a huge and dark Silverado, on its door, I could see from here, the bold white letters *DNR*, above it the round logo: the search and rescue truck.

I hung back in the shadows on this side of the house, watched for more neighbors rolling up, saw none. And of course as I stepped out, started across the yard, here came the headlights of another vehicle pulling into the drive, and I ducked down into a wax myrtle at the edge of the grass, made myself small as I could.

Yet another Silverado, those letters and logo again. The DNR agent Tyler'd called in.

He edged up to the bumper of the Crown Vic, and the dome light in the cab came on. Then I heard the door slam shut, the cab dark again, and saw somebody moving off quick to the hubbub ahead.

I ran across the lawn and the gravel drive, headed right on up and past the tee box, the camp chair I'd been sitting in still parked there. I slowed down, turned and sort of jogged backward a few steps, looked at the chair and the lights and carts and vehicles all beyond it: a circus, the center ring a body.

I let out a hard breath, edged up on it something like a cry for how sharp had been in me that feeling in my chest, the pressing down and pushing out. Not long ago I'd been sitting in that chair, watching golf balls go places I wouldn't go, being pissy about Unc and his life now, pondering the architecture at Stanford. And thinking about Tabitha.

But that was then.

I turned, headed for the dark line of trees past those kidney bunkers and the thirteenth green I could barely see up ahead for how dark it was. Those trees, the avenue of live oak leading to the original plantation house—planted by Landgrave Elliot himself in 1679—bordered the eleventh fairway. From there I'd have to walk that hole's length, then cross the tenth, make it past the clubhouse without setting off the motion sensor on the floodlights all over it, next head on through the ninth and eighth, careful all the while to steer clear of the couple dozen houses sprinkled everywhere out here. Then I'd be at the seventh, where at the far end, just off the left-hand side of the green and looking out on Goose Creek toward the Cooper River, was our cottage.

Our home. Or at least where we wrong elements—my mom, Unc, and me—all lived.

More days than I care to count I miss the old house on Marie, back before we ever lived here, and even farther back, even before all of what'd happened out to Hungry Neck so long ago. Too many times since Unc, Mom, and I had gotten here I was sorry I wasn't a kid anymore and hanging out with my old high school cohorts Matt and Jessup and Rafael, LaKeisha and Polly and Deevonne, us there on the tracks beside the Mark Clark high up on its concrete pilings, enjoying ourselves for no better reason than parking our butts on the railroad tracks. We'd sit and pass around Colt 45s and talk about teachers and who we liked and didn't, about grades and how we didn't care or did, about what shits other people were, ourselves included. We were black and white, stupid and smart, good grades and bad grades. We were just us.

But the idiot thing was that back then I couldn't wait to get out of there, that house where it was just my mom and me living, counting out the days until whatever would come of our lives would come.

Back when I thought Unc was my uncle, raised my whole life to call him Unc and to think of him that way and that way only, what I'd always thought my real daddy a man who ran off after Unc had been nearly killed in the fire.

Mom and Dad had lived out there in the trailer when I was little, Dad the one to run the hunt club, and when Unc's house burned down in Mount Pleasant, Mom and Dad had no choice but to take him in, to nurse him back. And where Dad would have to face, as I wouldn't find out until I was fifteen, the fact of what Unc and Mom had done, the news of my real patronage nothing my dad hadn't known. But which he'd chosen to ignore, until, finally, he'd taken off one morning, and all that'd been left was Unc, and Mom, and me.

Unc: that was his name until I was fifteen and found out he was my father, and the name I'd be using for the rest of my life. Trying to call him Dad or Pop or anything remotely close to those sounded wrong. Because he was and always will be Unc. Plain and simple.

And though it might seem logical that once the divorce was over, me just a kid still and wondering why my dad had left, that Mom and Unc would hook up, they never married, and never carried on anything between them, either. Unc'd loved his dead wife, Sarah, just too much, and Mom'd put too many years into trying to make up to my dad for the mistake she'd made with Unc—a mistake that'd resulted with me.

But she never made me feel as such my whole life long. Sure, she was the first one to give me hell for sneaking in and out of my bedroom window at night, and the first one to sit me down to study harder if my grades even fell a hair below straight A's. But she loved me, and I always knew it. Always.

Not but six months after Unc'd healed from the burns that blinded him, Mom moved the two of us to North Charleston, to the house on Marie. She went to Trident Tech and became an LPN, later on an RN. We set up our lives there, and I started in to meeting the friends I did, and discovering the tracks at the end of the street and the fine diversion they could be from the life I was living.

We had a house she was providing us with, and we had food on the table. Each afternoon she wasn't on shift at the hospital, she met me at the foot of our oil-stained driveway, me fresh off the block-and-a-half walk from the bus stop, and despite how embarrassed I might have been for fear of someone seeing us, she'd hug me hard, and ask after my day, walk me into the house. Every time.

Yet all I'd wanted was to live out to Hungry Neck, and Hungry Neck only. Unc had stayed out there in that trailer, and'd taken over running the hunt club despite his being blind. With the help of Miss Dinah Galliard, the woman who, with her daughter, Tabitha, cooked for the members of the club each Saturday hunt, the whole operation worked just fine.

Because Unc knew the land, knew it better even, I came to understand, than my dad had: he knew by smell how far off the creeks we were, knew by where I pointed his arm out toward a star at night where we were too. He knew where the two-track roads went to muck when the highest tides were in, and knew by the tick the tide made on its way out how far to throw a cast net for mullet. He knew, and knew.

Mom and I went out there every weekend those first few years—we were a family of sorts, after all—and then, once I'd gotten my learner's permit, it was nothing for her to let me drive out there alone and tend to him, and to help with the tract out there, the blue bloods who showed up in the fall for deer hunting season, and turkey in the spring.

Through it all, I came to think back then that the only home I wanted was that trailer, the single-wide Unc seemed to fill one end to the other with his just being Unc, and the spotless way he kept the place, the shag carpet always fresh vacuumed, and the orange and brown plaid foldout sofa—my bed—it was my job to have made and put away by 6:30 A.M. no matter what day of the week it was. Back then home had also been Miss Dinah Galliard and Tabitha's place, the house the two of them lived in only a couple miles away from Unc, a half-trailer, half-shanty concoction painted haint purple, the inside stacked with more books per square inch of living space than I've ever seen, Miss Dinah homeschooling Tabitha from day one.

Home had been Hungry Neck itself and that land I thought I'd worked out my self-inflicted therapy on, and home'd been the long low white dining cabin we called the clubhouse out there, with its screened windows and picnic tables jammed with those lawyers and doctors on Saturday morning hunts, at one end of the room an old iron stove where Miss Dinah and Tabitha cooked up the best grits and bacon and eggs and biscuits and fried chicken in the world.

But if I were a smarter person back then I would've seen my home, just as much as all of Hungry Neck, had been that house on Marie, and my mom inside it, trying to make a life for the two of us in North Charleston, and I would have understood that even those railroad tracks at the end of the street, that place where we kids gathered and did nothing but look at the steam off the stack of the paper mill, was home.

The same stack you could see from the fifteenth hole here at Landgrave Hall.

Tabitha gave up on me our senior year of high school. Of course I'd like to blame it on the whole thing about her being black and me being white, that stupid star-cross'd Montagues and Capulets business. Or I'd like to blame it on what seemed the remnants of the whole master-slave thing: Unc the landowner, her mom the cook.

Sometimes I'd even like to blame it on what might've seemed to anyone else the biggest dog on the porch between us: the fact Tabitha was deaf and dumb, though political correctness would have me call her simply hard of hearing, because—believe me—she can use those vocal cords when she wants to. But the whole hearing thing was never a problem between us. Ever.

She was smart. And beautiful.

Turns out it was me with the handicap. Me the one who was impaired, my pride—the same sort that made Unc golf at night—like some congenital defect lodged deep in me that kept me from seeing clearly, and from walking upright, and from listening to sense. It was my brain that was the biggest problem between us, and whether or not I'd ever see my way to using the one I'd been given to figure out I needed to deal the right way with the what-all shit I'd seen. Those bodies. And the man I'd killed, the one I'd made into nothing more than yet another of those bodies.

I thought I got over it.

She went on up to Duke, me to my glorious tenure in Chapel Hill. Though she'd been homeschooled, Tabitha'd accrued so many AP credits she was up near being a junior when she walked in the door. Her first semester she was in upper-division courses with names like Topics in Data Compression, Computational Linguistics, Numeric Artificial Intelligence.

Me? I was busy racking up D's in English, Spanish, Karate, and

Intro to Computer Programming, laying the solid foundation of getting my ass kicked out.

By then, too, she'd met up there the son of the owner of that monstrosity of an orange house in Mount Pleasant, where Unc plays poker every Thursday night. Thomas Warchester Whaley the Fifth. Five, for short. They ended up lab partners in—what else?—some computer course, and last I saw on Facebook was that they were both "in a relationship." Hence the bit of history I have with ol' Five. Why I sit in the Range Rover figuring routes to Palo Alto on my Maps app instead of hanging around inside his dad's ugly manse on Thursday nights while Unc loses or wins at Texas hold 'em.

And then, my second year to college, the *next* shit started, the tricky shit it seems I'll never get scraped off the bottom of my shoe for the way it's led me to here, and enjoying the life of luxury, replete now with yet another dead body:

Unc sold off a 130-acre chunk of Hungry Neck to developers, the parcel a wide swath of land that butted up against that precious island where all that booty had been discovered, and the access corridor through the woods to get out there. All because Charleston County was gearing up to lay claim to it by eminent domain due to the "historical magnitude" of who and what had been buried out there three hundred years before: the Mothers and Fathers, the first slaves to land in Charleston.

Talk was big about turning the tract into some kind of Williamsburg, Virginia, but different. This place wouldn't celebrate the whites who'd owned the land but the blacks who'd worked it—those original slaves who dug the dikes and culverts and races for the rice plantations by hand, landmarks you can still see easy as day just driving down 17 and across any of the causeways you will. Next came the condos and a small "towne centre" outdoor mall—what the developers'd really wanted to put in there all along. Condos and shops, they figured, was the only way to get anyone that far into the woods to visit a burial site. The world, they decided, needed one more retail and residential zone.

Then, finally, the real estate bubble popped like a bathtub fart.

Three-fourths of everything had been built when it all went bust four years back, scattered now through that tract of woods like bones picked clean four dozen three-story condos and that mall. Tar paper on roofs stripping off piece by piece every time a storm comes through. Faded green Tyvek peeling away like dead skin. The whole thing shut down. Nothing but a chain-link fence surrounding the Mothers and Fathers.

And Unc, and Mom, and me all left holding bags of money. Because Unc had gotten ours when the getting was good, sold that tract two years before Freddie Mac and Fannie Mae and the whole banking world marched straight into hell.

Suddenly we'd gotten rich, and since then the closest I came to anybody from those days up on the tracks was Jessup Horry, who I see—other than nights like these when he escorts us off the course and into the jon boat—when he happens to be on shift and I'm pulling up to the gatehouse on my way in from wherever I've toted Unc. He leans out the little white-brick building, gives a wave and smile, opens the iron gates for us. If the weather is nice I'll have the window down and say hey. But if we have the air-conditioning on, pretty much nine months out of the year, or the month or so when we have on the heater, I never even bother to roll down the window, only nod, smile, and drive on through.

That's the kind of friend I ended up being to Jessup, even though I miss so much those olden days of high school: I couldn't be bothered enough to lose a moment of either cool air or warm for him.

I made it to the avenue of oaks, crossed the gravel street—they were all gravel out here, nothing paved—and started down the right-hand side, parallel to the eleventh fairway. From here the live oaks stood in two columns ten yards apart and stretched a half mile ahead, all the way to where the plantation house had once stood. In this dark the trees made a black and heavy canopy over the road, hanging everywhere in it hanks of Spanish moss like the gray beards of men long dead.

Landgrave Hall is one of the original Lowcountry plantations, a thumb-shaped piece of land that juts north out into marsh, Goose Creek snaking along its outline, the parcel a mile wide and a mile and a half long. It'd already been around for twenty years when the Yemassee War started in 1715, Landgrave Elliot's son, Thomas, putting together a militia in the front yard of the house, then riding right along this avenue on his way out to fight the Cherokee and Yemassee busy massacring every settler they could. Both Francis Marion, the Swamp Fox, and his mortal enemy Banastre Tarleton had stalked each other through here during the Revolution, and George Washington rode this gravel track in 1791, when he'd made his southern tour, had lunch with Thomas's grandson Charles Prioleau Elliot, then spent a couple hours touring the grounds. P.G.T. Beauregard, not but a week before he gave the go-ahead to fire on Fort Sumter, attended a ball in the house that had been at the end of this road, and four years later the same P.G.T. Beauregard, once he'd given the order to evacuate Charleston before the Union troops arrived, sat in its parlor and cried like a little girl at losing the city.

It was fire that finally took the old house down in 1892, an ironic fluke that usually made me smile for how it happened: former slave George Murray, a customs inspector down in Charleston, was running to represent the district in the U.S. Congress, and there'd been a rally against the whole idea of a black man doing so, right here at Landgrave Hall, all under the direction of Henry Manigault Elliot, then the descendant in residence. It'd been a get-together that featured a cross twenty feet high burning away in the ellipse garden behind the house, there on the bluff that overlooked Goose Creek, meant to send a signal to every black in the district what a vote for Murray might mean.

And a rebel ember caught a whiff of wind, wandered inside an open window of the place to land at the foot of the curtains of an upstairs bedroom. In a glorious conflagration that lasted all of an hour, the plantation house was swallowed whole, nothing left of it but two charred chimneys, a brick foundation, and a rubble of slate shingles.

George Murray won the election. Henry Manigault Elliot, penniless for thirty years afterward, sold the empty tract in 1922 to an assemblage of blue bloods with the revolutionary idea of a gated private community with a golf course.

But thinking on that didn't make me smile at all tonight, and I only walked along the avenue, looked up in those trees. I was breathing easier now, though there was still a body not far from here, yet more history being poured out on these grounds that'd known so much of it. And there'd be even more history to come soon enough, though of a more private sort: I'd have to hide the goggles and face the wrath of Mom. I'd have to tell her why I was coming in the front door and not in from the dock off the back, and why I was alone and not with Unc.

I hunched my shoulders in close, looked down from those dead men's beards to the road, cut between two live oaks on my right, crossed in front of the tee box of the eleventh.

Coming out from beneath that canopy, I could see the sky again, the all of it caught in a kind of bowl, the rim of it the black trees that bordered this fairway. There were places like this out to Hungry Neck, clearings in the woods where the ground lay too low for pine to grow up, and sometimes back when I was working out what I thought I'd worked out I'd take nighttime walks deep into the forest, and I'd come on these sorts of places, and look up at that sky above me, endless and filled with stars.

But out here the sky was made up of only those thin stars I'd been able to see out on the water, that wash of them behind and above Unc. Sure, there'd been a half-moon out earlier, gone beneath the tree line now, but around here even on a moonless night I was lucky to find Orion for the pale film of light that filled the sky.

There were the lights off the paper mill to blame, of course, and the freeway lamps that ran all along the Mark Clark, and the lights at the port terminal sitting on the Cooper River, where all those container trucks on the freeway were always headed, and heaped onto that just the general blast of light the whole of Charleston gave off.

But the worst of it was from the stadium-like lights a hundred feet above the Navy brig, not a half mile south of this piece of land. Where supposedly they keep those terrorists Unc was hollering about us being treated like when Harmon and Stanhope pointed their guns at us.

At the bottom edge of the thumb Landgrave Hall sits on, there runs an eight-foot chain-link fence, three strands of barbed wire above it. Just the other side of it starts yet more Navy property, our gated golf community of cottages sandwiched between the Weapons Station land across Goose Creek to the north and that Navy land to the south. In winter, when you're on the green at sixteen or the tee at seventeen, you can see through the trees that fence, just beyond it Perimeter Road, the paved single-lane that encircles their whole property.

The only way I can figure these posh old houses and this golf course are even here and not a part of Navy land is because the money got here first. The Naval Shipyard, a couple miles south of here on the Cooper River in North Charleston, started up under Teddy Roosevelt, and as the Yard grew north and south along the river, bits of property were bought up and built on. Until they hit here. That's when the blue bloods must have drawn their line in the sand, and the Navy obeyed, leapfrogging Landgrave Hall to just north of Goose Creek, where the Naval Weapons Station is, the land sprawling out big and wide so the government could take up all it wanted. That's where they store the bombs, everyone knows, in the ammo dumps you can see on Google Earth. That's where, too, the nuke school is, the training center for every sailor ends up inside a submarine, and where when I was a kid the nuclear submarine base was. That place where Trident missiles got loaded onto subs and sent out to sea.

But to the south of us there's other buildings than the brig—there's SPAWAR, the Navy's charming acronym for Space and Naval Warfare Systems Command, the building filled with brainiac engineers working on secret stuff nobody talks about; and there's an Army transportation battalion headquartered out there, the whole complex butted up against the Cooper River itself so that ships can be loaded with sand-colored MRAPs, those giant Hummers-on-steroids they built specifically to make it alive through the improvised explosive devices in Iraq and Afghanistan, and with tanks and transport vehicles—and of course the requisite ammo for all—you can see being hauled in on trucks out on Remount Road and riding in on the trains.

There's a heliport over there, above the trees now and again one of those big Chinook helicopters with their two sets of rotors lifting up or coming down, toting whatever it is they tote in those things. There's even a half dozen or so jet fuel storage tanks over there, just inside the fence beside North Rhett, six or seven huge tanks you could hit with a slingshot from the sidewalk if you wanted.

But the United States Naval Consolidated Brig is Hanahan's claim to fame. It's the only place in the U. S. of A. where terrorists are kept—Jose Padilla was holed up out there for four years before the government moved him on, and Kahlah al-Marri was there for six.

And it's also one of the main places always being mentioned when any talk of closing down Gitmo is afoot, though it was built back in 1989 for nothing more than medium-security risks, sailors and marines gone middle-ground thug while in the service of our country.

There's always rumors going on about terrorists nobody knows about being kept inside, and when those two Egyptian kids got hauled in a few years back, engineering students from the University of South Florida who got caught driving near the Naval Weapons Station with what they called *fireworks* in their trunk, talk was those two would end up at the brig for the duration, keeping whoever else was camping out in there company. Though one of them was acquitted, the other convicted for making a video that taught you how to make a radio control toy into a detonator, neither ever did any time in there. Still, who knows what really goes on inside other than the guards standing watch.

Maybe there's terrorists over there. Maybe not. But it just isn't a part of what the blue bloods here think on or worry over: it's the golf game they have coming up tomorrow or the next day, and the stock portfolio falling and rising and falling again, and their table at the clubhouse and who'll get the one looks out onto the pond once its present owner keels over.

Terrorists? That's somebody else's problem.

All the United States Naval Consolidated Brig means here to Landgrave Hall is that light seepage over the land, and yet one more layer of history, one I'm certain nobody, from Landgrave to Henry Manigault, could have ever foreseen: a prison less than a mile from where the old plantation house once stood.

I jogged across the fairway, beneath that bowl of milky dark. Somebody up at this hour in any one of the three cottages along the right side of this hole could see me plain as day right now, and so I sort of ducked low, made for where the cart path cut through even denser trees for the tenth green.

Jessup'd come through here in his golf cart only a while ago, but in the opposite direction, headed for me and Unc, and I wondered what he'd thought he was getting into on his way to roust us out yet again. On the one hand he must have been ticked at us for breaking the club rules, for making him have to haul out there and write up whatever report he'd have to turn in—there was always a report drawn up, Unc the one to sign off without a word on the breach when the smiling club manager, Cliff Somebody, showed up at the house the next day in his straw Greg Norman hat and teal blue *LHGC* logo shirt, the clipboard in hand, report typed and ready. But on the other hand maybe Jessup'd thought this was a welcome break, his having to climb on a cart, say so long to Segundo at the front gate, then cruising through the dark to handle the dimbulb antics of the Rich and Stupid.

Jessup was one of the good guys I'd known in school, and not just because he was a part of the non-crowd hanging out and drinking Colt 45s on the tracks. He was the kind of kid who was smarter than he'd ever let on, seemed to ace all his tests without ever studying, but kept quiet the fact he got those A's. So it'd always seemed to me he'd be going on to college, too.

But then, when we were juniors, 9/11 happened. He dropped out of school the next day, took his GED, and joined the Army, all before the smoke'd literally cleared at Ground Zero, then served two tours in Iraq, one in Afghanistan. He was a Ranger, and'd made it to staff sergeant and gotten a Purple Heart and been awarded a Bronze Star before he'd gotten out. His story, these thin bits of it, had come to me through the fog of my own wallowing out to Hungry Neck back then, and later through the even thicker fog of a failed college career: now and again I'd hear words at me from Mom about how she'd seen somebody at the Winn-Dixie over on Rivers who'd heard about his medals, or how one of the nurses she worked with down at MUSC had heard he'd re-upped.

Charleston, finally, was about as small a world as you could get.

Now I wished he was with me, or me with him, riding in his cart back to the house. I wished I didn't have the goggles on me for whatever garbage it meant for us to have them, and wished we were buzzing along here on the dogleg left the tenth hole was, because somebody had to have seen I was gone by now. Most likely Harmon with that M4, but if my luck held out—and it seemed it had thus far—all the cops and DNRs and recovery scuba dudes digging up the body would keep him distracted enough.

And if he wasn't the one to spot me gone, more than likely it would be Miss Quillie Izerd Grimball, her cracker radar always on. Every second after I'd taken off was a second closer to her seeing one less blip on the screen and calling out like it was a bingo win that a redneck had fled the scene.

When the blue bloods bought the land, in 1922, the eleven families that anted up the dough made a pact among themselves that no one other than the families involved could ever live here. If somebody wanted to sell a house—there were only nineteen to start with, though it's grown to thirty-three since then—they had to offer it first to a member of the family selling it; if that member wasn't interested, the place could only be sold to a member of one of those other ten families. And if nobody in any of the families was interested in buying said cottage, then and only then could the place be sold to someone from Off, but only if all eleven families agreed. For one reason and another, there are eighteen families spread through those thirty-three homes now, all of them, for one reason and another, still with just the right blood.

We weren't supposed to be the kind of people to live out here, because these were the rules of Landgrave Hall.

But damned if it didn't turn out we had the right blood, too. And damned if we weren't a family willing to live by those rules.

Ol' Dupont—Judge Beauchamp Redfield Dupont—was the one got us in here. Judge Dupont, the man whose cottage we always put in at, the one whose creek held fast a woman's body right this second, and through whose French doors I'd met the eyes of his Guatemalan nurse. He'd been the one ushered us into the whole ordered universe that was Landgrave Hall, him the one responsible for opening the gilded door and hauling us all in.

He and Unc'd known each other through the court system for years, since Unc'd first graduated from the police academy up in Columbia and'd returned to the Lowcountry to be a snot-nosed cadet, Judge Dupont back then a criminal court judge. Unc had testified at enough trials in front of the judge to let him know Unc was a good and reliable man, a man who meant to be a good cop and meant to be one for life. Unc tells stories now and again of how back in the early days, back before he'd been blinded, he'd taken the judge out to Hungry Neck for turkey or deer, or out to the trestle to fish for spottail bass, and tell too of how the judge, already an older man by then, always scolded him for the conflict of interest this might seem, a judge and a cop out hunting together. "But he was a good judge," Unc always finished those stories, "fair and just and tough."

Through the years the judge'd been promoted and promoted, until he'd ended up a bigwig U.S. district judge, only to retire a couple years ago for Alzheimer's kicking in hard. But he'd always kept an eye on Unc through his career, and'd thought Unc good at what he'd done, too.

But four years ago, once all the dust'd settled over the sale of the land out to Hungry Neck, once a pile of money bigger than any one of us—Mom, Unc, or me—could have imagined that piece of dirt out there could have been worth, Unc'd gotten a call from Judge Dupont, who clued him in on a little bit of news he hoped Unc would appreciate.

It just so happened that some neighbors of the judge's out here to Landgrave Hall were going through a divorce right then, a nasty one in which a Prioleau (he) was pitted against a Grimball (she), a husband and wife from two of the founding families. A couple who'd united twenty-seven years before in wedded bliss, only to end up childless and in a nuptial smackdown so fierce that Prioleau wanted to sell the house out from under his wife before she could have a say in it—it was, according to the rules, his cottage to sell, come down to him through his own Prioleau side—and thereby head off any miring up of the monies were the place to be tied up in court.

The judge'd done the research—he was himself a member of the Society of the Cincinnati, and'd had access to the right genealogists—and, having seen of Unc's good fortune played out in *The Post and Courier* over the months it took to secure the burial site and then for Unc to decide to sell it, and knowing Unc for the man he was, informed him that he was a Prioleau on his grandmother's side, and would he care to put in a request to buy what was his rightful fiefdom?

Unc'd proposed the idea while we three were on our way home from the closing of the sale of the property out to Hungry Neck at the lawyer's office on Broad Street downtown, headed up Meeting Street and away from those huge Charleston mansions behind us, with their gardens and carriage houses and piazzas with joggling boards. Though there was now stashed in Unc's bank account a wad of cash with what seemed enough zeros to keep afloat a third world country, there lay before us only the sad fact of the house on Marie, with its oil spots on the driveway, front yard rubbed to bare dirt in places.

I was driving Mom's Corolla—Unc's Range Rover, my Tundra, and Mom's BMW 750Li were still a month or so away—beside me Mom, Unc in the back, and I pulled to a stop at the light at Columbus Street. Though Broad Street was only a couple miles behind us, this might as well have been a different planet, so quick was the decline in neighborhoods the farther north of Broad you got. Outside my window stood the Piggly Wiggly up here, scene of enough robberies and shots fired to give it its own reality show.

That was when Unc said, "Got a call from Judge Dupont," and I glanced in the rearview. "Turns out some element of our blood runs blue. Prioleau, somehow. He wants to know if we want to buy a place out to Landgrave Hall."

By this time it'd been already decided that Unc would live with Mom and me, once we'd closed on the land. It wouldn't be a single-wide he'd relocate to, we knew, but a big place, a place he'd need help navigating, and so it'd simply been seen as a done deal Unc would live with us, and that we'd have a place big enough to let him feel like he was living alone. Not to mention the ease and convenience of having me there to take him where he needed when I was home from school.

"You game?" Unc said to Mom. "You think we could pull off living out to Landgrave Hall?"

"Yes," Mom said.

She hadn't moved a muscle, only sat beside me, her black leather purse in her lap, both hands holding tight to it. She'd dressed up for the closing, had on a black suit with a purple silk blouse. She was smiling, her eyes straight ahead, so that I'd only been able to see this side of her face. She was still pretty, still petite, though the wrinkles beside her eyes were getting on past the point where you could call them laugh lines. But her eyes were still that same sharp green, her red hair still in its soft curls, that same spray of freckles across the top of her nose what somebody'd think was cute.

"Let's go look at it," she said. "Right now."

"Sort of hoping you'd say that," Unc said, and I could hear him move a little, then the quiet tap of him punching in numbers on his cellphone.

Of course we'd talked by then of different possibilities for the place we'd all end up living—everywhere from Kiawah to Pawleys Island to South of Broad itself.

But here Landgrave Hall had been served up, that mysterious land of secret wealth and importance. Kiawah and Pawleys were only cheap knockoffs of this place, the original enclave of the haves. Even South of Broad paled, made the neighborhood seem like a parade of dioramas for some giant science project, with its plague of tourists always wandering the streets and peering in windows of those homes.

Still Mom was smiling. But it was a different smile, I could tell, one I couldn't remember having seen on her face before. "Landgrave Hall," she whispered. She nodded once, said, "Yes."

In this manner, the issue was settled.

I could see out her window the bus stop at this intersection, always a busy one being so close to the Piggly Wiggly. A couple dozen people out there at the curb, all waiting. Blacks mostly, but some Mexicans in there, and a few whites.

But there, right in front of them all, stood a white family: the father, a guy no older than me with a cowboy hat on, no shirt, and a pair of jeans; beside him the mom, in a rainbow-colored tube top and short shorts, long straight hair parted in the middle and down past her shoulders.

And in front of them, right at the edge of the curb and happy for it, him smiling and smiling, stood a toddler, three years old at the most, wearing nothing but a diaper and a pair of kid cowboy boots. He was looking back the way we'd come, watching like everyone else for the bus to come, and now he put his hands up, and clapped.

"We're on, Judge," Unc said behind me, and I looked in the rearview again, saw Unc with his cellphone to his ear. He nodded, said, "Tell Cousin Prioleau we'll be there in twenty minutes, driving a tan Corolla," and slapped it shut.

Still Mom smiled, her looking straight ahead.

A bus rolled up just then, filled her window, that family and everyone else gone.

Twenty minutes later we were turning right off of North Rhett up in Hanahan and onto a two-lane I'd never ventured on before, because I and everyone else who knew what lay at the end of this simple piece of pavement knew it led to a place some of us were allowed, and most of us weren't.

Trees edged in thick on either side of the road, and I saw up ahead a white-brick gatehouse, a closed wrought-iron gate. And a person I thought I might recognize, someone maybe I knew, leaning out the gatehouse as we neared.

Jessup Horry.

The gate swung open.

Five weeks later, me home for spring break, I helped Mom pack up what little we'd be taking with us to the new house: a few things out of the fridge and pantry, my old kid stuff—books, models, a bit of old clothes—and nothing else. Everything in the house had been sold

with it, from the silverware in the drawers to the garden hose out
back.

I'd watched as she'd tossed into garbage bags every bit of her
clothes, from the least pair of those little footie-stocking things you
wear with a pair of shoes to her series of ten sequined cocktail dresses,
every one way too short for any mom to wear. Though they had cost
half a paycheck each—she'd been a pediatric nurse at the Medical
University for the last ten years by then—she'd worn each dress only
once, to the annual Med U Christmas party. Ten dresses, stuffed into
trash bags along with every other piece of clothing she owned, me
the one to haul it all out to the curb.

Except for the nurse's outfits themselves. These she'd set in a separate pile on her bed, and once all her clothes were gone, she'd gathered them all up, those sadly colorful scrub outfits with their balloons
or flowers or rainbow pinstripes, and went out to the kitchen, then
through the back door to the yard, where she tossed them in a pile,
doused them with lighter fluid from a rusty can next to the hibachi
on the stoop—we left the hibachi too—and lit them up.

We'd stood there in the backyard watching them all go, set atop
the pile her two pairs of white nurse's shoes, my mom hugging herself
and smiling at the show of this all, and I looked at her.

Here were those freckles, that smile.

For a moment I'd felt good right along with her, just us two saying
goodbye to the job she'd held all those years to make our lives here
close to bearable, saying goodbye too to this life lived out next to the
Mark Clark, a neighborhood where at any given moment you could
hear from the freeway the shriek of Jake brakes on eighteen-wheelers,
and where sometimes at night the smell of the paper mill a mile away
was so bad you'd think a cat had crapped in your pillowcase.

The rest of my semester, with its failing grades in Biology and that
History of the South course, the D's I would get in my Spanish III and
English classes, was still somewhere past the horizon but looming all
the same. But suddenly I felt good. After all those years of our living

in this run-down neighborhood, with its cars up on blocks in the driveways, front yards rubbed to bare dirt, and random shootings at the Aquarius Social Club three blocks away or armed robberies at the Hot Spot gas station and mini-mart over on Murray, I saw we were going to escape. We were going to make it out of this place alive, and my mom was happy.

Black smoke wafted up from those burning clothes, the soles of the shoes curling up like they meant to start walking off and escape themselves. Mom looked at me then, still hugging herself and smiling—she had on a new top, a green silk thing with no sleeves, and new jeans, culled from the new wardrobe in the bags and boxes she had piled up in her bedroom, all of it from the boutiques on King Street downtown—and said, sweet as anything I'd ever heard her say, "Landgrave Hall."

I'd only smiled back at her, then turned to the fire, watched the black smoke of those burning shoes and uniforms, her old life and the toil of it disappearing just like that.

6

I cut through a thin buffer of trees to the right of the cart path between the eighth tee box and the seventh green, and stepped out onto
our gravel drive. Here stood our house a good fifty yards away, every
light in the whole thing on, like a 4:00 A.M. party set to start.

It was a big white clapboard colonial, a covered porch stretching
the whole front of the house, all of it four or five feet off the ground,
built over a crawl space. All the windows had Charleston Black shutters, the roof above the second story steep-pitched with three dormers. The gravel drive swept off to the left, on that side of the house
the separate garage big as the house on Marie, just past it the dock
out to Goose Creek. To the right of the house and a good thirty yards
away lay the seventh green.

A place Unc wouldn't be caught dead trying to golf, even if it
was only putting. Because the chance existed he might be seen by

Mom herself, who, he feared, wouldn't let such a ridiculous thing as a missed putt by a blind man go without comment.

The pride thing again.

Like every time Unc and I left for one of his nocturnal golf jaunts, the place had been dark save for the single flood at the peak of the garage, where all three of our vehicles and the golf cart were safely tucked away for the night, the driveway empty. But now every bit of the landscape lighting was on out here, the twin palmettos at the front corners of the house lit up like two torches blazing, the crepe myrtle and sago palms and Indian hawthorn that littered the front walkway all perfectly highlighted, little explosions of light and growth that charted the tabby path to the broad set of stairs up to the porch.

The lamps were on inside the windows on either side of the oak front door, too, the library on the right, the living room on the left, along with the porch lights blasting down on the wicker chairs and little side tables up there, outdoor furniture that cost more than all the furniture we'd left in the old house when we moved out. The up-stairs windows were all lit, even the dormers, and I pictured Mom going room to room to room, flipping switches on everywhere. The landscape lighting all shut down at midnight, their timers inside the laundry room at the back of the house, so she'd had to go in there and make it a point to turn all of it on, too, and for about a second the idea crossed my mind that maybe she was afraid of something. Maybe she'd heard already about a body over at the Dupont place, and so she'd gone around and turned all this on in some attempt to fill time and quiet and being alone until her idiot son and her pride-ful ex-brother-in-law made it home to tell her everything would be okay.

Maybe she was afraid in there.

But the thought—a dumb one—only lasted just that long, because I knew my mom. I knew her.

I've already called your momma, Huger, Mrs. Q had said not a minute after she'd gotten to Judge Dupont's. *She's on her way as we speak,* she'd said.

Mrs. Quillie Izerd Grimball: mother of the Grimball daughter whose Prioleau husband had sold this fine house out from under her before the sale could be tied up in divorce court. Mrs. Q, the arbiter of good blood and bad, still riled and certain to be the rest of her days that her daughter hadn't gotten this house, a clutch of rednecks soiling up the place instead.

And I knew, just like I'd known the first second I'd come through those trees to find this Roman candle of a lit-up house, that Mom'd turned on every light to make a point: she was up, and waiting to give Unc and me the hell we were owed.

I made it to the foot of the drive, peeled off to the right on the tabby walkway through the planter beds, then stopped at the bottom of the stairs, looked down. I closed my eyes, slowly shook my head, and thought, *What am I going to tell her?*

We'd found a body? That the Navy was involved, and something called a master-at-arms and his sidekick had drawn their guns on us, ready to fire? That I was toting a set of night-vision goggles it seemed Unc was hell-bent on keeping close?

That we'd found a *body*?

Then I remembered. I opened my eyes, looked up to the porch and that oak door and whatever it was waiting to happen inside.

Hide the goggles, Unc'd told me just before I'd taken off, headed here, to this moment. *Tell your momma we'll all be all right.*

I could do that. Both those things.

I hitched the book bag a little higher on my shoulders, started up the stairs, the hollow slug of each step I made what seemed loud as a hammer in the quiet out here, and then I was on the porch and across it, my hand out for the bright brass door handle.

But the door opened, all by itself.

I looked up: Mom, her mouth and eyes open wide, and here were her arms up already for me, the trembling word "Huger!" out of her like it was some tremendous gift she'd been given even to utter it, and I stepped in to her, closed my eyes and felt her arms around my shoulders and her crying now, and for a moment I knew that, yes, everything was going to be all right. That Unc's words weren't any sort of fake promise meant to placate either Mom or me. He'd given us the truth: We'll all be all right.

Mom moved her arms, eased off, and started to step back from me, and I opened my eyes.

First, I saw her eyes and the wet of them, her quivering chin, and heard out of her the broken-up words "What took you so long? What took you so long?" and already I felt bad for whatever I'd caused her. That worry, that pain. She'd already known there was a body involved before I'd said a thing. I knew that, just from her chin and the way she let out these words to me.

That was the first thing I saw.

But then I looked up, past her shoulder, and saw next, there behind her and a few feet into the foyer, a man in a khaki uniform, smiling.

I tensed quick at him, a shot of cold surprise through me, and held harder to Mom in just that moment, nearly clutched her in to me.

"Huger," the man said, and nodded, and now I saw the gold at his collar, the four narrow bands of bright colors above his left shirt pocket. I knew already who he was, even before Mom in that next second pulled away from me and linked her arm in my elbow, turned to him and, gathering together what she could of herself, said, "Huger, this is Commander Prendergast." She took in a quick, broken breath. "He's been here keeping me company until you and Leland got back."

I could hear on Mom's voice a forced ease about this whole thing—a Navy officer in her house in the middle of the night—and I glanced down at her, saw her chin still trembling, saw her quick swipe at her eyes with the back of her free hand. But I saw too that she was smiling, giving this man her best shot at trying to get herself back together.

"Good to finally meet you," the man said, and took a step toward me, put out his hand to shake. "Though I think I've laid eyes on you a time or two out to Warchester's place."

I said nothing, still too startled at who was standing here inside our house: Prendergast: the one who'd lost the goggles to Unc.

"Poker night," he said, and tried at a little bigger smile. "I see you now and again bringing Leland in."

His voice was higher than I'd thought it would be, and he stood a good six inches taller than me. He had dark hair in the standard officer cut: nearly shaved above the ears, thicker on up, parted on the side but the hair so short the part was more an idea than anything else. He was tan, and every crease in his shirt and pants could've cut stone.

He smiled, nodded again, and now here was my hand out to him, slowly, and I could feel of a sudden the book bag on my shoulders, the weight of it.

He squeezed hard my hand, shook it once, let go and stepped back, put his hands behind him like he was at parade rest. He looked down at Mom, nodded at her, looked at me again. "Surprised we haven't met before," he said. "Not just because of our shenanigans on poker night, but because—" And he stopped, tilted his head a little toward Mom and looked at her again, gave another quick smile.

"Jamison and I go way back," Mom said, and I looked at her, saw her smiling at him still. She seemed not to hold on to my arm so tightly, and now I saw that she was dressed, had on a white turtleneck shirt and a blue sweater, a pair of jeans, and not the robe and pajamas I'd expected. She looked up at me, smiling. "Jamison was a year ahead of me at Stall," she said, and nodded. Maybe she was smiling too hard now, I couldn't quite tell, but she went right on, "Everybody knew him because he was a receiver for the football team." She looked at him then. "Of course he'd never give me the time of day, all the girls chasing after him, and me—"

"If I'd had the nerve, Eugenie, I'd have asked you out. But you had your own cadre, if you'll remember. There was Tommy Sanborn and Trace Suggs and Alton—"

"Why are you here?" I cut in. The words were too loud, I could already hear. But Prendergast was in my home. The exact man I had to keep these goggles away from, and Unc's words—*Hide the goggles*—came to me again, as though he'd known already this man would be waiting for me here.

They both stopped, caught in the nothing of this squirrelly nonsense talk about high school and who knew who when, and I stood there in the middle of it, the book bag hanging on my back, while what we weren't talking about—where the goggles were—lay square in front of us all. Because that's why Prendergast was here. Plain and simple.

"Had the men drop me off first, just in case you were already here. I ended up staying just to make sure your momma was all right, and let the men handle things down at the Dupont residence," he said, still at parade rest, still with that tight smile, and I realized only then there hadn't been a vehicle out front of our house, the driveway empty. "We had a report," he went on, "that there was some trespassing going on at the Weapons Station, and one of my men said he saw the two of you. That's all I know, and all we're here for, but—"

"Nobody trespassed," I said. "Nobody. We never even came close. We only—"

He shot out a hand from behind him like a traffic cop: Stop. "But our men found otherwise, once they were on scene," he said, and here was that same stupid smile of his, that same tan tightness to his face. "But no one dispatched out here knew anything about a body, and so we'll be on scene for a little while longer, just to make sure everything's all right."

He nodded again, and I felt Mom's arm slip from mine, let go altogether, her getting hold of herself like I thought she would have all along—there was still hell to pay, and I knew it—until finally she took a step away from me so that we three stood in a kind of triangle there in the foyer, the doorway still open behind me. She put her hands in front of her, laced her fingers together, and started sort of bouncing in the smallest way: how she lets you know she's done with you, that you ought to move along now before she blows up.

It wasn't lost on Prendergast. Still with his hands behind him, he nodded hard this time, said, "Well, I have to be heading out, now you're home safe." He turned to Mom, leaned in and kissed her cheek, brought a hand from behind him and put it to her shoulder, like the evening'd been some simple get-together. I stepped back and away from the door, let him pass between me and Mom, his hands at his sides now, and saw a radio clipped on his belt at his back.

Mom and I both followed him, stepped out onto the porch. He took a step down the stairs out there, then another, and stopped, half turned to us.

"The police will be over here pretty soon, and SLED," he said. "They'll be asking questions. Feel free to let them know about Master-at-Arms Stanhope and Petty Officer First Class Harmon, why they came over to Judge Dupont's for a visit." He took a breath, held it a moment, then said, "And we'll find out what happened and who that is over there. The body. I'm thinking you're safe, though. That's what's important."

I said nothing. I knew what would happen next, who'd be showing up at the door. But I hadn't actually thought of what I'd be saying to them, and especially about Stanhope and Harmon. I only knew the cops'd be here, and want some answers.

And it was a relief, if only a small one, to hear somebody say something about the body. About her.

"Fine," I said, and Mom, leaning against me again but this time, I knew, for only an effect—this piece of the family was safe at home—said, "Thank you, Jamison, for staying until he got here."

And it hit me: I could play along too, just like Mom was doing already. She didn't lean into me like this when I was in trouble, and I knew I was in trouble.

"You want," I said, "I can drive you in the golf cart over there. To the judge's house."

He'd taken another step, but stopped again, slowly turned to me. Here was that smile, still and always there: tight and determined.

"I'll walk, if you don't mind." He nodded over his shoulder, just a touch of a move, his eyes right on me, his face clear as day for the landscape lights out here. "Petty Officer Harmon here will take me back the same way you two came in."

I blinked once, felt my face start into some kind of a question, but then I looked past him, down to the left of the foot of the stairs.

There on the tabby walkway stood Harmon, that M4 pointed down. He was looking at me, and nodded.

"See you tonight," Prendergast said.

I blinked again, felt Mom stiff beside me.

Harmon had followed me the whole time.

I said, "What's tonight?"

"Poker!" Prendergast shot out, and now he laughed, a high-pitched thing that sent a kind of black twist through me. "Over to Warchester's," he said and shook his head. "It may be four in the morning right now, but it's a Thursday."

He took the last two steps down, and turned one more time. "I imagine I'll be seeing Leland over at Judge Dupont's," he said, and it seemed that smile of his was even tighter, that laugh he'd given as fake as Mom's leaning into me right now. "But in case I forget to tell him, you let him know I'll be taking him to the cleaners tonight." He paused. "You tell him to bring only what he's willing to lose."

He nodded again, and turned. Harmon stood at attention, saluted him, but Prendergast did nothing, only started on the path toward the drive, away and to our right. Harmon fell in right behind him without looking back up at us.

And I'd gotten the message: Bring the goggles. Prendergast would get them tonight.

But then, as if all of this weren't enough, Prendergast and Harmon only made it to the end of the walkway and a step or so out into the drive before they both stopped, sudden and sharp, as though they'd been scared by something.

I felt Mom beside me jump for it, felt too the blitz of hot blood to my face and neck, the rush of it, all in an instant, and looked past them off into the dark on the other side of the drive, there past where the landscape lighting blazed down.

A man stood there, maybe fifty feet away from the two of them.

Jessup, in his black ball cap, black windbreaker, and black pants.

"Thought I'd tag along, just in case," he said, and I saw the ball cap nod at them. He looked up at us on the porch, called out, "Huger, Mrs. Dillard. How you doing?"

"I'm sorry for all this mess Huger and Leland are putting you through," Mom called out quick as that, when I hadn't even got my breath yet, hadn't any words even to answer back.

"No problem," he called out, and nodded again, a dark figure down there. "Just doing my job," he called, then looked back at Prendergast and Harmon. "Think I know a little quicker way than the one y'all came in on." He turned then, started away down the drive, and into the black out there.

I looked at Prendergast down at the edge of the drive, saw he was turned to Harmon behind him, his head cocked to one side, eyes open wide.

You know he was there? I could hear loud as a brick on an aluminum hull for the look he was giving him, that tilt of his head.

Harmon shook his head, just once, and they were gone, walking fast across the gravel drive, following a security guard who'd been there all along.

Mom wouldn't talk to me, only went to the kitchen at the back end of the house, pulled the coffeepot from the maker, turned it upside down in the sink and rinsed it out. Two empty cups sat on the glass-topped breakfast table, two of the four wrought-iron chairs pulled out, too, the ones that faced the picture window to the dock and marsh and creek out there.

I didn't egg her on, didn't ask her the dumb question what was wrong, didn't volunteer any apology. Whatever was coming would come, and so I stayed quiet, only went around the table to the far side closest to the window, and took off the book bag and leaned over, slipped it beneath the glass tabletop.

I turned then, looked out the window at the dock lit up every few feet with the knee-high solar lamps we had running the whole length. The lights were dimming down now, night almost over and the solar power nearly bled out.

From here the creek made an arc away to the left and right so that I could see a good long stretch of it, maybe a mile altogether, our dock off the back of the house, maybe twenty yards out, at the bottom of the sweep of it all. Even in the dark out there and the light in here, I could see the water, the silver run of it, like a thin ribbon lying in the uneven lay of blacks and grays and silvers of the marsh. Out there, farther now, a couple miles off and to my left, sat the Weapons Station land, on it nothing I could see, just that ragged black tree line, to my right the far spread of marsh that led out to the Cooper River. From inside the kitchen it was all a guess what exactly it looked like, the broad void out there filled in with my memory of being on my boat, or at the end of the dock and just throwing a cast net for mullet to bring along with me fishing somewhere. But I could see from here the creek, the curve of it away on both sides. I could see that much.

Of course Mom and Prendergast'd known I was on my way here. Harmon had followed me every step, radioed in, and I hadn't known it, thought myself alone out there among the ghosts. But Harmon hadn't known *he* was being followed, and there was something to that: the fact a Navy dude was following me without my knowing, while *he* was being followed by someone *he* couldn't hear.

And I thought of my mom, and how quick she was to answer Jessup calling out to us, how fast she'd been with an answer when Harmon and Prendergast both had been stunned at him standing there.

I smiled. For the first time that night.

I heard behind me one of the chairs move against the heart-pine floor, and I turned, saw Mom sit down at the table, those two empty coffee cups gone now.

She didn't look at me, only put her hands on the glass tabletop, her fingers together, and looked down, like she was ready to start in on a prayer.

I turned from the window, pulled out the chair across the table from her, and sat.

"I'm sorry," I finally said, though I wasn't quite certain about what. The fact, of course, was that I'd taken Unc out to golf, so I was the one who'd had a hand in getting caught, and Mrs. Q was the one to call us in. There was that humiliation for starters.

But there was also a dead person involved, one I'd been the first to lay eyes on, and I felt like I had to ask forgiveness for that too, for whatever reason. Maybe because the woman'd been trumped by concerns over some shitty game about Unc and the commander and me and night goggles, the idea of a dead woman taking a big backseat to the cat-and-mouse crap these goggles were causing.

Still she said nothing, and so, just to fill the quiet, like maybe she'd done with turning on all the lights, I said, "That's something, huh? Jessup scaring those guys like that." I paused, still got nothing. "And I didn't know you knew Prendergast. That's funny, because Unc sees him every—"

Mom lifted her head at that, and I stopped. I could see her chin set hard, no more trembling, her mouth a thin line, her eyes nearly closed.

She unlaced her fingers from in front of her, reached behind her with one hand. She moved that hand a little, fishing for something, then brought it from behind her, and lay on the glass tabletop a pistol.

A small one, but serious. Black, semiautomatic, maybe six inches long, less than that tall. A little handgun, tough and smart. And my mom had it.

"Mom," I whispered. "How did you—"

"A Beretta," she said. "Px4 Storm subcompact." She stopped, swallowed, and I looked from the gun to her. Still her eyes were almost closed. She wasn't looking at me, but at the gun. "I have my concealed weapons permit," she said. "I've done the training."

Her eyes cut to me, that look cold and hard.

She whispered, "I got my first one when we still lived on Marie. After what happened out at Hungry Neck." She paused, and I could hear my own heartbeat for the quiet. "This is my third one. I get a new one every couple years. And do the training again."

She bowed her head a moment, like she'd given up of a sudden, but then she looked at me again. "I don't give a damn about you and Leland golfing," she said. "I really don't. When Mrs. Grimball called me I thought she'd do best for us all by just dropping dead. I thought maybe I'd just ignore the whole thing and let you two come on home and I'd chew you out then. Turned on every light inside the house and out just so you'd know how mad I was whenever you two showed up back here." She paused again, closed her eyes, bit her lips together. "But then when I hear a car out in my drive," she whispered, "and I'm up in my bedroom and look out the window to see a black Suburban, and see him climbing up my front steps and hear the knock at the door—"

She stopped.

I looked down and away from her, as though what she was telling me was something I ought to be ashamed about hearing. Too personal. Too real.

But now I was looking at the gun, the matte finish on it, the little notched sight at the rear of it, the single blade at the barrel tip so you could line up fast what you were aiming at. A Beretta. My mom with it, and a concealed weapons permit.

A real thing. A third party to everything we were saying, like some unimpeachable witness in the room that could testify to what all was going on tonight.

I looked up at her. I said, "I didn't know any of this was going to happen. I didn't know any military were going to come over here and talk to you. And we didn't trespass. I can tell you straight out we never even set foot over there. Never. And there's no way we could ever know there was a body involved in this whole thing. No way."

There was more I could tell her. About the goggles, and what I'd seen looking back at me from the Weapons Station tract. And about Unc warping up the body, and her face. What had happened to the woman's face.

Mom opened her eyes, looked straight at me. She swallowed, and it seemed maybe the quiver in her chin was starting up again.

She said, "It's not the Navy coming here, or anybody in a uniform." She paused, swallowed. "It's Jamison Prendergast." She let her eyes fall to the gun, whispered, "I never want to see Jamison Prendergast here again. Do you understand?" and her eyes came back to mine. "He's a bad man," she whispered. "A very bad man." She paused. "He's why I got the gun out."

Now I was certain of her chin, the muscles across it contracting her mouth into a taut frown, and she reached a hand up to her eyes, wiped at first one, then the other, and took in a quick sniff.

I wasn't sure what I was supposed to say, and thought of Prendergast, and the tightness of his smile. I thought of his kiss on Mom's cheek, as easy as anything I'd ever seen her take, and of that nod behind him out on the porch steps, the ace card he thought he was playing by revealing Harmon had followed.

I thought of Jessup, standing there all the while, and the look Prendergast had given Harmon for the real high card of an unarmed security guard following him in without his even knowing it.

I looked back at the gun. I didn't like Prendergast. I'd known it from the moment I'd laid eyes on him till the last words he'd given me, that warning to Unc through me of how he'd better bring the goggles to poker night.

But this in Mom was something else. This was different, what Mom was talking about. This was something personal.

"Do you want to tell me why?" I said. I thought I sounded old enough— adult enough—that she might give me an answer, and I looked up from the gun to her, there in her white turtleneck and blue sweater. My mom.

But her eyes were past me, over my shoulder, her eyebrows together, straining to see something out the window behind me, and I turned in my chair, looked out there.

Two boats were coming down the creek, I could see from here. Maybe a hundred yards off and to my left, just motoring along that silver arc toward our dock, and though there was this light from inside reflecting off the window, I could see now it was a Boston Whaler towing a jon boat, and I could see two people standing side by side at the console about halfway back on the Whaler, two shadows coming up the creek.

"Here they come," I said. "Looks like Major Tyler's towing Unc in."

"Who?" Mom said behind me. "Who else?"

"Alton Tyler," I said. "A DNR guy. Showed up right after the Navy—"

Mom's chair pushed back fast, and I turned around at the sound.

She was already at the sink, reached to the strainer and pulled out the coffeepot, flipped the water on and started filling it. She took in two or three quick breaths, still gathering herself, wiped once more at her eyes with her free hand.

The gun was gone from the table.

Mom stood sideways to me, and I tried to see if she'd tucked it back behind her again, underneath the blue sweater. But I couldn't tell. It was only my mom standing there at the sink, filling a coffeepot.

"Unc knows him," I said. "I don't." And then, because they were the words that came to me and because I think I knew already, I said, "You know this guy too?"

"Yes," she said, and turned off the water, stepped to the maker to her right and emptied the pot into it. "Yes, I do." She slipped the pot into the maker, popped open the coffee canister and scooped beans into the grinder at the top of it, closed the lid, pushed the canister back to where it always stood beneath the cupboard. She reached to turn on the coffeemaker, the grinder about to fill the whole house with its burring wail. The reason Unc and I always made instant in a thermos at two in the morning.

But before she turned it on, she stopped, turned to me, said, "How do I look?"

For a second I said nothing. A moment ago she'd been calling down a curse on the man she was sipping coffee with for as long as it'd taken me to get here, no matter how many people I was leading in. But now here she was: my mom, thinking about a man.

I said, "You look like a mom packing heat."

"You can't see that, can you?" she said, and reached a hand behind her again, touched back there. "I didn't have time to put on the pancake holster I bought for it. But you still shouldn't be able to see that," she said. "Can you see it?" and she turned sideways to me again.

"Mom," I said. Then, "Mom."

She stopped, turned to me. She looked down a second, took in a long slow breath, let it out. "We all went to high school together, and then he worked with Leland."

"With Unc?" I said. "He's known Unc that long?"

She quick looked up. "Yes," she said. "And he knew Parker, too." She paused, screwed up her mouth a little, tried at a smile. "Your father. Those three were all good friends of mine. We were all good friends."

Parker Dillard. The man I'd thought until I was fifteen was my father. The one who'd left Mom and me when I was seven and we were still living out to the trailer at Hungry Neck. The man who'd taken off only a few months after Unc's wife had killed herself, Unc living with us in that trailer, getting better, and getting used to having no eyes.

She never talked about him, never brought him into any conversation. But now here he was: a kid in high school, good friends with Alton Tyler.

"Oh," I said, and turned in my chair, looked out the window to where Major Tyler, the old family friend I never knew I had, was slowing down for the dock, and now, off to the right, far and away to the east, I could see the very beginning of the next day we'd have to walk through: a thin thin band of violet, hanging over the Cooper River, and all this marsh.

"I'm sorry," Mom said behind me, but I didn't turn to her this time, only watched the shadow that was Tyler step off the hull of the Whaler, kneel on the dock out there to cleat off the bow line.

Then I saw Unc, a shadow all his own, make carefully for the stern, stand on the gunwale a second, take his own step off, kneel there and do the same with the stern line. From here, you'd never know he was blind.

I turned from the window. Mom was still standing there, her arms crossed now, her head down.

I said, "You look fine, Mom. You look good." And I meant it.

She looked up at me. She smiled, turned on the coffeemaker, and here came that machine wail, dark and solid and loud.

I touched the toe of my boot to the book bag there at my feet beneath the table. As if it had a mind to take off on me.

7

Mom went out the door onto the back deck and to the dock, and I watched them talk a minute or so out there, the coffee bubbling through behind me. Then she turned, walked Unc and Tyler back to the deck and into the kitchen, and I stood from the table.

Tyler seemed even taller now he was inside, and I could see he had light brown eyes, salt-and-pepper hair. He took his hat off once he was inside—he had a tan line on his forehead where the ball cap sat—then shrugged off his windbreaker, though Mom had to coax him some to do it. He had on his olive green DNR uniform, the gold badge above his right shirt pocket, his metal name tag above the left, and wore a thick leather duty belt with three or four pouches, a radio, and a holster for the service revolver he was carrying.

And of course I could only think about Mom, carrying her own gun.

Unc closed the door behind him, took a couple steps to his right,

leaned a little until he just touched his walking stick there in the corner of the breakfast area, right where he'd left it. The move was his
own little tic: he needed to know where that stick was at any given
moment, as though it were some magnetic north. He turned from
the stick, took off his *MtPPD* windbreaker and tossed it on the counter a few feet away in the kitchen proper, then traced his hand along
the edge of the table to his usual seat looking out on the marsh, that
Braves ball cap of his never coming off.

Unc and I sat down while Tyler hung his windbreaker on the back
of the chair across from me. Mom was at the counter and pouring out
coffee, but just before she got to the fourth cup she stopped, turned
to Tyler and said, "Still just black?" and Tyler nodded, said, "Still just
black."

He stood waiting while Mom brought the cups to the table, then
sat down herself before he took his seat, and I glanced at Mom, saw
the quick look she gave me and Unc both: we weren't the gentleman
Tyler was.

But I didn't care about any assessment Mom was making right
then of manners and bearing. Even if it was somebody here who
seemed some weird mix of old family friend and law enforcement
agent. I figured he was here to ask me questions. I figured he was here
to find out what I knew about a dead woman being tended to at this
very moment.

But once we were all sitting down with coffee cups in front of us,
Unc and Mom set right in on small talk about the old days, Tyler
quiet and just sort of smiling all the while. Now and again he let out
a small laugh, shook his head at what Mom and Unc threw at him of
days gone by—Mom talked of when they'd all gone shark tooth hunting out on Drum Island in Charleston Harbor once, Unc and Sarah,
Tyler and a woman named Jenny, Mom and my father—she'd had to
pause before she'd said the word "Parker," a tiny stutter to it but there
all the same—and how they'd gotten so carried away with looking for
teeth they'd missed the fact the tide had up and gone, their boat sit-

ting in pluff mud. They'd had no choice but to bake out in the sun for four hours until the tide came in enough to get the boat free.

Unc told of the time he'd gotten a brand-new boat, a twenty-foot Sea Ray Amberjack, and wouldn't let anyone help him trailer it at the boat ramp down at Remley's Point after my father, Tyler, and somebody named Mitch had spent all morning fishing with him at the jetties outside the harbor. Unc'd backed his truck and trailer down the ramp, the others only watching because Unc had to do this himself, he had to do it himself. He got the trailer down into the water, waded in, climbed aboard the boat and motored it onto the trailer, settled it perfectly. No need even to use the winch line for how faultless he'd eased it in. He'd climbed off the boat and walked around the whole thing, proud of the job he'd done centering it in the cradle of the trailer, then got into his truck, gave it the gas and got up on the ramp, only to have the whole boat slide off, smack on the concrete. He'd forgotten to hook the winch line in and the safety strap at the bow.

"There's a picture of that somewheres," Unc said, and laughed. "My brand-new boat sitting high and dry on the ramp at Remley's. Don't know if I ever been more embarrassed in my life." He shook his head, both hands around the coffee cup on the table in front of him. "Mitch took a photo with a little Instamatic he had with him, and soon as he gets the prints back he's over to the house and showing them off to Sarah like it was a picture of a twelve-point buck he'd shot."

"Easy to laugh now," Tyler volunteered then. "Back out on the ramp, no way any of us was going to say a word, you stomping around and swearing like a sailor." He shook his head, smiling. He held his DNR hat in his hands by the bill and facing him, then eased off on the laughs, shook his head again. "Old Mitch," he said. "I miss him."

"Mitch," Unc said, his eyes down. He stopped smiling, took a sip of his coffee, set the cup down. "Wonder where that old picture is."

I looked at Mom beside me, saw her with her arms crossed, looking down, her head slowly shaking too.

"Mitch who?" I said. "What happened?" The way they'd all gone quiet I was ready for something about cancer taking him, or his running off same as my father had, never heard from again.

Unc shook his head one more time, said, "Mitch Claussen. Lost him in a bust out near Awendaw in 'seventy-nine."

"A good man," Tyler said. He'd set the cap on the table, took a sip off his coffee, set it down on the table. He put his hands in his lap, leaned back a little bit in his chair, and I could hear the leather creak of his belt and holster.

He looked up at Mom then. "Thank you for the coffee, Eugenie," he said, and got this small and careful smile. He nodded, said, "You look good as ever, too."

"I'm a wreck," Mom said and looked down, pushed a strand of hair behind her ear, tilted her head.

Unc still sat there, the cup in both hands, no look on his face at all, and I couldn't tell if he was thinking about this Mitch, or whatever was up with Mom and Tyler, or about a dead woman in pluff mud.

"You look just fine for this early in the morning," Tyler said, that small smile still on him.

But then he lost the smile, took hold of that cap and looked at the bill again. He didn't see, like I did, Mom glance up at him an instant, her head still tilted.

"I know," he started, "all y'all been through a lot in the last few years. But I need to talk with Huger here—"

His eyes cut to me, a quick nod, then he looked back to Mom, who'd sat up straight, quit with that tilt of her head. "I'll need to ask him a few questions, just like I already did with Leland on the way over. And there's going to be a whole lot more people coming over soon enough to just keep on asking them. State Law Enforcement Division ought to be here in a few minutes, then the sheriff's office. Hanahan police will be here too, though most of this'll end up handed off to SLED. Seems we got at least four sorts of jurisdictions involved here, and everyone likes to put his oar in on this kind of thing. But SLED'll be the ones to handle it all."

He paused, looked over at Unc. "Beat about all the info I could out of this bull shark here," he said, and reached out, gave a soft punch at Unc's shoulder. Unc smiled, nodded sharp. "But tell you the truth," Tyler went on, and now he was looking at Mom again, "I'm not even sure how much the DNR'll be involved in the end."

He stopped, looked down again, slowly shook his head, but this time in some other way. No rueful sort of pondering the loss of a comrade in a bust, but a puzzled kind of regard. He said, "Seems somehow the Navy's gotten involved, too, for whatever reason." He looked at me now. "Unc tells me you both never even come close to the tract, but here two seamen were, acting all kinds of put out, like they—"

"Jamison Prendergast was over here," Mom said flat-out right then, and both Unc and Tyler looked at her.

"When?" Unc said, cold and hard.

"Not fifteen minutes after Quillie Grimball called me," Mom said. She sat up even straighter now, crossed her arms again. "His boys dropped him off here and went on over to where you were." She paused, bit her lip. "Then he stayed here. To keep me company. He said."

"And you let that son of a bitch in here?" Unc shot out, his hands on the table already in fists, and I wondered for a moment why he'd be so pissed. He played poker with the man.

"What was I supposed to do?" Mom said, and though I'd expected on her voice some fire, some pissed off Mom-ness about whatever even deeper shit we were heading into here, she was quiet, her voice just like it'd been when she'd laid that gun on the table. "A black Suburban rolls up at three in the morning," she nearly whispered, "and out pops a man in uniform and a second later I see it's him and I don't even know what—"

"Eugenie," Unc whispered hard, shook his head.

"She's right," Tyler said, and looked at Unc. He laced his fingers together on the tabletop: all business. "She did the right thing, Leland. Nothing to worry about, either. Prendergast gets a report you two are wandering around on the tract—"

"But we—" Unc started in, but Tyler said "Leland," sharp and low.

Unc stopped, his teeth clenched. He let out a short breath through his nose, and Tyler went on.

"Somebody's been spotted out on U.S. Navy land, and he has the job of making sure it's secure. He knows you, Leland, which is a fact no one can say isn't true, and so his first stop with his support is to come to your house in case you and Huger are in transit via the jon boat, then dispatch his men to the scene itself." He stopped, looked at me, at Mom. Then he looked at his hands. "It's a man doing his job. Doesn't matter what history somebody brings up a set of stairs," he said.

From where I sat it seemed suddenly like his eyes weren't looking at his hands at all, but straight through the glass tabletop, and to the book bag still here at my feet. Both my feet were touching it now, though I hadn't known I'd done this, hadn't realized I'd pushed my toes right up against it.

And I wondered: Had Unc told him about what we'd seen with the goggles? Had he told him about the goggles at all?

Was he looking right now at the book bag beneath us, his words about what somebody brought to the table a signal he knew everything?

And for the ten thousandth time in my life, here was Unc, looking at me now, a blind man reading me better than anyone on the planet, though I hadn't said word one since I'd asked about this Mitch Claussen.

Unc said, "You're right. Better we don't bring any of that old history to what's going on here tonight." He nodded. "Because what matters is a woman's been killed, and everybody's just trying to find out how to get the piece of trash did it."

And I got it: shut up about the goggles.

"It's all right, Eugenie," Tyler said, and I glanced at him, saw his head tilted, his eyebrows drawn together. His eyes were on Mom now, and I turned, looked at her.

She was crying without a sound out of her, her chin on her chest, her shoulders heaving up and down, arms crossed in front of her. Already I was up and out of my chair, and I touched her shoulder, said, "Mom, it's okay, we're here. It's okay," even though I still had no idea what I was comforting her for. Prendergast was a bad person, and everyone here at the table knew why except me. But right now that didn't matter at all, and now I was crouched beside her chair, ran my hand across her shoulder and arm. She leaned into me, and I put my arm around my mom.

No one said anything for a minute or so. Unc only sat with his cup, looked inside it like it could tell him something. Tyler looked up at us now and again, then down to his hands, still laced together in front of him. Then Unc finally said, "Another cup of this coffee sounds good to me," and stood from his chair, turned straight for the kitchen counter two paces away, and touched its edge, traced it to right where the maker sat.

He reached in, pulled out the pot, and like always held the handle of the cup so's his index finger was hooked over the rim, his way to tell how full the cup was, and he poured.

"Alton?" Unc said, and turned to him, still in his seat. "You want a refill?"

Mom took in a couple deep breaths, touched my arm with a hand, patted it. She nodded, a signal to me all its own: I'll be okay. I'll be fine.

Suddenly she was standing from her chair, and here she was wiping an eye again. She gave out a crumpled smile while Tyler and I both stood. She said, "I'm sorry, Alton, for this fit I'm pitching. I just can't seem to—"

"No apologies necessary." He squared himself up at this, hooked his thumbs into his duty belt, that creak of leather again. He nodded, and it seemed he was trying now to be an agent of the Department of Natural Resources, this talk about a boat dumped on a ramp and sharks' teeth a mile behind us.

At least he was *trying* to make it feel like that. Because now I could see in his eyes, and in the stiff nod he gave, and the posed thumbs-in-the-belt, just a boy, a kid standing here.

He liked my mom.

"I have to go," Mom said, and she turned, started away from the table and through the sitting room for the front of the house, and the stairs. "Anybody needs me I'll be upstairs," she called out, and I could hear her trying to make herself sound all right, make us believe she'd be fine. "In case anyone has to ask me any questions. I'm okay." Then she was gone.

Unc stood in the kitchen looking toward us, the pot in one hand, the cup still on the counter with his finger hooked inside. Tyler stood with his thumbs in that belt, his eyebrows a little up for the surprise of how quick she was gone.

I said nothing, only looked out past Tyler to the sky out the window, a dull and dark purple gearing up for daylight.

"Now we get to the questions," Tyler said, and turned to me, nodded. He reached behind him, pulled from his back pocket a thin black notebook.

I couldn't sleep much at all the rest of the day.

Morning wormed in through the blinds in my room, for starters. Every time I took Unc out to golf it was like this, me trying once we were home to sleep and failing at it. Whatever time I'd get up, the rest of the day always had this fuzzy hot edge to it, like I was watching myself from inside a low-grade fever as I did whatever that day called for.

There was poker night tonight to think about, and my job of having to make certain Unc brought to the house in Mount Pleasant the goggles to hand over to Prendergast. And there was Prendergast himself to think about, and whatever it was made Mom into the mess she'd become for his showing up to the house.

There was that gun she carried with her, and how long she'd been carrying it without me knowing anything at all.

And buried at the bottom of it or heaped at the top was a woman pulled up from pluff mud by me, and by Unc.

So I lay there in my room, pretended I was sleeping, rolled back and forth under the covers in my pajamas—a pair of basketball shorts and one of my old Bass Pro T-shirts—and did nothing but think, and think.

Tyler's questions had been only routine, his demeanor suddenly nowhere near a kid with a crush sitting at a table and drinking coffee in the predawn dark. But he wasn't any kind of menace, either, once we were left sitting alone there at the table, Unc with his coffee heading to the library and his recliner in there.

They were only questions, a good couple dozen of them, among the standouts Why were you there? What were the circumstances involved with finding the body? How long had you been out there? Was it Unc or you to wedge it up? Did you know anyone at the Dupont house?

Anything else you care to tell me?

Of course it was that last one that made me into a liar. I could answer every question he'd thrown at me and not have to mention anything about the goggles, or those IR illuminators shining at us from across the marsh, and know I was giving him the truth. But when it came to that last question, all I knew to do was to shake my head, look Tyler right in the eye, and hand him a good solid flat-out no. The question made me into a liar, because there was plenty more I wanted to tell him about.

The interview had taken about a half hour altogether, and then he smiled, nodded, put the black notebook he'd been scribbling in back in his pocket. He stood, the light behind him out through the window gone now a heavy blue, and he took in a deep breath, looked past me toward the hallway to the front of the house.

"Leland," he called out, "how'd I do?"

"Couldn't hear a word y'all said," Unc shot right back from where he'd been sitting and listening the whole time.

Tyler let out a small laugh, looked back at me, and now I was standing, put my hands on my hips. "You think of anything else you want to tell me," Tyler started, "you just—"

"Tyler, ten-eighteen, Tyler, ten-eighteen," cut in from the radio on his belt just then, sharp static yelps of sound. He quick reached down and pulled the thing off his belt, held it up to his mouth.

"Tyler," he said, and turned from me to the window, looking, I figured, for some private way to talk.

"Nine seventy-seven," came the voice. "All the way up here to Wambaw Creek at Echaw Bridge Landing. You still working with recovery?"

I could hear Unc move in the recliner, his steps on the hardwood floor back toward us now. But I didn't turn to him, only stood watching Tyler, and listening.

"Negative," he said into the radio. "Interviewing witness, but we're done." He paused. "Nine seventy-seven?" he said.

"It rains, it pours," the voice crackled out. "Charleston County recovery already on the way. Sure could use a hand up here. Vehicle in the water, body in the trunk."

"Campbell," Tyler barked, then said a little easier, "Quiet." He paused a moment, put the radio back to his mouth. "ETA one hour. Over."

A couple seconds later came this Campbell and his single word, "Over."

Unc said from behind me, "He got that right about when it rains it pours," and Tyler turned to us, already had the radio clipped back on, a hand pulling his windbreaker off the back of the chair.

He put it on, said, "Two in one night. All I'd planned was putting in at Bushy Park Landing and motoring up Flag Creek, see if I can't park somewheres and hide out until a couple duck hunters who've baited the place back in there show up, start banging away." He shook his head, let out a low whistle. "Planned on having a nice quiet morning, just enjoying the sunrise and writing tickets. But no."

He stepped to the door off the kitchen, pulled it open, but turned to me, looked me in the eyes. "I'm sorry for what you saw today. Everyone involved's going to do their best to get who did it." He nodded, glanced at the floor a second. He drew in a breath, and looked at Unc. "Leland," he said, "you make sure and give Eugenie my best. And tell her I hope we can all get together over better circumstances sometime soon."

"Will do," Unc said, and smiled, nodded. I could see his coffee cup was empty, and then came three sharp knocks at the front door.

Tyler nodded at us both, and he was gone.

It'd been South Carolina Law Enforcement Division at the door, two crew-cut thick-necked boys with windbreakers all their own, *SLED* in bright yellow letters a foot high across their backs. Same questions as Tyler'd asked, but neither Unc nor I sitting down to answer them. We only went into two separate rooms, Unc staying there in his library with one of them, the other following me back into the kitchen. A half hour and we were done, and when we opened the front door to let them out, two sheriff's deputies stood at the bottom of the stairs up to the porch, waiting in the gray light out there, Smokey Bear hats on.

A half hour after that it was the Hanahan police at the bottom of the stairs, though not Poston and Danford, the two who'd arrived on scene at the Dupont house. These were two slightly older dudes in jeans and sweatshirts, detectives who'd obviously been asleep not that long ago, their hair still wild, the two unshaved. Unc knew them both, had fished with one of them's father when they were kids, had dated the other's mom when they were in high school.

And when we opened up the door to let them out, the sun just touching the tops of live oaks across the drive, of course I thought I'd find the ones I'd been expecting all along: somebody from the United States Navy, here to interrogate. I figured it wouldn't be Prendergast—he'd made it clear he wouldn't be seeing me or Unc until tonight at poker—and didn't think, either, it would be Stanhope or Harmon. But somebody. Somebody.

But this time there was nobody. Only the black Charger the detectives'd parked in the drive.

We said goodbye to the Hanahan detectives, we'll call you anything comes to mind, thank you, thank you, and closed the door.

Unc put a hand to my shoulder then, turned to me, said, "You did fine. We told them everything we know on how we come about finding this body. We just left off a couple details is all. Things we'll wrap up tonight at poker." He paused, took in a breath. "As for this woman," he said, and slowly shook his head, looked down. "The body." He paused again. "All these boys are doing their jobs. They'll find whoever did it." He looked back up at me. "Go on up and get some sleep now." He let go my shoulder, turned from the foyer, and started back toward the kitchen.

And I'd done what he told me, climbed the stairs, turned to the left at the top and went to the second door on the right, opened it to find things exactly the way I'd left them at two o'clock this morning: bed unmade, dirty clothes in a pile in the right corner of the room, bookcases jammed with books and DVDs and games, Xbox booted up, the forty-two-inch plasma TV waiting to engage.

Though it didn't seem enough to me, what was happening about the body, and Unc's words on it. It didn't seem enough for Unc to just say somebody'd figure out who did it.

No doubt Unc'd poked around in the kitchen after I'd gone up to try and sleep, him looking for my book bag, just to make sure all was well. I imagined he pulled out of there the thermos and my travel mug, gave them a rinse and set them in the strainer beside the kitchen sink, good citizen that he is, and I wondered where his own travel mug was right then, if it was in the jon boat out at the dock, or maybe sitting on the wrought-iron table out back of the Dupont place. I saw him sipping at it again, right before I'd made my big escape with not one but two parties in tow, Harmon and Jessup both. My Covert Op.

Once he knew where the goggles were, he'd take a second to touch at that stick leaned in the corner of the breakfast area once more, just to make sure. Then he'd be on his way to try and catch a nap in his own room down off the library, where he kept his bed made from the moment he rolled out of it—usually 5:00 A.M.—and where he had his own plasma TV mounted on the wall, the thing always on the History Channel. He claims the sound is why he bought the thing, though I know it's the fact he'd been able to afford it after all his years of living in the trailer out to Hungry Neck.

I imagined, too, my mom—we hadn't heard a word from her since she left us there in the kitchen—trying to sleep in her room at the opposite end of the second floor from mine, her there in the master suite with its Jacuzzi spa tub and stone-tiled shower with four showerheads and steam jets too. A bed the size of her whole bedroom on Marie. A walk-in closet the size of our old garage.

And with a Beretta subcompact, and a concealed weapons permit. Something called a pancake holster. I'd never heard of that before, a pancake holster. But it made sense: you had a gun on you, you wanted that thing flat as one so nobody'd see.

8

Eventually I'd found a piece of crappy sleep, and came out of it into late afternoon light. I stood from the bed and stretched, then leaned into the blinds, fingered them open for a second to find just another day going on out there, but with the added bonus of that fuzzy hot edge to everything for having stayed up all night: flower beds with their tabby paths through them still lay out there, and an empty driveway, past it all the gravel drive I'd walked in on, Spanish moss in live oaks like the same old dead men's beards.

The weird thing was the way the world just kept moving on. At some point this evening we'd be turning on the television, seeing about the body the same shit everyone sees every time something like this happens: somebody finds a body, and there's video on the five, six, and seven o'clock news from a camera in someone's yard across the street or down the road. Yellow crime scene tape snaps or doesn't snap in whatever breeze or still air was out there when the cameraman set up. Vehicles jammed in a driveway. Men in uniforms and not in uniforms busy about the house or woods or marsh or wherever, talking to each other or with hands on hips or moving in and out of said house or woods. Somebody in the studio drones on about who what where.

Then you turn the channel, or crank up the TiVo, or just wait until sports or weather or whatever else comes on. And the world just keeps moving.

Same thing with a woman pried up out of pluff mud, it felt right then. After we'd watch the news, I'd drive Unc out to Mount Pleasant for poker, and we'd hand over goggles to solve the particular drama we'd been involved in with Prendergast and whoever saw us from over at the Navy tract. And now there was another, more pressing drama here in the house, with his showing up and Mom and Unc and Major Tyler's reactions to that fact, something I didn't know how to solve because I had no idea what it was all about. But a drama that'd made Mom get out a gun.

There was all of this. But beneath it that woman, levered up by Unc and me. And out my window the same old world going on.

Mom's bedroom door was closed, and I went down to the kitchen, saw she wasn't anywhere around, figured maybe she was asleep. But out the windows in the breakfast area, the same windows I'd watched the gradual light of this day come up on, I could see Unc down at the end of the dock, sitting in one of the lawn chairs we kept folded up in the marine storage locker out there.

He was parked facing the setting sun, him looking back up the creek toward the Dupont house, though you couldn't see it from here for the arc the creek made. Once you reached the tip of the arc, the creek turned around the point, and it was still a half mile to Judge Dupont's from there.

At the right end of the dock stood the boathouse, pylons with a roof over it, the jon boat cradled up in the rafters, all put away neat and clean by Unc alone. His walking stick was leaned up against one of the pylons, and I saw him lift his hand to his mouth now. He was smoking one of his cigars: a Hoyo de Monterrey Excalibur II. The only thing he smoked.

I reached for the door out onto the deck, started to pull it open, but stopped, turned to the breakfast table behind me. Beneath the glass top sat my book bag, exactly where I'd left it last night, and there seemed for this second something good about its not having moved. But in the exact same moment it seemed totally wrong. The goggles'd been what brought Prendergast here to the house, and so whatever piece of Mom's past with him. But tonight Unc'd be handing them back to Prendergast, and maybe whatever shard of glass Mom'd had pressed into her hand for all this might disappear.

I turned to the door, opened it, and went out onto the deck, careful to close it quiet as I could for fear I might wake Mom.

The deck was wide as the whole back of the house, the half of it to the right under a pergola, a built-in gas barbecue and range and sink against the far side, wooden benches built right into the deck railing. The other half, right out the kitchen door, had railing, too, but had a wrought-iron table and chairs of its own. Big ceramic garden pots sat beneath the railing, filled with petunias and snapdragons. All very elegant, all right out of *Southern Living*, all very Landgrave.

But centered on the table was a bright blue and definitely ugly ceramic thing big as a bowling ball, a thick spray of rosemary growing out the top of it: something I'd made when I was on a field trip in third grade. I'd meant it to be a lidless cookie jar that looked like an apple, had painted it with a glaze that seemed at the time something like red. But when it was delivered with all the other kids' creations from the kiln back to Miss Picken's class a week later, here had been this hideous bright blue thing. I'd carried it home in my yellow nylon *Jurassic Park* backpack, the padded shoulder straps cinched down tight—the jar was heavy as a bowling ball, too—and had given it to Mom. I lied to her, told her it was a giant blueberry, then watched as she fussed over it and fussed. "What a beautiful planter!" she'd said, and bent to me, kissed me on the cheek.

I had no idea what a planter was, and so, because I'd already lied about its being a blueberry, I nodded, acted like that was exactly what it was. It'd sat on the front steps of the house on Marie from then on, was now in residence in the classy digs here. Still a blue apple just as ugly as the day I'd brought it home. But still displayed by Mom.

Our place had no backyard, so when you stepped off the deck onto the dock you were already in the marsh, sawgrass and salt-marsh hay on either side. When it was quiet you could hear the tick and dribble of the tide crawling in or out, filling in or emptying out the billion tiny crab holes in the pluff mud all around. The sun lay straight out in front of me a couple fists above the tree line over at the point on the creek, the tide already back on its way in for the second time since this morning, and as I walked out toward Unc, I could see the cordgrass on the edges of the creek already swallowed up in water. The world just kept moving on.

I waited for Unc to say something to me as I came closer to him. He'd have heard me from the second I opened the back door, figured he'd ask after how well I slept, or what Mom was up to. Some small talk as a means not to go headfirst into talk about last night. But he was quiet, only sat there with the cigar to his mouth.

I made it to the end, headed for the marine locker in under the roof of the boathouse, unlatched and lifted the long white lid of it, reached in and pulled out a folding chair, all still without a word. I closed the lid, parked the chair a few feet to the right and behind him, and sat down.

The air was a little thick today, the distance between the dock and the tree line over at the Naval Weapons Station the slightest white. Already I was sorry I hadn't grabbed a ball cap of my own and a pair of sunglasses, though the sun was fast on its way down.

The marsh had hit that color in mid-spring when the brown of winter was being hustled out by the sharp green of new growth. Even with the thin white pall of the air I could see the hard push of colors one against the other out there, beneath it all the creek and cold green water. The sun was already too low to bang its reflection off the creek and up into my eyes, and for the same old reason I ever had I wanted right then to drop the boat in, head out on the water.

"You remember," Unc said then, his voice quiet, "that first night I played cards with those gentlemen over there in Mount Pleasant?"

His voice had been an interruption, but not a surprise. But still, with just those words, here was triggered in me the surprise tremble of my mom's mouth last night, and her tears. Here was the surprise of her gun on the kitchen table, and the stunned look of both Unc and Tyler at the news Prendergast'd been at the house with Mom, all of it crashing down on me. No tick and dribble of a tide secreting its way in, but a wave that slapped hard from high above, and I shut my eyes, felt myself holding tight the arms of the lawn chair, felt my feet flat on the boards of the dock and pressing down.

I said, "Yes," and did my best to conjure up some picture of the first few times we went to poker night. But all I could see was that huge orange stucco house in Mount Pleasant three stories tall, a grand set of stairs up to the front porch on the second, the front doors up there a huge arch that looked more like the entry to some sort of church than anything else.

"I thought I could play without reading the cards," Unc said, and I heard him draw in on the cigar, only now realized the smell of it in me, the comfort of it, the predictable acrid ease of it. I took in a breath.

"Thought I could win," Unc went on, and shot out the smoke. "Before we got in there that first night, I was thinking all I needed to do at the table was listen to the people around me and how they bet, their voices. Only how they called or checked or raised. I thought, Who the hell needs cards to play poker? Just play the man at the table."

My eyes were still closed, but I could see him, gray smoke wisping up from his cigar, sunglasses under the bill of his cap, the setting sun yellow and gold on him. I could see this all, and had no reason to open my eyes. None.

"I remember," I said, and suddenly I could see the inside of the place that first night.

This was the summer before what would be my last gala semester at Chapel Hill, maybe four or five months after we'd sold the parcel out to Hungry Neck and moved in to Landgrave Hall. That night the owner, Thomas Warchester Whaley the Fourth, a doughy-faced real estate agent with silver hair and a close personal friend of Grange Cuthbert—the one who'd told Unc of the gathering in the first place—had given Unc and me the grand tour of the establishment, introduced us to all the doctors and lawyers and brokers and bigwigs of one sort and another, all of them slapping Unc on the back and welcoming him, though he already knew half of them for being the same clientele he'd been serving for years out at Hungry Neck. About the only difference I could see in the crowd was that instead of the crisp and clean camo outfits they all wore out at the hunt club, these same people were decked out now in Tommy Bahama and Nat Nast shirts.

And one other difference: even though he had on his khakis and suspenders, Braves cap and sunglasses, now Unc was one of them.

The whole operation was on the bottom floor of the house, the area most people used for a garage and storage. But Whaley'd finished all the interior off, then set up five professional poker tables in there, those long oval things padded with leather all the way around, chip trays and green felt tops and a dealer's position, all built high so you had to sit at a stool or stand to play. The place was all carpeted, paintings on the walls, chandeliers from the ceiling.

A kind of chip cage was at one end of the room, more like a closet with a half door, behind it always a chunky Filipino woman in a white shirt and black vest, in there with her the money box and chips. At the other end of the room was a full-length bar, brass toe rail, mirrored shelves behind, working it a big tanned dude dressed the same as the cashier, biceps big as that stupid planter I'd made. Somebody you wouldn't want to argue with over the pour you got. Ever.

Each table had a dealer, too, men and women dressed in those same white shirts and black vests, all like some sort of bad TV show, like what you'd *expect* to expect an in-home casino in a suburb to look like. One of the paintings on the wall was of a huge martini complete with two green olives and an onion, another a croupier's rake and two huge dice. Cheesy, to say the least.

And all of it illegal. Not because there was a five-hundred-dollar buy in, or because of the amount of cash flowing through there every Thursday night, the limit for loss five grand, after which you'd be sent home in the kindliest way by that big dude behind the bar.

No. It was all illegal, because games of chance, no matter it was Uno or pinochle or five-card no-peeky or Texas hold 'em—the one they played all night long at the Whaley establishment—were illegal in South Carolina. Period. You could buy lottery tickets fast as you could hand over a dollar, sure. But a two-man game of war? You're a gambler.

Yet none of this was a worry for the crowd at the Whaley place, as they had among their regular players not only the tried and true of Charleston society, but also three city councilmen—two Mount Pleasant, one Charleston—a Summerville police lieutenant, a vice president of the College of Charleston, and a member of the Charleston County School Board, all of whom provided a kind of civic force field for the night's activities.

And there was a Navy commander in there, too: Prendergast.

"That first hand I sat there with my two cards," Unc said, and paused, drew in on the cigar again, let it out. "But I wouldn't let you see them," he said. "Now how stupid was that?"

"Stupid enough to lose the hand," I said, still with my eyes closed. He'd sat starch upright on the stool that first night, me just behind him, waiting for him to show me his cards so I could tell him what he had. But he'd only lifted one edge of them a quarter inch, then set his hand flat on top of them. I'd leaned in, whispered in his ear something about needing to show me so I could help, but he'd only waved me off with the other hand. I'd stepped back, glanced at the table and all the players watching the whole thing, eyes wide open, dealer included, and the strange moment of a blind man playing cards without knowing what he had.

"One of the stupidest moments of my life," he said now, and I opened my eyes. He was slowly shaking his head, a thin strand of smoke rising off the end of his cigar. "Totally forgot there'd be other people playing *me*. That I wouldn't be the only one playing the people at the table. Didn't figure in, too, it'd be clear as glass that every hand I'd ever play would be a bluff, even if I had a royal flush." He shook his head again, gave out a kind of sad laugh.

A six-inch mullet jumped out in the creek just then, a silver slip of color ten yards away, gone as soon as I'd seen it.

Unc'd been about fourth or fifth at the table that first hand. When it'd come to his turn, he'd sat there for a long second or so, even stiffer on the stool. Everyone was still looking at him, and from where I'd stood I could see him swallow, try at some sort of smile. But then his hand on the cards had made a loose fist, and he'd knocked once on them, said, "I'm out," calm and smooth as could be.

He'd spent the rest of the night grimacing every time he showed me his cards, his jaw clenched and lips tight between his teeth, as though with every deal he were being forced to drop his drawers to show the room a boil on his butt. All he did was tip the cards up for me to see, and I whispered to him. Though he ended up winning a couple hundred dollars that night, I'd figured the whole endeavor was over once we were ushered out with the rest of the rabble at two that morning, Unc quiet the whole ride home.

But the next Thursday night at around 9:30, here was a tap at my bedroom door. Unc pushed it open, stick in hand, said, "Let's go," and then we were parking a hundred yards down the street from that house, the Range Rover in line with all the other cars. Once at the door into the garage, we were promptly met by a grinning Whaley, who held up close to Unc's face three decks of cards still in their wrappers.

"Braille cards!" he hollered out. By the look on his happy realtor face, you could tell his ingenuity startled even him, as though he'd in fact invented Braille itself and tonight was the big reveal.

But a moment later he lost the grin entirely. "Oh," he let out. "You read Braille, don't you?"

Though I'd figured on Unc's being testy for this accommodation someone'd made to the fact he was blind, maybe even ticked off for the conventions of the rest of the blind world he'd have to observe when it came to playing cards, he actually smiled, nodded sharp. With all the genuine goodwill I'd ever seen him muster, he said, "Well enough to kick the house's ass."

"Then kick away!" Whaley said, and with his free hand slapped Unc on the shoulder. He took hold Unc's arm and turned, started to lead him off between tables and players, me already wondering what the heck I was supposed to do now that I wasn't going to be needed. But then Whaley stopped, turned to me and smiled. "Somebody here wants to meet you, Huger," he said. "Says you got a mutual friend."

He nodded over his shoulder, off to the left of the room. I turned, saw leaning against the bar over there a tallish guy with black hair and skin so white you'd think he'd only heard of the sun. He seemed about my age, and had a martini in his hand, his elbow on the bar. He wore a Nat Nast shirt, bright blue with a wide white stripe down the left side. Peeking out the top of the shirt pocket on the right were three pens, tucked tight in a tight row.

"My son," Whaley said. "Thomas Warchester Whaley the Fifth. Five for short." He smiled again, headed away with Unc on his arm.

I turned back to Five for Short, saw him hold up the martini glass, give me something of a toast. He sipped at it, and I started toward him.

That was when he called out, "Tabitha Galliard is my lab partner in Numeric Artificial Intelligence. Up at Duke." He grinned, nodded. "Said she's heard of you."

Tabitha.

I paused for an instant, though flinched might be a better word for it. I made a sort of a stutter sound, too, a hitch in my throat that heaved out in the form of a word that might have been *oh*. And suddenly I was blinking too many times in a row.

I made it the rest of the way to the bar, maybe five or six feet and only as many seconds. But time and distance enough to make me feel like I was maneuvering my body between the molecules of a lead wall.

I put my hand on the bar, saw the big bartender looking at me like I would know what it was I wanted to drink.

"Look like you could use a strong one," the bartender said and smiled, nodded.

I managed a nod back at him, said, "What he's having." As soon as I said it I knew how lame and stupid I sounded.

I took in a breath, blinked a few times more. *Tabitha who?* I wanted to retort. I wanted to say, *Can't place that name,* or *Sounds familiar.*

Or even *Tell her I love her and that I've never stopped loving her.*

These were the words, however equally lame and stupid they were, that came to me as I stood at the bar that first time I met Thomas Warchester Whaley the Fifth. But I said none of them, only watched the bartender pour off a martini from a pitcher and drop in an onion and an olive.

"Enjoy!" he said, and smiled happily, nodded. The word had seemed a preposterous thing coming from such a big dude, and coming at this particular moment, when the idea of enjoying anything at all pretty much ever again seemed not even a possibility.

I picked up the martini, nodded back at the bartender, and turned to Five for Short.

I held the glass up, like I was about to make my own toast, and saw them again: that tight row of pens in the front pocket of his fancy silk shirt, the international sign for a Poindexter. And now I saw what I could say. I had some words, ones that would knock him down, give this pasty-faced turd a thing to think about.

Tabitha said she'd heard of me. Right.

I nodded at the pens, said, "You forgot your pocket protector."

"Did you pass Intro to Computer Programming this time around?" he said right back, smiling.

I turned, set the martini glass on the bar without taking a sip of it, put both hands on the bar top. The bartender raised his eyebrows a bit, as though I hadn't liked what he'd given me, or to wait for the answer I was supposed to give back to Five for Short.

But I had nothing more, only nodded at the bartender, said, "Thanks." I turned, headed back out the door and onto the driveway to the same warm summer night Unc and I'd left out here only a couple minutes before. Tree frogs droned, cicadas whirred, the moon shone.

I walked back to the Range Rover, turned it on, sat with the AC on me, then listened to a few different programs on XM. Eventually I plugged in Durham on the Maps app. Eventually, too, the phone buzzed: Unc, calling to tell me he was waiting for me to come get him.

I'd seen Five for Short only a few times after that, bumped into him as I was ushering Unc into the orange palace now and again. Sometimes I'd hang around inside for a while, if I knew school was going on and he wouldn't be around.

And Unc won at cards. Usually around a grand a night.

Thus began, with only the break that fall of my last pathetic semester of college, the routine of Thursday nights.

"I was thinking," Unc said now, "maybe I've been playing cards too long even to ponder the man behind the man I was playing." He paused, took another pull on the cigar. The sun was low now, almost touching the trees out at the point, the marsh everywhere even sharper in its colors. "I've been playing cards and only thinking about the man there at the table with me, what he's going to do with the hand he's got."

He tapped the cigar on the end of the lawn chair arm, on the dock board directly beneath it a tidy heap of ashes. He had only about three inches or so left on the cigar, almost time to give it up. "Works well enough to win money," he said. "But you tend to forget there's a man behind the man at the table. Prendergast, for example. I know from playing him he's a little desperate at times. He goes bust, then waves around a set of goggles to cover a bet." He paused. "Gives up something ain't his in order to get what he wants. I know when he's got a hot hand his voice tends to go lower, him trying to stay cool but trying to stay cool the signal he's hot. I know when his voice goes high and tight he's got nothing better than a pair, because he wants you to think he's all excited about a good set of cards. But—"

He stopped. His hand with the cigar was still on the chair arm, and he sat there, quiet.

I said, "But."

"But what does any of that matter when you're at a table with someone you know is fundamentally bad?" He shook his head again, this time even slower. "What does that say about the man *you* are, sitting there at the table?"

Still he didn't move the hand with the cigar.

I put my hand up to my forehead, squinted hard across the marsh to the Navy tract over there. Like I could see anyone at all.

"I feel like we got a good hand," he said, quieter now. "There's no bluff involved in our having that set of goggles and his wanting it. He knows what we have." He tapped the cigar again. Nothing came off it. "But I can't help but wonder what the man behind the man at the table wants them so bad for. All he's got to do is write the missing pair up as a Field Loss, and they disappear. Can't help but figure, actually, that that was what he'd done after I won them off him in the first place. Mark a piece of equipment off as a Field Loss, and all questions cease. Equipment destroyed in the field of action. End of story. Don't even matter what happened. And he's got plenty of access to the kind of paperwork all that involves." He paused. "But what I'm wondering is what does it say about me, that I've been playing him every Thursday night all these years?" He shook his head again. "That it's been me winning what I could off him, and your momma here at home and . . ."

"And what?" I said. "What happened between him and Mom? And what do you and Tyler have to do with it?" I blurted it out, no better word for it: the question.

He started to bring up the cigar, but stopped halfway, slowly looked over his shoulder at me, as though he might could see me sitting behind him. Then he turned back to the sun, touching the trees now.

"Another day," he said. "I'll tell you that another day."

Finally he drew in on the cigar, let out the smoke. With the sun just touching the trees on the point, the smoke out of him was in shadow, dark gray and thick, and now I knew I wasn't going to get an answer from him about Mom, or about Prendergast and Tyler and him either. At least not with asking point-blank the question I did. So I decided to let him in on what I did know, and throw in all I had.

I said, "Did you know she has a gun?"

He gave out a small laugh. "Thinks it's her big secret," he said, and shook his head again. "But I used to smell it on her every time she came home from the shooting range."

He held the cigar in front of him sideways now, like he could see it. Like he was reading that gold and brown Hoyo cigar band, thinking on it.

I'd tried. Of course he knew everything. Of course.

"You never smelled her coming through the door once she'd been

over there?" he said, and there seemed on his words a kind of reproach, and a kind of surprise. I'd smelled gunpowder plenty before.
But just not on my mom.

"She used to go to the range up at ATP Gun Shop on College Park.
Back in the day, right after she bought the thing. Started maybe only
a month after what all happened out to Hungry Neck." He stopped,
took in a deep breath, shook his head again. "Knew a couple boys
used to work up there. Used to give me a call whenever she was out
there." He gave a kind of shrug, that cigar still in front of him. "Told
me she was a pretty good shot, too. But this was all a long time ago.
She ain't shot for years now, far as I can tell. Be surprised if she ever
even—"

He stopped, put his hand with the cigar back on the arm of the
lawn chair. He sat that way a few seconds, quiet, then turned to me
again, said, "Why are you asking? And what is it you know I don't?"

"She had it on her last night," I said. "When Prendergast showed
up. Had it when you and Tyler were talking to her, too." I paused, and
found in me a kind of strange pride somehow: I'd known something
Unc didn't.

"A Beretta subcompact," I went on, bent now on exhausting the
secret stash of facts I owned. "It's her third one. And she still goes
to the training. Which means she's still shooting." I paused again,
the sun behind the trees now, and in the miracle way they always
had, the colors out in the marsh—the green and brown, the gray and
yellow—all seemed to flare open, all seemed more alive and genuine
than at any time of the day. "Which means maybe you've been missing a step or two," I said. Then, a moment later, "Old man."

He said nothing, only lifted up the cigar, took one long last pull.
He let out the smoke, pinched the butt between his thumb and middle finger, shot the stub out off the dock a good ten feet, a quick arc
that ended with a sharp spit of sound when it hit the creek.

He stood then, crossed in front of me to his walking stick leaning
against the boathouse pylon to my right. He took it, turned, started

off across the dock. "Fold up these chairs and put them away," he said, the words not gruff but short all the same, and I wondered if I'd made him mad. A part of me in just that instant was sorry if I had, but another part of me thought, Too bad if I did.

But he was already halfway up the dock, me with the chairs folded and marine locker lid open, stowing them away, before it finally came to me what I'd wanted to ask all along, this whole time we'd been out here. What had been inside and under and through me the whole while we'd been talking, but that'd disappeared somehow, like that smoke off the end of his cigar: there, and gone.

"What about the woman?" I called out to him.

"Let's watch TV," Unc called back over his shoulder, him tapping out the boards with that stick, headed for the house.

9

The lead story was about a tractor-trailer wreck up on I-95 that shut down the freeway for four hours. The video showed a line of cars as far as you could see, then the steaming hulk of the jackknifed truck on its side, the cab off the edge of the roadway and bent at an ugly angle, like some giant animal with its neck broken.

Next came word of a former teacher for the Charleston County school district who'd been found not guilty of molesting a student thirty years ago, the white-haired man and his wife crying into each other's arms inside the courtroom right after the verdict was read, and comment then from his attorney about how justice had been served.

Then came the happy news that tourism was up in Charleston, the mayor delighted at the upswing, and file footage of a horse and carriage making its way along some oak-lined street south of Broad, and lines of tourons out front of Hyman's Seafood on Meeting Street.

And then, finally, came word about the body.

No video. Only the anchor, a guy with slicked-back hair and a too-bright tie, reading off the teleprompter about an unidentified body found in Hanahan early this morning. Behind him was the stock graphic of a white outline of a body on a bright red background, what they used when they had nothing else. There wasn't even mention of Landgrave Hall, or a marsh. "Authorities are investigating" were the last words on the issue from the anchor, the same old sign-off that meant the station didn't know a thing.

That was it.

We were in Unc's bedroom, him in his recliner—he had one in here too—me on the edge of his bed, watching the wall-mounted television he had in there. We'd come straight here from out on the dock and'd turned it on just as the opening shots of the evening news began: video of the Morris Island lighthouse, waves at the beach, Fort Sumter with that huge American flag flying over it, inside it all a cheerful and serious voice announcing, "Live from the Lowcountry, it's News Four!"

It'd been halfway through the story about tourism before I finally pieced out how he knew exactly when to shut down on the dock and come up here for the news. He'd known to the minute what time sunset was, checked it on the weather radio he had on his nightstand first thing when he woke up every morning, then kept close the whole day long everything the station had given him: weather forecast, winds, temperatures, tides, sunrise and sunset. His own sort of predawn survey of the world, all handed to him in that slightly jerky machine voice of NOAA. He'd only had to figure how long before true sunset the sun would touch the tops of those trees out on the point of the creek, then sit in a lawn chair and feel the light disappear on him inch by inch until the shadow cast by those trees told him what time it was: Let's go watch TV.

Now, the non-news item about the body over, he sat looking up at the set, mouth a little open like he was a kid and this was cartoons.

He had the remote in his front shirt pocket, where he always kept it when he was watching in here.

I said, "Not much to go—"

"Quiet," he cut in, the words a hard whisper, and lifted a finger from the armchair to signal me to wait.

I turned back to the TV. A white car sat up on the back of a flatbed tow truck with its yellow and orange lights flashing, then the truck pulled away into the dark outside the camera's light. I'd missed the first couple of words, but heard now "in the trunk of a 2002 white Toyota Corolla recovered from Wambaw Creek near Echaw Bridge in Francis Marion National Forest early this morning."

I blinked. That was Major Tyler's call. Where he'd had to head off to last night.

"Investigators from the South Carolina Law Enforcement Division have identified the victim as Robert Mazyck of Goose Creek," the anchor went on, while here now was video of a low concrete bridge over water, still only seeable from the light off the camera, then a shot of crime scene tape across a wide gap in a line of trees, beyond it nothing but black. "Authorities have determined that Mazyck, a 2005 graduate of Georgia Tech with a degree in chemical engineering, has no surviving family. News Four has also found that, according to state records, Mazyck was born in Iraq in 1983 and moved here with his mother, father, and sister as refugees during the first Iraq war in 1991. The family changed its name when they moved to the United States."

Off to the right of the shot of the row of trees, at the very edge of the picture and standing in front of the tape, were two men in uniform, hands on hips, looking away from the camera and out into that black.

One of them turned a little, crossed his arms.

Tyler.

"They're showing Tyler," I said. "Up on the riverbank, where they must've driven the thing off into the water. Showed them towing a car away too."

Now came a quick clip of an EMS without its lights going—the coroner's vehicle, toting off a body—then a shot too close up of a good ol' boy with three or four chins, a ball cap pushed high up on his forehead, his face washed too white for the camera lights on him. "We's up here fishing off the bridge for striped bass other side from the landing," the man said, "and my boy Tick snags on something wasn't there last night. We shine the flashlight down there and seen two-three feet down to a big ol' white something, and I says 'That got to be a car down there,' and so Tick gets on his cell and calls up the nine one one." He reached up to his ball cap, pushed it even higher on his head, let out a deep breath. "This is a certain tragedy, I tell you what, no matter who it is in the trunk of that Toyoter."

Here was the anchor again, and that same stock graphic of the body outline. "Investigators from the South Carolina Law Enforcement Division, the Department of Natural Resources, and Charleston County Sheriff's Office are continuing their investigation of the case," he said. He made a quarter turn at his desk, looked to another camera, though the one he'd been talking at stayed on him, the body outline still behind him. "The annual Blessing of the Fleet and Seafood Festival on Shem Creek in Mount Pleasant happens this weekend," he happily read, and here came footage of a shrimp trawler cruising past Crab Island out in the harbor.

The TV shut off, and I turned. Unc was looking at the floor in front of him, the remote pointed at the set for a moment before he slipped it back into his front shirt pocket.

He said, "Front gate wouldn't let anybody in here with a camera is what that's all about. Why they got no video of anything." He paused, pinched up his mouth a second, considering. "Segundo up at the gate's just doing his job not letting in film crews and reporters and whatnot. No law says a news crew's got a right to come on in here and start to filming. So, no video, no story, far as the station goes." He turned his head a little toward the window beside him, the blinds down and closed like he kept them. "We can watch channel five at six, two at seven, see if there's any other word." He stopped again, turned a little more toward the window. "But I doubt there'll be anything."

"So," I said, "the difference between news about one person getting murdered and another is a piece of footage. They can haul ass all the way up past McClellanville, fifty miles for a bubba and his boy who get a hook on a wiper blade, and the world knows the life story of a dead body when there's a woman whose face has been mutilated and anchored into the mud like she was a—"

"Listen," Unc said, that finger up again, him turned full to the window.

"Most likely nothing but some sort of meth lab turf war out there," I kept on. "Wambaw Creek's out in the middle of BFE. Who knows if My Boy Tick isn't some compatriot of whoever's in the trunk and just wanted the body of his fellow chemist turned up quick so's SLED would start making arrests, shut his competition down fair and square."

Unc quick looked at me, said, "You watch your mouth, son."

I could see by the set of his jaw I'd made him mad with that BFE crack. I'd never been up Wambaw Creek before, only knew it for being off the South Santee River on the way to Georgetown, Wambaw a sizable branch that wandered up past Hampton Plantation. I'd gone there on yet another field trip when I was in fifth or sixth grade, the old plantation house about as classic a one as you could get, perfect white columns and clapboard, an avenue of live oaks. Yet one more place, too, where Washington stayed when he made the tour down south. But what I most remembered about the whole thing was riding in a sweaty school bus for what seemed like days up there and back, kids screwing around making paper airplanes and throwing pencils and nodding off in the heat only to be shoved awake by a bump in the road. Wambaw Creek really was the middle of nowhere.

And inside just that sliver of memory, the one time I'd been up to that plantation all those years ago, I saw Jessup three or four rows in front me on that bus, him just sitting there, no havoc out of him whatsoever. Just a kid sitting still on the same bus I was on, and behaving. A kid—a friend of mine—years before 9/11, and his quitting high school to serve his country, only to come back a security guard standing out front of my house at four this morning in his black ball cap and windbreaker and pants, and I saw again how stunned Prendergast and Harmon were at seeing him there just past the landscape lighting.

Thought I'd tag along, just in case, he'd called out.

And now I heard it, what Unc wanted me to listen to: the crunch of gravel on our drive. Unc turned back to the window again, and I stood from the bed, crossed to the blinds, lifted up one of them to see outside. Maybe it would be SLED come back to ask us something else. Maybe it would be Tyler.

Maybe, I thought, somebody gave a shit about a dead woman.

But it was Mom's BMW—Moonstone Metallic was the color, though it'd always looked nothing other than a shiny beige to me—and for an instant I wondered who the heck had taken her car out on a jaunt and was bringing it back, the garage door opening right now to let in whoever it was.

Mom was supposed to be in her room, asleep.

"Is that Eugenie?" Unc asked, and I glanced down at him in the recliner beside me. He had an improbable look on his face, one I didn't often get to see from a person who could judge time by the tilt of the earth, the touch of a shadow: he looked stunned, what eyebrows he had high on his forehead, mouth open even wider. He, too, had thought she was here and sleeping.

I looked back out the window. "It's her," I said, "unless some joyrider's putting her car back where he found it." She was almost in the garage all the way, the rear tire and trunk all I could see, Mom inching it in like she always did, even with that tennis ball hanging from the ceiling to signal her exactly where to stop. The brake lights flared again and again, the vehicle twitching more the farther in she got.

But then it stopped, the vehicle all the way in. The brake lights went out, the garage door started down.

Unc stood, started for the door. I turned from the window, said, "You didn't know she was gone, did you?"

He stopped inside the doorway, one hand to the jamb. He stood there a second, said, "Guess I must've dozed off downstairs earlier." He paused. "Can't keep track of everything, now can I?"

He looked back over his shoulder at me, and I could see a sort of half smile on his face. "But now she's home," he said, "you see if you can't smell a shooting range on her. Even if it's slathered in that lavender hand lotion she's all the time putting on." He tapped the doorjamb once, stepped on into the library. "Because I'm betting that's where she's been, no matter what camouflage she brings in with her."

Her camo: a roast chicken, gallon of milk, bag salad, and loaf of bread.

And a perkiness off the Richter scale.

"Hello, sleepyheads!" she nearly shouted on her way in the door off the breezeway between the kitchen and the garage. I was in the foyer, Unc already coming through the sitting room next to the kitchen, and I heard plastic grocery sacks settling on the island in there, then Mom call out, "Mama Bear's brought home dinner!"

By the time I made it in there she had the chicken in its plastic container out of one Bi-Lo grocery sack, was pulling the milk out of another. "Took advantage of you boys and your naptime to go over and see Deb Bloom at the Med U. She's senior pediatric nurse-practitioner over there now, and today she—"

She stopped, looked up at us, quiet and side by side across the island from her. "What?" she said, and smiled, tilted her head, finished peeling the sack from the milk jug. She turned to the refrigerator door, pulled it open, her back to us now. "You two know Deb Bloom.

She was my buddy back when I was working down there. My shift supervisor for three years."

She'd changed clothes since last night—or this morning—from that white turtleneck and blue sweater to a white cotton blouse a little snug on her, snug enough so that with her back to me I could tell she wasn't wearing that holster. She set the milk on the shelf inside the door, then turned, reached for the bag salad. "Deb's the boss lady up there now and I just wanted to pop in, give her a big hug for all the hard work she's had to go through all this while."

She opened the crisper drawer, dropped in the salad, then closed the refrigerator, turned back to us. "You know Deb," she said, still with that smile. "Deb Bloom. You met her a few times when you were little, Huger. Over at the Med U." She nodded.

Maybe it was nothing more than the power of suggestion, or maybe it was the truth. But I thought I could smell something on her, the smallest tinge of an idea of the sharp edge of smoke, nothing more than a match strike three days ago, a burnt-out sparkler from last Fourth of July. But it was there, buried beneath that lavender always on her.

I said, "I remember her," and nodded, smiled, though I couldn't for the life of me bring anything to mind.

Unc was already coming around the island, reached out into the air above the granite and landed it right on the third white plastic bag. He reached in, pulled out a loaf of bread. "Let me help," he said.

We ate dinner, there at the breakfast table in the kitchen, that same table we'd all sat at last night, and where still my book bag lay at my feet. The sun was down now, the water on the creek gone silver for the fading light, the greens and browns only going deeper. Then here came a pinprick of light out there in the pale orange: Venus.

We talked a little, Unc about commercial shrimp season starting up and maybe this fall we ought to go out and shrimp bait for ourselves, me about heading out to Hungry Neck one day next week to take a look for some turkey. But mostly we listened to Mom carry on, trying her best to convince us of how she spent the afternoon with this Deb Bloom who'd been at the Med U for twenty-eight years now and was the first nurse Mom had met her first day and who had a married daughter my age living up in Bloomington, Indiana, getting ready to have a baby in June, and wasn't it funny Deb's daughter's maiden name was Bloom and she lived in Bloomington?

No one said a word on a body in a marsh, or on poker night creeping up on us by the minute. And when we finished, Unc and I carrying the plates to the sink to do our nightly duty—I washed what couldn't go in the dishwasher, Unc dried—and after Unc wiped down the island and I did the counters and table, we thanked her like this were a cotillion lesson and we were penitent students, then told her we were going to watch the news up in Unc's room.

"I'm just fine," she said, though neither of us had asked her. But she wasn't stupid. Not by a long shot. She knew we were worried about her. And she knew there was news we needed to see. She winked at me, picked up the glass of white wine she'd been sipping at all through dinner. "You boys don't need to worry a whit about me," she said. "I'm fine."

"Good," I said, and nodded at her, smiled. Unc echoed, "Good," and we left her there.

And watched at six and again at seven the same empty announcements about a body in Hanahan, then a story and footage about a body in a Toyoter in Wambaw Creek. Both channels had also interviewed the sire of Tick, who gave the same story we'd already heard; both channels had a fleeting second or so of Tyler and a couple other men in uniform, hands on hips or arms crossed as they spoke to one another.

Yellow crime scene tape hung in the still air out there. Somebody in the studio droned. And the world went right on.

10

Like always this time on a Thursday night—10:08 by the numbers on the dash clock—there were plenty of cars already parked on the street, the usual BMWs and Audis and Lexi. But I lucked out, saw up ahead a spot only two doors down from the Whaley manse.

Already I could feel my neck going hot, my palms on the wheel the smallest bit sweaty.

Prendergast was in there.

A parking spot two doors down in this neighborhood meant we were still a good fifty yards away. This was Hamlet Square, a high-end development out on Rifle Range Road here in Mount Pleasant, the Beverly Hills of South Carolina. Home of big black SUVs with MY KID IS SMARTER THAN YOURS bumper stickers, plastic surgeons by the score, and a kind of residential sprawl that'd let this suburb across the Cooper River from Charleston bleed north for the last twenty years until it seemed almost to touch Virginia.

The streets here were all half-acre lots plotted out with raised houses. Clapboard siding and Charleston Black shutters, front porches with rocking chairs or joggling boards, three-car garages underneath each house: all predictable. And somehow allowed in this the wild hair of Thomas Warchester Whaley the Fourth's orange stucco place, dropped smack in the middle of it all.

I know I was being snarky about this neighborhood, and all of them over here. I know I was being shitty about those highlight-haired and Botoxed women behind the wheels of their tanks, and about the husbands who drove these luxury cars over here on Thursday nights to throw away money like it was peeing in a ditch.

But there was nothing I could do for feeling that way, because I was a piece of the shit I smelled: here were Unc and me in his black Range Rover, pulling into a place at the curb. Driving here from our own posh digs in a neighborhood more exclusive than this place could ever hope to be.

This is where it'd gotten us: meeting up to play some sort of game that involved a set of goggles and a man who'd blowtorched a piece of my mother's soul.

And there was a dead body involved here. One it seemed, if our talk on the way over was any kind of pulse check, Unc was having second thoughts even thinking about.

We pulled into the spot, parked behind a silver Mercedes CL550, the paint job almost too bright in the headlights. I sat there a second, squinting at it, and the row of cars in front of us and across the street. And that orange house up there, all lit up and ready to go.

I turned the engine off, looked behind me to the backseat, where the book bag lay there in the dark. Right where I'd put it.

"It's going to be all right," Unc said beside me, and I looked at him. Just his shadowed profile, him looking straight ahead. "Everything's going to be just fine."

My neck went even hotter, no matter how much I wanted to believe him.

We'd left about 9:30, Mom already in her pajamas and in bed. Of this I was certain, as I'd seen her into her room, gave her a hug, told her not to worry about us and that we'd be back early. She'd smiled, nodded, flipped on her own TV to start watching her TiVoed *American Idol* results show: her Thursday night routine.

Tyrone was working security up at the front gate. We'd pulled up to the white-brick gatehouse, the wrought-iron gates in my headlights making their slow push forward to let us out, and I rolled my window down. Usually I just eased on through, but there seemed this night something better I could do, something different, for no other reason than that Jessup had been out front of our house last night, watching. Just in case.

Tyrone, smiling and with his hands in his pockets against the cool night air in through his open door, stepped out of the gatehouse, leaned forward toward the car. "Mr. Huger, Mr. Leland," he said, "how you doing tonight?"

"Good," I said, and Unc said, "Just fine."

"Bad night last night," Tyrone said, the smile gone now. "Heard about what you found out there. And about Segundo having to fight off the news crews." He shook his head, grimaced. "Told me he had to threaten to call the cops if they didn't turn around and go on home. Three vans showed up here." He looked to his left, out front of us where the gate still stood open. "Sad piece of news, whatever it was happened."

He looked back at us, shook his head again. Then he opened his mouth, on him what looked a kind of surprise. "Oh!" he said, and turned quick back to the gatehouse, stepped in and reached down beneath the window. Then here he was with Unc's golf club, the camp chair folded up in its bag. "Jessup brought these up before he went on home this morning," he said, and held them out, an item in each hand, like they were prize fish. "Wanted me to bring 'em on over to you, but I clean forgot, what with all the buzz going on."

I popped open my door, stepped out and started around to the back of the Range Rover, Tyrone right behind me. "We can put them in here," I said, and Unc called out from inside, "What is it?"

"Club and chair," I said, the tail door open now, Tyrone settling them inside. "From last night."

Unc said nothing, and Tyrone stood up, brushed his hands together like this was the end of a job well done. I closed the door, and he stepped in front of me, headed for the gatehouse door.

I came around to my door, put one leg up into it to climb in, but paused a second. "Jessup did a good job last night," I said. "If you talk to him before I do, let him know I want to thank him." I climbed in, pulled closed my door.

"He'd of been here tonight," Tyrone said from the gatehouse door, hands back in his pockets. "This was supposed to be his regular shift. Supposed to be me working last night, but a couple days ago he said he had something coming up and couldn't work tonight, and we traded." He shook his head again, looked out front to those open gates, glanced behind us. He let out a small laugh, and looked at us. "I'm not gonna lie, I'm sort of sorry I missed all the action. This is a good job and all, and I'm sorry somebody was killed. But, well . . ."

He stopped, blinked, swallowed. He glanced down at the ground and back up to me again, and I could see he'd realized he'd walked too far into the sentence he'd begun, one that was going to end with what a boring job he had. This to a couple people who lived out here: his employers.

He stood up a little bit taller, took his hands out of his pockets, and now Unc called out from beside me, "Can't imagine what it would be like having the job you do." I turned, saw him leaning across the console between us and looking up and out the window. "Just wanted to stop and say thank you for that." Unc nodded once, and sat up, faced forward. "We have to head on out now," he whispered then, low and just the least bit sharp. Just loud enough, I guess he figured, for only me, and I turned back to my open window to see if Tyrone'd heard him.

But he was inside the gatehouse again, reaching down for something else beneath the window. "Almost missed these," he said, and stepped out, held a Ziploc bag out to me, inside it four golf balls and a few tees. "They were out with the chair and the club." He nodded. "With Jessup's best," he said, and I took the bag, dropped it in the console tray. I smiled back at him, nodded. "Thanks again," I said, and pulled forward through the gates.

We'd driven then that same old quarter-mile spit of asphalt edged with overgrown trees to the light at North Rhett. The road into Landgrave Hall we were on was meant to look like a dead end to anyone driving by, even a yellow ROAD ENDS warning sign up at the head as soon as you made the turn off North Rhett so that anyone not in the know would think they were headed into the marshy unknown.

I turned left, headed for the on-ramp for the Mark Clark a couple miles down, and just like that we were in the lower intestine of Hanahan: on the right sat an industrial park and its prefab metal buildings with their oddball array of business signs on the sides—CHARLESTON RUBBER AND GASKET, THE ODLE GROUP, MOTION INDUSTRIES, NORANDEX DISTRIBUTION—while on the left stood those jet fuel storage tanks, each one big as an airplane hangar, out front of them all a chain-link fence eight foot high with three strands of barbed wire above it.

More Navy land.

This was the same fence that separated Landgrave Hall from Perimeter Road, the paved single-lane that encircled the whole Navy property. That fence you could see in winter when you were on the green at sixteen or the tee at seventeen. Here was where it came out of the woods to meet the public proper, cordoning off these storage tanks, and corralling in Space and Naval Warfare Systems Command, all those SPAWAR nerd-spies at their computers, and keeping from the civilian world the Army transportation battalion fitting out the never-ending convoy of MRAPs for Afghanistan and loading those bad boys onto the Navy ships moored at their wharf on the Cooper River.

Just then I saw out my window and off to the left past the tanks the snapping blink of lights on some kind of aircraft, and knew in just that moment, with how slow it was, and the way it was easing straight down, it was one of those Chinook helicopters, making a night landing at the heliport over there.

And out my window too, off to the right and looming high above the fence and a half mile away, stood the stadium lights of the Navy brig, illuminating the world just like they had the fairways when I'd walked them home last night, their light washing the stars out of the night sky.

We passed two more warehouse-like buildings on the right, these for something called Blackhawk Logistics, then Lee Distributors on the left, with its rows of Miller Lite trucks in the lot out front, waiting to be filled for tomorrow's deliveries. All this military and all this industry, hiding the fact of the homes we lived in, the manicured greens, the docks and picture windows and marshes, and the ghost beneath it all of a history three hundred years old.

And though my head was jammed tight with what we were heading out to do tonight, no matter how ridiculously minor a black-ops mission it was for a blind man and an unemployed rich kid to hand over a pair of goggles, it came to me the fact that someone right then was thinking on an order of gaskets and how to get them boxed and shipped in time tomorrow, and someone else was tallying up the cases of beer to load into one of those trucks. Someone, too, was working through his head the spy specs of the schematic on his SPAWAR computer back at the office, where tomorrow morning he'd pick right back up working on it once he passed through military security at the gate off Remount Road.

And just then, if the rumors always going around were any of them true, a terrorist or two or three were sitting in a cell beneath those lights right over there, running off in their heads wisdom from the Koran.

Terrorists who wanted to kill any and every American they could get their hands on, only walking distance from here.

All this going on, while my mom sat at home in bed, skimming through commercials with the remote in one hand, in the other, I felt pretty certain, a subcompact Storm. The entire pastoral world out to Landgrave Hall wrapped in the disguise of industry and military, my mom gated inside its refuge.

But only a knock on the door away from practicing what she'd preached out on the shooting range.

We bumped over the railroad tracks just past the beer distributor, passed next the rec baseball field and the Kangaroo mini-mart. The light at the intersection with Remount turned yellow, and I gunned through it, just ahead the on-ramp for the Mark Clark and our path to Mount Pleasant.

That was when Unc said, "Just don't know what one has to do with the other."

I moved to the right lane, made the slow swoop onto the ramp and started up, and let myself glance at him even inside the tight circle we were making up to the elevated freeway. "What do you mean?" I said.

He was turned to his window, shaking his head. We were at the top of the ramp now, and I moved left out onto the freeway, ahead of us the metal cage of the Don Holt Bridge shooting high over the Cooper River toward Daniel Island. Below us to the right I could see the 84 Lumber, to my left the paper mill in all its nighttime glory: lights and towers and that smokestack chugging out steam. On the highest tower flew an American flag, lit up with a floodlight from below.

"For some reason I keep tangling these two things one in another," Unc said. "But it's two events. Two things." He paused, and I could see him face forward, above and around us now the beam-and-girder skeleton that was the bridge. "One is a murder," he said, "plain and simple. We were the ones who found her. That's all. The other is, somebody's out on patrol over to the Naval Weapons Station and sees you wearing a set of goggles civilians aren't allowed to have. Prendergast'd have to grab his ankles and hold on the rest of his life for the ass-kicking he'd get if someone higher up finds he's giving out equipment in a poker game, so he sends a couple of his men to get them back. They come on over to Judge Dupont's place for the goggles, but walk in on a late-night patio party with all these people who weren't there when they first saw us from over on the weapons tract. The Cuthberts, Mrs. Q. That screaming nurse of Dupont's." He let out a quick breath, shook his head again. "Stanhope and Harmon got no choice but to improvise then. That's when it all turns into this haul-you-in-for-trespassing hoo-ha. Prendergast figures maybe the best thing to do is to make like he's arresting us, confiscate the goggles, then let us go on home. All there is to it."

I looked at him. "But somebody was killed," I said, and thought again of the green scope of sight I had, the woman's teeth bared and grimacing, the swirl of her hair in the water. That blue crab, there at her ragged jaw. I swallowed, said, "A woman was murdered, and the body was anchored in the pluff mud at Landgrave. Does it matter if it's only a coincidence?"

"What do you propose we do?" Unc said, on his voice a kind of edge that made me feel twelve years old again, a kid too dumb to reason with. We were off the bridge, the freeway now a long concrete chute four lanes wide and crossing the dredge-dump flats this side of Daniel Island. Above the tree line up ahead I could see the lit-up arc of the bridge over the Wando a couple miles away, the long hump of it that dropped down into the promised land of Mount P.

"We were interviewed by three pairs of detectives," Unc went on. "Plus Tyler. It's not like nobody gives a damn. So what if there's nothing on the news about it. That don't mean nobody's working this." I could see out the corner of my eye him turn full-on to me then. He said, "Do you understand, son?"

"But I saw her," I said, as though that would explain anything and everything. As if this were the only thing I understood about why I wanted something done to find whoever killed her: I saw her.

Unc faced forward again, folded his hands in his lap. "I got no help for you on that one," he said, quiet. "And for that I'm sorry. But it's Prendergast the one we need to deal with right now. It's him we have to think on." He stopped, turned to his window again. "It's him we have to keep from your momma," he said, "because if we don't, I'm afraid for what she'll do to him. Not that I give a damn about Prendergast. But because of what it might mean for your mom. And the law against what she's got every right to do."

He looked at me then. "You smelled the range on her, I hope."

I looked back to the freeway. We were already almost across Daniel Island, on the right the tennis center and its boxy stadium, just ahead the Grace Bridge rising over the Wando. Just ahead, too, lay poker night in Mount Pleasant, and whatever hand we'd play to see this to its end.

"Yes I did," I said.

A car slowly cruised past us, a black Audi trolling for his own spot on the street, though there couldn't have been any more of them this close to the Whaley house, and I leaned forward, looked in my side-view mirror to see how far back the line of cars went. Here behind us was another set of headlights easing up same as the Audi had: yet another player.

I felt a drop of sweat carve its way down the back of my neck and into my collar, and sat back, forced myself to take in a deep breath. There stood the Whaley place fifty yards away, inside it Prendergast. And we were going on in there.

It was a black Suburban coming up on us, slowing down even more the closer he got, and I imagined his Botoxed wife had gotten the Lexus tonight for her Pampered Chef party. He edged past us, touched the brakes a second in front of the house, almost like he was giving a thought to pulling right up on the lawn, to hell with all this street parking. But then he moved on, prowling for the sacred spot that meant he wouldn't have to work up a sweat in the armpits of his silk shirt before he stepped into the casino. He'd end up parking on past the house, of course, and I saw beyond him the brake lights on the Audi flare a half dozen houses away, pull to the left and to the curb.

I popped open my door then, the dome light cutting on above us, and turned to climb out.

"No," Unc said hard beside me, his hand a vise on my forearm just that quick.

I turned to him. The bill of his Braves cap hid his face beneath the dome light, but I could see in the darkness the reflection of me in his sunglasses. Two of me, right there in the dark of his face.

He wasn't letting me go with him.

"Close the door," he said.

"Unc," I started, and made to pull away from him. But his hand on my arm went even tighter.

"Huger."

I looked at him a couple seconds longer before I slammed closed the door, the two of us in darkness again.

"You listen," I started in, and felt my jaw go tight for the fight I was going to give him over this. He wasn't going to leave me out here. No. "You listen," I said again. "You need me in there. You need me. I'm not just your chauffeur. I'm not just your boy to drive you around and watch you do what you have to do without me there, too. I didn't come all the way out here to—"

"Huger," Unc said again, but this time in a whisper.

I took in a breath, surprised at the sound of just that one word. "You need me in there," I said again, but already there was nothing in it, whatever words I'd lined up already breaking down.

Because he didn't need me. I knew that. He could just walk along this line of cars, a hand trailing rear fender to hood on each one, leaving two gaps for the driveways of the houses between us and the Whaley place, then head up the third one, his stick tapping out the length of it. With any luck either the driver of the Audi or the Suburban'd be hustling to the driveway at the same time, help him on up. They all knew him. And once inside he was, like every poker night, his own man. That was when I always went back to the Range Rover anyway, started in on my Maps app wanderings, my cellphone solitaire.

Though I wanted to go in, I knew he was right. He could handle Prendergast all by himself.

He let go my arm, and I took in a couple defeated breaths, closed my eyes.

And then I asked it, one more time. Because it was what I wanted to know of the deep down of all this. It was what I wanted to know, the why of the fact I couldn't go with him, but Unc had to do this alone.

I thought of my mom, and that gun centered neatly on the table between us.

"What did he do to her?" I whispered.

He took in a deep breath, held it a moment, let it out.

He said, "Back in high school, seven boys on the football team got four girls to go with them after a game to a trailer up past Moncks Corner. Eugenie was one of them."

He said it with no measure to the words, no emotion at all. Only words out of him.

He paused, took in another breath, and I fit my tongue in the side of my cheek, bit down hard for the feel of it, the pain. It was something I'd done since I was a kid, a distraction I gave myself when I knew the world was about to crash in. Here it came.

"Prendergast the ringleader to it all," he said.

I'd asked for this. And already I didn't want it. I didn't want it, and I bit down harder.

"Got them up there and drugged them. Give them something

in their beers. This was back in 'seventy-six. Before roofies. But this stuff has been going on forever." He paused, and inside the pain in my tongue I saw up ahead the driver of the Audi come around the tail of his car, cross the street for the house. "The girls wake up the next morning alone in the trailer," Unc went on. "No car to get them home. Of course no cellphones back then. So they have to walk. And from that point on all four of them have a reputation. All four of them get known for being sluts, because Prendergast and the boys are already home on a Saturday morning and bragging to any school chum who'll listen what they done to four girls in a trailer out to Moncks Corner."

I let up on my tongue, the pain no distraction at all. Only pain, already a kind that meant nothing at all. I said, "But couldn't they report—"

"This is thirty-five years ago," Unc cut in. "This is four girls against seven boys, all of them first-string seniors on the Stall team. This is North Charleston, and girls with no proof they could know of other than the feeling of it."

He gave out a breath. "It's only one girl, Gloria Deedham, decides she's going to fight them," he went on, only this time with his voice pitched in a strange way. Quieter, but given up, too. As though the words themselves had surrendered to the work they knew they had to do. "Gloria Deedham decides she's going to report them to the police. And she does. Gets her momma and daddy to go down there with her and file the report, but this is already a month after the fact. Still, she tries to charge these boys with rape, though it means admitting to going out to that trailer, and that she knew better than to go out there in the first place, and that she has no proof. Other than the feeling. The same feeling all four of the girls said they had when they went on home from that trailer." He paused. "Gloria Deedham won't name the other girls with her, either, because she wanted them to report it of their own accord, and because she didn't want to bring them down into what she had to know could happen after she started this thing going. North Charleston police start asking questions, get nowhere, and meanwhile that girl and her family ends up with the tires slashed on the two cars they own three times in a month, some-body shitting on their front porch one night, and a word I won't say painted in red full across her garage door. At school everything you can imagine. While the other three girls don't say a word."

He paused, shook his head. "One of them transfers to a differ-ent school. Another one drops out altogether. But Eugenie stays on, though she won't file, won't say anything to any of the authorities. And does her best to talk Gloria Deedham into dropping the charges." He took in a breath, sat quiet a second. "I know all this because it was your daddy and me and Alton Tyler she told what happened, when what Gloria Deedham was going through was at its worst. She told us because we were her friends, and had been since we were kids in junior high. She knew she could trust us, and trust us not to tell." He stopped, and I could hear him swallow. "She wouldn't even tell her own momma and daddy, your grandparents. They passed never even knowing."

"Unc," I said. "Please. You don't—"

"The football team," he went on, "ends up regional champs. The police get no one who matters to the whole thing to talk. And Gloria Deedham—" He paused again, leaned his head back to where it just touched the headrest. He took in one more deep breath, let it out slow.

"One afternoon," he whispered, "just before Christmas break, Gloria Deedham steps in front of a train out on the tracks behind Sunset Memorial, the cemetery up off Ashley Phosphate. And your momma there with her when she did it."

He swallowed again, and I closed my eyes tight. No need now to bite down on my tongue. No need for that ever again. Because there was no distraction for what I knew now. There was no going back ever again. And I'd been the one to ask for it.

"Your momma and her was walking home after school that day,

Eugenie still trying to talk her into dropping the charges," he whispered. "And then Gloria ended it. Eugenie's lived with that her whole life. Her whole life, and Prendergast showing up on her porch last night."

I saw again the reaction Tyler and Unc both gave when Mom told them he'd been at the house, the shock of it. And I saw Unc out on the dock, asking why he'd ever play poker with a man fundamentally bad.

My eyes still closed, I whispered then, "How could you?"

The words came out through clenched teeth, though I didn't know I'd clenched them. My hands squeezed hard on the steering wheel, though I didn't know I'd taken hold of it.

I whispered, "How could you play cards with him?"

"I didn't know he was there, back when I started up," he said, then went quiet, took in a breath through his nose. "All I know is that one night maybe a month after I started Warchester introduced me to a man he figured I didn't know, we three halfway through a hand already. 'Don't know if you know Commander Jamison Prendergast,' Warchester says to me, and Prendergast says before I can blink 'I know who he is.' His voice all smiles." He paused. "I played out the hand. And after that first one, the next one was a little easier. And then the next one. He was easy to beat. Easy to read, like I told you." He paused. "None of that's anything but an excuse. A sorry one. Though it's no consolation, the day after Gloria's funeral, Alton Tyler and your daddy and me showed up at Prendergast's house and beat the living shit out of him and a couple-three of those boys over there with him." He paused again, took in another breath. "And after all that, the whole thing disappeared. Those boys all seemed to just walk away. Seemed from then on to bow their heads and swallow hard and walk away. Not a word come out of anyone after that." He stopped again. "I don't know what come of those other two girls. Couldn't give a shit what happened to any of them boys. But Prendergast ends up an officer in the Navy. No charges filed, no record." He paused. "The

Navy. I've known a thousand good people in the Navy. But here's the one shows up at a poker table. The one shows up to our door, too."

I heard him turn in his seat then, toward me. "Your momma's had this on her heart her whole life," he said, his voice thin and ragged. "She's had all of it. The fact of what happened with those boys, and the fact she was there when Gloria killed herself, and the fact she still kept quiet once that girl was gone. She's had to live with that. And it's me brought it all back to her with these goggles, and with this poker house."

He stopped, sniffed. He whispered, "I have to ask her forgiveness. And I will. Once this is all over. Because I have done the wrong thing. I have done the wrong thing here, and all the years we've been playing cards like this. To be playing with him." He paused. "I just wanted to beat him at something, even if it was just cards. But that's me being the selfish shit I am. It's me doing the wrong thing all this while. But this will be the end of it."

He took in a breath, then said, "And I need to ask your forgiveness, too. I ask your forgiveness. Because I've been playing cards with this same man. Forgive me for sitting across the table from him, betting against his voice for the sake of nothing other than a game of cards and the pitiful joy of a handful of cash. But I aim to end that now. And that's why you have to stay here."

I opened my eyes, felt the wet of them and the hot, and I turned, saw his shadow waver in the dark of the car.

I said nothing.

He leaned over to me, put his hand back on my arm, but softly, gently. "Huger, where I need you is out here," he said. "You know I need you, but what I need is for you to stay right here and to stay put. I'm going in there and get this done."

He sat up straight, turned to his door and popped it open, the dome light on again, self-appointed and dull. Then he turned back toward me, and here was his face hidden in the shadow of his bill once more, inside it again those two reflections of me. Like nothing had changed between the first time I'd seen them tonight and this moment, here, now.

"You stay put, you hear?" he said, and reached a hand into the pocket of his windbreaker, pulled out his cellphone, set it in the console tray, there with the bag of golf balls. He leaned a little forward, pulled from his back pocket his wallet, set it in there too, all while I just watched, nothing making much of any sense right now. Not much sense at all.

He turned to the open door, climbed out and closed it, then opened the backseat door: darkness for a moment, then the dome light again. He reached down to the floorboard, picked up his walking stick from where it lay down there, took hold of the book bag.

He looked at me again. "You stay in here, and just stay put. No matter what. Because that's what I need from you."

I swallowed, nodded.

"Okay," he said. "Good." Like he'd been able to see me.

He stood, started to close the door, but leaned in again.

He looked at me, said, "I love you, Huger."

"Okay," I said, my voice barely loud enough for even me to hear.

He stood there a moment longer, then closed the door, moved alongside the Range Rover up to the hood, crossed to the silver Mercedes. He held the book bag in his left hand, in his right the walking stick, then shrugged the book bag over his shoulder. His left hand now free, he touched the rear fender on the Mercedes, started off, the walking stick in his right hand tapping out the curb.

A moment later he was gone, hidden for the cars. Next time I'd see him from here he'd be walking up the drive of the house.

I breathed in, wiped at my eyes with the palms of my hands, then opened them wide, blinked and blinked. I took in another breath.

No wonder Mom'd leaned in close to me last night when I finally showed up. No wonder she'd held on tight, her arm crooked at my elbow while we three stood there in the foyer of our home. No wonder she'd gone to the shooting range.

He'd kissed Mom on the cheek. And she'd taken it.

I leaned forward to rest my forehead against the steering wheel, as if that might do anything for me at all.

And saw in the side-view mirror a set of headlights again: that same dumbshit black Suburban, sweeping through from behind us one more time, as though there might have been a spot open up since the last time he drove by.

For a moment I thought of giving him this one. I thought of starting the engine, then rolling down my window and waving him in as I gunned on out, swerved up onto the Whaley driveway and crashed right through those garage doors. Then I'd find Prendergast and do my best to beat the living shit out of him.

The Suburban passed by, tapped its brakes again out front of the Whaleys', moved on.

II

I stayed put.

I leaned my head against the steering wheel again, rested it there for what seemed an hour, then sat up, stared at the Whaley house for another hour. I stared for one more at the moonlit silver of the Mercedes in front of me, then leaned against the steering wheel again, closed my eyes.

I tried not to think of anything, tried only to take in one deep breath after another.

But of course I was thinking.

What happened had been thirty-five years ago. Thirty-five years. And I wondered: How do you continue? How do you go on with your life after what's happened to your life has happened? After you watch someone you know step in front of a train? After you've been drugged and bad things done to you, and after you've chosen to stay quiet for the shame of it all, then live with the guilt of knowing you didn't help her when she was alive or after she was gone?

How do you end up, after what Mom'd been through, anywhere *but* at target practice, and imagining the black silhouette fifteen yards in front of you is the evil shit who'd kissed you on the cheek in the foyer of your own house?

I knew where those train tracks were, just the other side of I-26 from Northwoods Mall. I knew Sunset Memorial Gardens, had seen it any number of times when for one reason or another we were driving Ashley Phosphate. There was a bowling alley we went to once or twice out that way when I was a kid, a Glass Masters I'd had the windshield on the old Chevy LUV changed out at one time. Mom used to shop at a Hamrick's up where Ashley Phosphate hit Dorchester, back before the money came in.

But the only reason I remember the cemetery is because it was such a plain place, just a spread of grass fronting on the four-lane street while I was on the way somewhere else. A line of sago palms across the front of it, memorial plaques flat on the ground, an asphalt entry without even a gated arch above it. Just that piece of ground, the green of it.

And just past it, crossing Ashley Phosphate, the train tracks.

I thought of Unc, and Parker, my dad, who'd left when I was a kid, and Alton Tyler, the three of them teenagers with their hands in fists, walking up the driveway of Prendergast's house in order to do to him and his friends what they could.

I thought of Mom.

I opened my eyes, sat up. I blinked a couple times, not certain if I'd fallen asleep. I pulled out my iPhone, checked the time: 10:26. Not even twenty minutes since we got here.

And because I had the same old nothing to do while I waited for Unc to come back, and because Tyler'd been one of those three to beat up Prendergast and his pals, and, finally, because it was my habit while out here to go somewhere other than where I was, I opened once more the Maps app on the iPhone, typed in "Echaw Bridge, Wambaw Creek SC." Where Tyler had taken off to last night, only to show up on the evening news.

Here came the gray map, a line for the road, a tiny blue squiggle for the creek, a red pin sticking up. I pressed Satellite, got the photos from space, and saw a minuscule bridge across a creek, green trees everywhere around. That red pin still plugged into the middle of nowhere.

For a moment, Tyler's job seemed like it could be a good one. To have a boat out at night and wandering around creeks, trying to get the jump on duck hunters baiting a blind. Or writing up shrimp baiters for hauling in too much catch, or stalking through a piece of woods to make sure turkey weren't being shot out of season. Just being outside, on the marsh or in the woods or on a creek, out in that middle of nowhere, and trying to make sure people played by the rules.

But then I thought of nights like last night. I thought of his silhouette in the searchlight of his boat, him kneeling way up on the hull and leaning over the edge, the Maglite in his hand moving back and forth on the creek as he looked at the woman. Then the call to visit a body in a trunk and whatever ugly surprise that had involved. I saw Tyler in his Boston Whaler speeding down Goose Creek to the Cooper, having to trailer it back at Bushy Park Landing, and driving like hell to make it all the way to Wambaw Creek in the one hour he'd figured it would take. Only to look down into a trunk, and one more body.

I thought of how sometimes when it rained it poured.

I heard a tap at the passenger window.

Unc, I knew, finally back. Package delivered. Now maybe we could head on home. And I decided, in just that instant of a tap on glass, that once we got back I'd spend the rest of the night on the floor outside Mom's door, then hold her close as I could the second she came out tomorrow morning.

"It's open," I called out, and put the iPhone back in my pocket.

The door opened, that dome light again, and here was Thomas Warchester Whaley the Fifth—Five for Short—leaning in, and grinning.

"Leland thought you could use a little company out here," he said. "Sent us to come visit you."

I blinked.

The last time I'd seen him was six months or so ago, me dropping off Unc inside. Whaley Five'd just gotten a job with a bank up in Charlotte, something to do with computer systems, and'd taken the opportunity to crow to me about it.

And to tell me he'd just been out to Frisco—he'd really called it Frisco—to visit Tabitha over at Stanford, and that her work out there was going great.

I'd nodded, seen Unc to the first stool available at the closest table, and walked out.

Now here he was again, wearing a navy blazer and pink button-down shirt, and with the way the jacket fell open for his leaning in, I could see in his shirt pocket three pens, tight in a row.

"Don't act so happy to see us," he said, and stood up, stepped a little aside. He leaned his head in again, said, "Brought somebody here wants to say hey."

Someone stood in the dark just past the dull glow from inside the car, and I squinted, saw in the same second Tabitha lean forward into the light, give a small wave.

Hey, Huger, she mouthed.

Tabitha.

I took in a breath, felt myself shake my head in disbelief over this: Tabitha. Here.

"Cat got your tongue?" Whaley Five said, and leaned into the light again, still grinning.

"Hey!" I said, and again, "Hey!" and felt my hand fumbling for the door handle beside me without taking my eyes off her, then the door popped open, and now I was quick coming around the hood. Whaley Five had closed the passenger door, stood at the curb with his arms crossed and leaning against it, Tabitha beside him. Though it was dark, I could see she was looking at the ground.

"Tabitha!" I said, and started to reach my arms out to her, but realized just then she hadn't been smiling when she'd leaned into the car. I could see in the dark she had on a light jacket, held a purse by the strap with both hands in front of her, the strap long enough to where the purse almost touched the ground. She was still looking down.

And it came to me, the idea that trying to hold her even just to give her a hug might be a very bad thing to do.

Because two years ago, in Palo Alto—the last time I saw her, after the text explosion we'd had on the phone, followed by me backing my Tundra out of the garage at the house and then driving fifty-two hours straight to a parking spot in the lot across the street from Lyman Graduate Residences, the Maps app leading me all the way—I'd tried the same thing. To hold her in my arms. And I'd also tried to tell her I loved her, and that I'd never stopped loving her.

She'd been out on the sidewalk in front of the building before I even crossed the street from the lot, behind her the four-story curve of windows and tan stucco and rust-red architectural beams of the apartment complex. What seemed more like a Spanish fortress at her back than anything else.

She'd stood with one hip out, arms crossed, jaw jutted forward, all exactly like she does. She was shaking her head, her eyes creased halfway closed, and had on an old pair of jeans, a gray sweatshirt, her hair pulled back with a white headband.

She was beautiful.

I stepped up onto the sidewalk, and she uncrossed her arms, pointed her index fingers a little above me and then straight at me, then with her right hand pinched her fingers and thumb together, touched the corner of her mouth, then her cheek.

She did it five times. They were quick moves, and sharp, and fierce, each point of her fingers two shots into my chest, each touch to mouth and cheek a fist to my face.

Go home go home go home go home go home.

The three years we'd been together—from my sophomore year until I was a senior—she'd taught me some sign language, enough for me to understand most of what she had to say, and enough that I wouldn't forget. The finer points she'd always had to spell out for me. Words like *traumatic* and *minimization* and *cognitive dissonance*. Those sorts of words the psychologists used, after what happened out to Hungry Neck.

She put her hands on her hips, looked at me hard, her chin still out.

That was when I put my arms up to hold her, took a step toward her. But she took a hard step back, shook her head.

You killed a man, she pounded out. *But you forget you saved me. You saved my mother, and your mother, and Unc.*

I let my arms drop then, looked at the ground. It was late afternoon, a cool March day. Leaf shadows from trees on the median behind me moved on the sidewalk.

I looked up at her so that she could read my lips, took in a breath to speak. I had the words ready, had practiced them a million times the whole way here. I was ready.

But nothing came.

She looked down. She let out a breath, her hands still on her hips. Then she looked up at me, her eyes the same perfect brown they'd ever been.

Slowly, carefully, she signed, *You have a purpose. Get through the past. Then be Huger.*

She closed her eyes, let her chin drop. Then she turned, walked away up the sidewalk to the rust-red and glass doors into the building, pulled one open, and went inside.

That was the last time I'd seen her.

I'd find out later it was Mom to call and tell Tabitha's mom I'd been on my way, Miss Dinah then texting Tabitha, so that all she'd had to do was wait for me to pull up the requisite hours later.

But I didn't even think of that, of how she'd been outside and geared up for me.

Instead, all I did was turn, walk back to the truck. I pulled open the door, felt breathe out at me the funk of a cab after that many hours of driving without stopping for more than an hour now and again, when sleep had screamed at me too hard to let me see the road. It didn't matter, though, that smell. Or the floorboard and passenger seat thick with Red Bull and Monster and Amp cans, Sonic and Burger King and In-N-Out wrappers.

None of that mattered. Because she was right, and I'd come all this way only to be delivered what I knew already: Get through the past.

I climbed in, pulled closed the door, sat there a few seconds. Then I said it, the line I'd rehearsed all those hours, those words I'd taken in a breath for out on the sidewalk. I said it, there in the cluttered and foul and Tabitha-free cave of the cab.

"I love you," I said out loud, "and I've never stopped loving you."

I looked at the apartment complex again, a Spanish fortress inside of which resided the woman those words were meant for. And I heard how cornball they would have sounded if I'd actually said them to her. But even worse, I heard how pathetic they were now that I'd spoken them to no one.

I started up the truck then, backed out, and headed for home.

Now here she was, a few feet in front of me.

"If I were you," Five said, "I'd consider at least saying hello." He still had his arms crossed, I could see, his head tilted in a way that said even in this dark, *She's mine.*

So I waved at her, the move big for the dark out here, and saw her look up, finally, and nod.

And then I remembered, inside the bang and jolt of seeing her face suddenly inside the Range Rover, and of Five the one to usher

her out to say hey, and of seeing her standing here, right *here*—inside the rush of all this shock and dark and panic that felt like I'd never even left the funk of the cab of my Tundra, never yet emptied the debris across the floorboard of my life, never yet moved an inch toward getting through the past and toward being Huger, I remembered: it hadn't been Unc at the window. That hadn't been him to tap the glass. The mission hadn't been accomplished, and it wasn't time to go home.

We were here to drop off goggles. We were here to walk away from Prendergast and the pile of shit we'd stepped in. We were here to finish something.

And I'd been given a story of my mom, that story still pounding inside me.

I looked over my shoulder, saw the Whaley house still there and lit up. As if it would have gone somewhere.

I turned back to them, said, "Did you say Unc sent you out here?"

"Yep," Five said, and pushed his hip off the passenger door. Tabitha hadn't moved. "He told me you were lonely out here, needed some company." He let out a small laugh, the sound a kind of squashed snort. "A couple minutes ago he comes up to me, says he heard my voice and didn't know I was here, then tells me I need to come and visit you. Then I introduced him to Tabitha."

I could see him uncross his arms, reach a hand to Tabitha's shoulder from behind, place it there.

Tabitha quick looked back at him in the dark, her hands in front of her and still holding tight the purse strap.

"Leland's a crazy old fart. He finds out Tabitha's with me, and he kind of goes hyper, hugs on her and smiles and all that, like they were long-lost friends, tells us we both need to go on out here and see you."

I could see his head move a little, look down at Tabitha, and I turned back to the house again. Maybe Unc was on his way out, I was thinking. Or maybe he was planning to stay the whole time. Why else would he send them both out here, if not to help me pass the time?

152 | Bret Lott

"Five," I said, looking at the house and hoping I'd see Unc walking back along the line of cars between here and there, "they actually *are* old friends."

"I know that," Five said, his voice a little indignant, and I turned back to them.

Here was Tabitha, right in front of me, and I started, felt myself nearly jump. I still couldn't make out her features for the dark, but I could see the whites of her eyes, her looking up at me.

She reached out to me, took my right hand in both hers, that purse at her elbow now. She held my hand palm up between us, then let go her right hand, settled it in my palm, the moves all gentle, her hands warm on mine.

Slowly she spelled out, *Too dark to read lips.*

I took in a sharp breath without even thinking on it, held it. This was how she'd taught me to sign, all those years ago back at Hungry Neck, whether sitting on the couch in the front room of Unc's trailer, him in his recliner and watching TV, or at her house and parked at the dinner table under the watchful eye of Miss Dinah, their ramshackle house filled with more books than the county library branch in Ravenel.

Or in the cab of my old Chevy LUV somewhere out on the property, parked and alone.

But always her hand in mine. Letters and letters and letters, each placed in my palm like a warm puzzle piece, each leading to the next and the next and the next, until here was a word between us, and another, me giving back to her words of my own then too, until there'd appeared like a lost continent language between us, made with our very own hands.

A language I still hadn't forgotten.

I breathed out, nodded: Yes, it was too dark out here.

She started in again, but this time even more slowly, even more gently: *How are you?*

I blinked, swallowed. I tried to smile, though I knew she probably couldn't see it. I turned her hand over, held it palm up in mine, settled my other hand in hers.

Fine, I lied.

Because how could I tell her any of what we were in the middle of just this second?

How could I tell her of a body? Or of my mom?

And how could I tell her of what it felt like, right this instant, to have her hand in mine, and Five a few feet behind her, bringing her here from inside his very own home?

She put her hand back in mine, spelled out even more slowly, *Liar.*

And I spelled right back, *Bingo.*

She shook her head, still looking up at me.

"No secrets," Five called out, and took a couple steps toward us, his hands on his hips, I could see, the blazer flared out for it. "What's she saying?" he said, the smug I'd only ever heard on his voice gone.

I looked past Tabitha at him. "She says she could never love a man who packed only three pens," I said.

Tabitha's shoulders moved up and down then, and I looked at her, saw her lean a little forward: she was laughing, and this fact made me feel good for what seemed the first time in a decade. We were still holding hands, and I spelled, *Light inside car, let's—*

But then it hit me. She'd read my lips, had to have in order to get the joke of those pens in Five's pocket, and only now did I take into account the pair of headlights only a few cars away coming up the street from behind her, toward us and the Range Rover. Yet one more straggler here for poker, those headlights as he approached enough light for her to see my face.

She stood up straight then, looked at me, and now I could see her face, her smile, her teeth and cheeks and her chin and the way it curved just so, just so. I could see her eyes, too, and the brown of them, all of her slowly going clearer, sharper, because now there was light on her from behind me, light growing and growing, and I realized there had to be headlights coming toward us from that direction, too.

"What the fuck?" I heard Five say, his voice quiet, and I looked up from Tabitha, saw him clearly now too. He was turned from us, looking down the street behind the Range Rover, and the fact it wasn't just one set of headlights coming up on us, but a whole string of them moving along the street, and I turned, looked behind me and back toward the Whaley place, where another string of headlights was moving toward us, too. A whole lot of headlights.

Then the lead one down there pulled right up into the Whaley driveway, and suddenly blue lights flashed on from the top of the vehicle, and the vehicle behind him turned his on, and now the headlights that'd been coming up the street from behind us, the ones that'd lit me up enough for Tabitha to read my lips, came even with us, and now blue lights blazed on right there on the other side of the Range Rover as the vehicle moved past, and I saw it was a black-and-white. A police cruiser.

Another behind him, and another, and another, all with blue lights flashing.

More vehicles pulled into the driveway of the Whaley place, that string of headlights and blue lights still coming down the street, now parking out there, and not just cruisers but black trucks and a couple black vans and now a big black thing pulling to a stop only a little ways past the house on that side. What looked like a UPS truck, and now these vehicles were all being emptied of people, all of them dressed in black windbreakers and black pants, a swarm of them in this moment, doors left open on vehicles as they hurried up the drive and around the sides of the house, and I could see too that they all had their guns drawn, sidearms out and pointed low in front of them, held with both hands, arms rigid.

All of this from where I stood at the curb out front of the Range Rover, all of it in only a few seconds, the whole neighborhood, the world, shredded up again just like last night out front of the Dupont house, when the red strobe on the EMS had made the whole world quiver.

Now the light was blue, everything blasted and broken with it, and even though I could see all these vehicles and all these people, all this frantic scatter and odd order as now more vehicles arrived, wedging themselves two across in the street—even inside all this I couldn't quite get what was going on, couldn't quite grab hold of this moment except to know that something terribly wrong must have been going on inside the Whaley place, that somebody had done something very bad, and I knew right then it had to be Unc and Prendergast, that something had gone down in there. Something had happened. Of course it had.

"Son of a bitch," Five said beside me, and I turned, saw Tabitha next to me and looking at the house, her eyes and mouth open wide, beside her Five, hands still on his hips, he and Tabitha both blasted over in that pulsing blue.

"Never thought this would actually happen," Five said, and I could see him slowly shaking his head.

I ran.

Unc was in there. And he was in trouble, and I was the one supposed to help him. Me.

He was my father.

I ran.

"Whoa," I heard behind me—Five calling out—but I was already across the yard and driveway of the first house between us, now running across the lawn of the second, and I heard behind me someone running too, and here right now was the Whaley place only a few yards in front of me, the driveway jammed with cruisers. I could see up there the door beside the garage door open, light coming out from inside, and now I heard shouts from in there, men shouting, and I had to get in there and help Unc, even if he had his walking stick and even if he were the least helpless person I'd ever known, blind or no, and then I was at the first cruiser that'd pulled in, and just like that and out of nowhere, a man stood in front of me, caught me and wrapped his arms around my waist, nearly knocked the wind out of me, and I felt him lift me off the ground at the same time I heard him grunt out for the force of the work this was, "Nobody goes in. Police barricade. Nobody goes—"

"Huger," I heard called from behind me, and those steps running behind me caught up, and I felt a hand at my shoulder as I twisted in the arms of the policeman holding me in his bear hug. "Huger, no," I heard, a winded voice but familiar, and I glanced away from that open door and those shouting men, more of them right now moving inside, and saw it was Five, of course it was Five, breathing hard and shaking his head.

"Huger, dude, no. Come on," he said, and nodded over his shoulder as he gasped in a breath, nodded again. "Come on."

"But Unc's—"

"Just come on," he said, his hand still on my shoulder but pulling at me now, and now I could feel the policeman set me back on the ground, ease off on the tight grasp he had around me.

"Police barricade," he said again, his face too close to my ear, "no one past this point."

"He won't be a problem, Officer," Five said, still winded. "His uncle's in there is all. We weren't involved with anything in there."

"What's happening?" I said, and felt now my own breaths hard in and out of me. "What's going on?"

Still the policeman held me, and I could see past him that things had changed now, that no more men were swarming in the door, and heard too that the shouts were over. A policeman stepped out of the doorway then, a black silhouette with his gun holstered, and called out, "Officer Lamb? You okay?"

"Situation under control, Sergeant," the officer holding me called out sharp, too loud in my ear, and though I thought maybe I could break out of this guy's hold if he believed I was going to back off, I thought better of it.

Because there was nothing I could do.

I let out a deep breath, gave up, and the officer let go, took a step back from me. He looked about my age, his hair buzzed nearly to the scalp, and had on the same black windbreaker and pants as everyone else involved.

"We're not going to have any problems, are we?" he said, and took in a couple breaths of his own. "This is a police barricade. If you try to get past here, you'll be arrested."

"Thank you, Officer," Five said from behind me, and I could feel his hand still on my shoulder. "Thank you."

"What's happening?" I said again, and felt again the tug at my shoulder.

"Move along," the officer said, and nodded.

"Sorry, Officer," Five said, and pulled even harder at my shoulder, so hard I stumbled a step backward, and had no choice but to turn away from the policeman, and the house, and Unc inside.

"Dude, what is your problem?" Five whispered to me, and I felt myself put my hands on my hips, take in a deep breath. My ribs hurt, I knew that, and I still hadn't gotten my breath back.

But that didn't matter at all, and I looked back over my shoulder at what seemed now a kind of calm settling in just that quickly. Officers stood on the street out front of the house every ten feet or so to guard the place, a cluster of them huddled at the door of the garage talking to each other. And all this blue everywhere flushing over the whole of it.

"Just leave it alone, Huger," Five said, and I looked at him, saw his eyes were on mine as we moved across his next-door neighbor's yard toward the Range Rover. "Let's just go on back to your car, wait it out." He still had his hand on my shoulder, and for a second—a very small one, one I didn't actually want to acknowledge I understood— I could see he was concerned about me, or at least seemed to be.

His head was tilted forward a little, his eyes open wide, look-ing at me. "Dude," he said, "it's a bust. Unlawful games and betting.

Magistrate-level offense. That's all." He paused, shook his head, eyes still on me, and I felt the breaths coming deeper into me now. "You okay?"

We were on the next-door neighbor's driveway now, and I looked away from him, still with my hands on my hips. I nodded once, took in another breath. Then I stopped, half turned from him, and leaned over, put my hands on my knees. To take in another good breath, sure. But also to get out from under his hand on my shoulder.

Five didn't know what Unc had in the book bag he'd brought in. He didn't know what kind of charge that might bring in, once these Mount Pleasant cops figured out what they had.

Or maybe, I thought, Unc had already passed the goggles off to Prendergast by now. Maybe that son of a bitch would be the one to end up charged with possessing a piece of government property he shouldn't have.

But how stupid was that idea. Prendergast was an officer in the U.S. Navy. He had all the permission in the world to have possession of the goggles.

No. If there was going to be trouble about the goggles, it would come down on Unc.

I looked at the Whaley place again. I couldn't believe the number of vehicles that'd been brought out for this, all filling in every possible space on the street and up into their driveway.

I still stood with my hands on my knees, looked down, breathed, and now here on the driveway beside me moved in a pair of shoes and pants—the same white Keds Tabitha always wore, and jeans—and I felt her hand on my back, felt her patting me. I glanced up at her, saw her eyes were to everything happening before us, her head shaking just the smallest way, as though she wasn't even surprised. Her as blue and pulsing as everything else out here.

"My dad's been worried for the last nine years this was going to happen," Five said, and I looked past Tabitha to him. His arms were crossed again, his feet spread on the driveway. "That's why he got the dudes he did to play with him. He's got city council members in there, and a Summerville police lieutenant, and all kinds of other big dogs. He's even got a Navy captain or something like that in there." He gave another small laugh, but this one quieter, and I looked down again at the driveway. "He figured that would make it safe," he went on, "if he had enough bigwigs playing." He shot out a breath, shook his head, and now I stood up, felt Tabitha's hand on my back rest there for just a second longer before she took it away.

She didn't look at me, and now I wondered why she was so calm about all this. Why she'd only now strolled over, looked like she'd known the whole thing would happen.

"Shit," Five whispered. "What are the chances? Come home for a long weekend and to see Tabitha while she's out here. Then this." He shook his head.

I touched Tabitha's arm then, and she looked at me. I nodded toward Five, and she turned to him, enough blue light out here, I figured, for her to see what he had to say.

"He told me a million times what to do if I was around when it happened. And if I wasn't inside with him. Otherwise, I'd just get hauled off with the rest of them." He shook his head again. "Stay out the way. Period. Then just post bail, if they don't let him out on his own recognizance." He paused, said, "He's got a wad of cash he showed me once in his bedroom. I'm supposed to follow the paddy wagon on down to Mount P jail, use that wad to bail out anybody gets busted. A kind of courtesy from the management."

He stopped. He shook his head more slowly. "I can't believe I'm even saying this. I can't believe this is really happening," he said. "Nine fucking years and it's never happened where—"

"Do you live here?" someone called from behind us, and both Five and I turned, then Tabitha.

A woman was walking fast toward us across the yard, and I could see in the blue lights she was dressed up, had on a jacket and skirt, a blouse that seemed to erupt at her neck. A little ways behind her was another person, a man, weaving between two cars at the curb.

He had a video camera on his shoulder.

"I cannot believe this!" Five said, and turned away, moved up the driveway toward the street. Away from her.

Tabitha looked at Five, then at the reporter, and turned, followed after him.

A reporter, and a camera.

She stepped out onto the driveway, said, "Monica Slater, Channel Four News," then asked again, "Do you live here?" and nodded at the house we stood in front of. Whaley's next-door neighbor. "Because we need to set up our camera here, if that's all right."

Here was the cameraman beside her now. The camera on one shoulder, he slipped off the other a strap attached to a long black metal something, and already the tripod was unfolding, sliding and clicking into place, and now the camera was on top of it, the man twisting here and there beneath it.

The camera light came on then, flooded us in a bright pool that nearly cleared out the blue, and I had no choice but to think of that white Toyoter up on a flatbed tow truck, sharp in the lights from a news camera out at Wambaw Creek.

"They're only here for the perp walk," Five called out, and I looked off to the end of the driveway at him standing there with Tabitha. The two of them pulsing in that blue.

"We need to know if it's all right to set up here on your driveway." She stood just far enough into that pool of light so that I could see she had too much makeup on, her lips a red gash. She gave a quick smile at me, fiddled with the microphone in her hand, turned to shake out the cord trailing away from her. She glanced up at me as she messed with it, said, "You live here, right?"

I looked back at the Whaley place, there in its strange calm, then at Tabitha and Five, down at the end of the drive.

I turned back to her. "Yeah, I live here," I said. I put my hands on my hips, said, "Get off my property. Now."

She flinched at the words, looked up from the cord, her mouth in a stunned O. She blinked, shook her head. "But this is for TV," she said, and blinked twice more, quick shook her head again. "I don't understand," she said, and looked back at the cameraman, at me again.

The camera light went out then, and I heard a sharp click, saw the camera sliding off the tripod and back onto the cameraman's shoulder.

"He does," I said, and nodded at the cameraman, that blue pulse on us all again.

12

We sat in the Range Rover, the dome light on so that Tabitha could read lips. She sat in the passenger seat, Five in the back but leaning forward between us. Out my window were two cruisers parked side by side, filling the street, in front and behind them more. All jammed here, and all with their blue lights on.

The reporter and cameraman had only moved off the driveway and set up between cars right in front of the Whaley yard, where policemen still stood guard. Two more channels had showed up— 2 and 5—and wedged themselves between other cars out there.

We'd been walking back to the Range Rover when those two reporters and their cameramen came jogging toward us on the grass and right on past us, no words out of them. We'd stopped then, watched them set up, those pools of light crashing down once the cameras were on. Three reporters, two women and one man, all dressed nice and bright, standing and talking into the cameras. While nothing much seemed to be happening at the house behind them.

Five'd said, "Let's go." I'd looked at him beside me, seen in the blue lights he was looking across the street, but with his chin down, hands in his pockets. I'd turned, tried to see what he did.

Neighbors were out of their houses now: a couple stood on the front porch of the house across from the Whaleys', someone stood out on the driveway of the house next to that, a clutch of people— a family, maybe—on the steps up to the front porch of another house three doors down.

"Yep," I'd said, and we three had turned, gone to the Range Rover, climbed in.

"I still can't believe this," Five said from between us now, Tabitha half turned in her seat so she could see him. "I just can't believe this."

Tabitha pulled from one of the pockets of the jacket she had on—it was a nice one, a light tweed blazer, the blouse under it white and simple—a small pad of paper and pen, set the pad on her leg and wrote. Same as when she and I were first together, and I hadn't yet gotten the whole signing thing.

She tore off the piece of paper, handed it to Five, and though it wasn't meant for me, I could see as she passed it the plain and square and perfect printing she'd always had.

Five looked at it, nodded. "Yeah," he said, and let out a sigh.

"What?" I said.

Tabitha looked at me, lifted a hand, her pinkie finger pointed out, and started to sweep it down, but Five quick looked up at me, said, "It's personal." Even in the dim light of the cab I could see his black eyebrows together, him incredulous, as though I'd asked to kiss his mom.

I looked at Tabitha, still with her pinkie in the air. She'd cut her eyes to him, looked back at me, shrugged. She put her hand down.

I looked out the windshield: still nothing up there but a lit-up orange house bathed in a flashing blue I'd grown beyond tired of. From here inside I could see the halo of lights of the cameras, too, but not the reporters, or the garage door. Only policemen standing along the property.

"So, Five," I said, "where's your mom? Is she in there too?" and wondered for a second what that would look like, to see your mom arrested.

"Huh," he let out. "No." He paused. "She's in Boca Raton. With a loser named Dante she hooked up with on a Celebrity cruise my parents took for their tenth anniversary."

I was quiet a moment, said, "Sorry."

"If she knew this was going down, Dad about to get arrested, she'd be dancing on a table," he said, then, quieter, "They got divorced when I was six. Haven't seen her in eight years."

I looked at him, his head and shoulders there between Tabitha's seat and mine, his eyes straight ahead.

I said, "Sorry, Five."

He shrugged.

Tabitha gave a wave at me, and both Five and I looked at her.

He doesn't like Five, she signed. *He wants me to call him War.*

She spelled out the last word, and I said, "Why?"

"Stop that," Five said, and let out another sigh. "We talked about this," he said.

Tabitha looked at him, at me again. *He doesn't sign.*

"Now come on," he said, and leaned back hard in his seat, shook the vehicle the smallest bit.

I turned, looked back at him. He had his arms crossed, and faced the passenger window. I said, "You want to be called War? Are you serious?"

He looked at me. "Short for Warchester," he said, and uncrossed his arms, set his palms on the seat either side of him. He gave a small smile. "Beats the hell out of being called Five my whole life. Nobody calls Dad Four." He paused, and now he leaned forward, put his elbows on his knees, looked out the windshield again for anything going on. "Just call me War," he said. "Seems pretty logical."

I sat back in my seat, looked at Tabitha.

Let's call him Cinco, I spelled.

She laughed.

"Not putting up with this secret shit much longer," Five said from between us. But this time he didn't sit back, only stayed right there.

"You need to learn to sign," I said, and before I'd even finished the words a piece of me—a big piece—was sorry for it. I didn't want him to learn this language. I didn't want him working out words between them that only the two of them would know. I didn't want his hand in her palm, or hers in his.

I looked at Tabitha. She'd seen what I said, and held my eyes for a second too long before she looked out the windshield.

I looked too. Nothing new out there. Only Unc somewhere inside. With Prendergast.

"Tried it," Five said. "Signing." And Tabitha turned from the windshield toward him, but just barely. She didn't want him to see she was watching him, reading his lips. But she wanted to listen all the same.

I'd been with her a long time. I knew how she was.

"Ordered a CD with these songs on it and a book for the signs," he went on. "Just couldn't get the hang of it. But I know every word to the stupid songs by heart. 'Who Knows the Alphabet?' was one. 'Opposites Are Out of Sight.' 'Up, down, big, small, young, old, short, tall,'" he sang, his voice bright but quiet.

He stopped. He took in a breath, let it out, and I could tell he'd heard himself carried away, singing inside a car while what was going on just outside was going on.

"I can't believe this is happening," he whispered. "And I wonder who the son of a bitch is called this in. Who up on his porch watching right now called the cops on us. I don't get it." He paused. "Maybe Adkins across the street. Maybe Mrs. Herron." He nodded ahead of us, as though I'd know which houses he was talking about and the people involved. "I mean, I know the cars out here every week are a problem," he went on, "but Dad sends everyone in the six houses on either side of us and the eight across from us this monster thing of Omaha Steaks for Christmas every year."

And now, with his bringing the whole thing up, I wondered about that too: why tonight this had been called in. I didn't care who had done it. But it was the fact of it that bothered me. Why tonight?

I looked at Five, him leaned forward between us, and saw Tabitha with her eyes on mine.

She looked at me, held it. She blinked, seemed to swallow. She glanced at Five, then out the windshield, and back to me.

I looked. Officers moved back and forth along the driveway. The world pulsed blue.

I turned back to her, still looking at me. "Why are you back here?" I said. "Why are you home?"

"Long weekend," Five answered, still looking out the windshield.

"No," I said. "Tabitha."

He glanced up at me, at Tabitha. He shook his head, looked forward again.

Tabitha looked down a second, then back up. She pursed her lips, signed, *See my mom.*

"She's here for an interview," Five said at the exact same moment. "She could tell you where but then she'd have to kill you."

Tabitha, thumb still at her chin and fingers spread wide for the word *mom*, froze, her eyes on Five. He looked at me first, had this smile on his face and raised his eyebrows, and turned to Tabitha.

Her fingers snapped together right at her lips, a tough little move it wouldn't take much for anyone to figure out: *Shut up.*

"I know that one," Five said, and looked at me, the smile gone.

Tabitha turned from him to the windshield again. She crossed her arms, settled in her seat.

"An interview?" I said, but she was ignoring me or couldn't see me, one. I reached across to her, touched her arm to get her attention, but she wouldn't look, only sat tight with her arms crossed.

"She's pissed," Five whispered. "Best to leave her alone when she's like this," and he shook his head. "Shouldn't have said anything."

For a second I thought to tell him I knew when she was pissed, believe me. But I was still stuck on whatever this interview thing meant. And the idea she could be moving here for a job. Moving back home.

"Whose are these?" Five said then, like nothing had happened at all, like there hadn't been any kind of turn just now for the possibility of her being home and why, no mystery to whatever she was here and interviewing for.

Because he knew things between them. He and Tabitha both knew about each other, and what could possibly be. I had nothing to do with either of their lives. He'd spoken out of line, she'd told him to shut up. Of course he'd moved on.

He reached between us to the console then, picked up the object of his interest: Unc's wallet from the console tray. "If this is Leland's," he said, "then he's . . ."

His words trailed off, and he set the wallet down, picked up Unc's cellphone, all before I could tell him to leave those things alone, that they weren't his to touch.

"Does he just have cash in his pocket when he walks in and when he heads home?" Five asked.

"Does it matter?" I snapped at him. "Leave it alone."

But even as I said these things, I began to wonder at what it was he was touching: Unc's wallet, his cellphone.

I thought of Unc climbing out of the cab after he'd told me about Mom, the hurry of it all while news of her life had pounded inside me, and the odd business of watching him pull out that wallet, set the cellphone there, and how nothing just then had made any sense at all.

He always had his wallet and cellphone with him. And even if he'd carried cash in his pocket and not in his wallet—which he never did—how else was he going to call me out here, like he did at the end of every poker night, to let me know to come in and get him, walk him back to the car?

"Doesn't he call you when he's done to tell you—" Five started, his voice low and with a kind of confusion to it.

But Tabitha started tapping hard at the dashboard in front of her right then, and I looked up from the console, and from Five's hand still holding the phone, to see her nearly jumping in her seat, and I looked out the windshield, saw it all start.

The perp walk.

Here came one man, and another, and another, a line of them headed along the driveway and away from the house, beside each one a man in a black windbreaker and pants, a hand up and holding the upper arm of the poker player beside him.

Every player with his hands behind him. They'd all been cuffed.

Five let go the cellphone, wedged himself up even farther between us. "I can't believe this is happening," he said.

A parade. A real parade. Men drenched in blue and dressed in those Nat Nast shirts and Tommy Bahamas all moved along the drive, some with their heads down, some with chins high. And more of them, and more, all easing along the driveway. All of them right toward where the cameras were set up, those halos of light.

The clutter of vehicles out on the street made it impossible to see what was happening to each one as he came off the drive, but I knew they were being fed into the back of the big black UPS truck down there: a prisoner transport. A good old-fashioned paddy wagon.

"There he is," Five said in the same moment Tabitha started tapping hard the dash again, jabbing at the air in front of her: *Look!*

Not Unc, or Prendergast, but Warchester Four. Five's dad, doughy-faced even from here, but blue, like everyone else. He was smiling, I could see, head up, nearly strutting down the driveway. Then he disappeared behind the cars strung along in front of us.

"What an idiot," Five said, and pulled away from us, his head and shoulders disappearing into the backseat. "You guys just wait here. Be back in a minute," he said, and popped open the door.

"Wait," I said, and looked down at the console, the wallet and cellphone, and pieced together, finally, what Five had been on the border of figuring out for himself.

You stay put, you hear? Unc had told me. *Where I need you is out here,* he'd said.

Unc had been the one to call this in.

"I need to get that stash up in his room, and to get my car," Five said, the door standing open. "So I can follow him over to the station."

"You think they're going to let you stroll in and just take a wad of money out of a house in the middle of being raided?" I said. "And if your car is in the driveway, you think they're going to drop everything and move all their vehicles for you?"

Stay put, Unc had said.

He'd known what was going to happen. That's why he'd told me to stay here, why he'd dumped these things, too: the police would show up, and now they wouldn't have anything of his, no ID, no cellphone, nothing but the book bag. And who knew if he'd even lay claim to that now? There was no ID in the bag either. As of right now, it was just something in the house when the cops had busted in.

And inside, when he'd walked in tonight, Unc had run into Five, and with him Tabitha. Two people who had nothing to do with anything. Two people who didn't deserve to get busted along with the rest of the crowd, for whatever reason he'd decided to call in the cops on this, and now I saw Unc back at our house this afternoon, me asleep and him figuring Mom to be doing the same, her bedroom door closed.

I saw him in our house, and making a phone call to the Mount Pleasant Police Department, maybe three more after that, each to a news station to let them all know at 10:30 tonight an illegal evening of poker magic would be in full swing, and everyone involved—the

MtPPD and all three stations—could take home a full cast net of big fish.

Among them a Navy commander, I realized, whose career would be tarnished big-time—whose ass would be kicked in marvelous new ways—were he to be paraded before television cameras, if he were to have a mug shot taken, if he were to have to make one phone call to get someone to bail him out.

All of this, I understood finally, Unc's middle-aged means of walking up Prendergast's driveway with his hands in fists to stomp, in a more public way, the shit out of him. Payback, I saw, for the story of Mom.

So what, I could see Unc reasoning, if he got arrested along with the rest of them? What did he have to lose, but the fact he'd been playing poker for years with a bad man?

And what did all these other people have to lose, too, I could see Unc thinking, if in this one evening of a pile of misdemeanor charges he could make a Navy commander who'd raped girls he'd drugged—my mom one of them, my own mom—do a perp walk in order to get him busted down a few ranks or even booted out altogether?

I felt, in a very small way, myself begin to smile.

Five climbed out the open door anyway, said, "I'm gone. Back in a minute," and before I could say anything else to try and keep him here, to make him stay put with me and with Tabitha, he closed the door.

Tabitha felt it close, and turned from the windshield to look behind her, then out her window at Five moving past, and toward the house.

She turned to me, raised her eyebrows and shoulders: *What is he doing?*

"Going to try and get bail money out of the house. Maybe get his car."

Her expression went from inquiry to utter puzzlement: her eyebrows came together, shoulders squeezed high, her mouth open. *Huh?*

"Go figure," I said, and looked out the windshield.

Still the perp walk continued—there must have been thirty people escorted down the driveway by now—Five walking toward it all with his coat flared out for his hands in his pockets. He got to an officer standing perimeter, began talking to him, Five's back to us.

Tabitha touched my arm, and I turned.

Unc told me, she signed. She tilted her head, shook it just barely. *Inside.* Took my hand, spelled fast POLICE COMING. HUGER OUTSIDE. GO.

I looked at her, nodded. I pointed to Unc's wallet and phone. "He told me to stay put," I said. "He didn't tell me, but I figured it out."

She nodded, looked back at Five, still talking, then back at me.

Why call in? she said.

"Forgot he knew how to spell," I answered. No answer at all.

Because I didn't want to go into it. There was too much involved with why he'd called it in, all of it stuff she didn't need any part in knowing: a body in a marsh, a pair of goggles. My mom, and the story of her life.

"Forgot Unc learned how to spell so's he could talk to you when you were a kid out to Hungry Neck," I said, and made my eyes go to Five out there.

But she reached across to me, took my hand again, spelled out for me there so I wouldn't have any choice but to know the question.

Why?

I looked at her. I took in a breath, swallowed. I felt the warmth of her hand yet one more time.

"To settle an old score," I said, and looked out the windshield again.

Five still stood talking to the officer, who had his hands on his hips.

Tabitha took her hand from mine, and I glanced at her, saw her looking out there too, and I reached to her, took her hand. She turned again to me.

Do you love him? I spelled.

She tilted her head, blinked quick a couple of times, her eyebrows working again.

Unc? she spelled back. *Of course.*

I smiled. *Five.*

She took her hand from mine, seemed almost to flinch, a kind of reproach on her face, if you could call it that. As if I'd asked a question too intrusive to answer. Or one too ugly to acknowledge. She looked out the windshield again, her own way of avoiding the question I was asking her now.

But then I saw her look down, at her hands. I saw her take in a deep breath, then let it out, and she turned to me.

He was my lab partner, she signed. *A good brain, and he was using it.* She paused, looked down at her hands again, then up at me. *He's funny. And he's moving ahead with his life.*

The last part stung. I knew what she meant, and she did too. I blinked a couple times, then did the best I could: I shrugged. "You still haven't answered my question," I said.

One more time she looked down at her hands, held them out in front of her palm up, like she might be expecting something magical to happen, some answer to materialize that she didn't yet know and that would surprise us both. Then she looked out the windshield, and slowly back to me.

He thinks it's more serious between us than I do. But I have things to do. I have a life to make.

"But Facebook," I said. "Your status and his both."

She looked at me, sneered almost. Slowly she shook her head as she signed *You believe Facebook?* She paused. *I just leave it so people don't bother me. I see Five maybe twice a year.*

She let her hands drop, turned in her seat without looking at me, faced forward.

Maybe, I thought, I could take her hands again, her words just now, I hoped, a kind of permission. I could spell out what it was I should have said back in Palo Alto, what had never yet changed.

I love you I could have told her.

But that was when she started tapping the dash again, and pointing, and I looked.

There now was Unc, hands behind him, moving out onto the driveway. Ball cap and windbreaker.

And Prendergast beside him, his hands behind him, too. He didn't have on his uniform, wore instead his own silk shirt, dark from here, same as everyone else. But I knew it was him: even from here I could see his officer haircut, nearly shaved on the sides, thicker on top. Tall and thin and military.

They were walking side by side, between and behind them one of the policemen in black, holding the upper arms of both of them. It seemed odd, that here would be one man holding two when every player in the perp walk thus far had had his own escort. Maybe they thought Unc a low-enough flight risk not to need his own private cop, figured a blind man wasn't going to run. Let's just walk him next to this other dude out to the paddy wagon.

They were halfway down the drive now, and I could see two more perps a few feet behind them walking next to each other, too, one cop assigned between them, just like Unc and Prendergast.

These two were different, though. One was a woman, short and squat, the other a big guy taller even than Prendergast. I could see, too, that they both had on long-sleeve white shirts, black vests, and I recognized them: the chunky Filipino woman who worked the chip cage, that closet with a half door at one end of the room. And the other was the bartender, the big tanned guy with biceps the size of bowling balls. The same guy who'd been present at my initial humiliation at the hands of Five, when I'd ordered the same drink he was having.

I touched Tabitha's arm, and she turned. "I'm glad Unc sent you out here," I said. "Wouldn't want you included in this."

Five was about to figure it out, she signed, her mouth in a kind of frown. She glanced down at the wallet, the cellphone, and back at me.

"If he gets ticked off," I said, "we'll let him know Unc got him out of there so he wouldn't get arrested. If it's any comfort."

She nodded, and we both turned forward again.

Right as something started happening.

There stood Five at the edge of the property, his back still to us, talking to the policeman, who had his arms crossed now. Unc and Prendergast were almost even with them, almost hidden behind them as the one cop pushed them along the driveway. But right then they headed away from us, off the driveway and across the grass in front of the house, all three of them—Unc, Prendergast, and the cop—with their backs to us now. Headed somewhere other than the paddy wagon.

And I could see from here the letters across the back of the windbreaker the cop escorting them wore: CBP.

Everyone else—everyone—had on MTPPD windbreakers. Even Unc, I could see as he was led away. The same one he wore everywhere when it was cool like this.

And right then, as those three pulled off into the grass, the woman behind them, that squat chip-cage worker in the white shirt and black vest, tore from the grasp of the cop walking behind her, twisted herself free and bolted straight this way, across the neighbor's grass and then driveway, right where Five and Tabitha and I had stood while I'd tried to get back my breath.

She bolted, and through the closed windows of the Range Rover I heard the short muffled word "Hey!" and again "Hey!" and saw the cop she'd wrested free of let go the bartender, and draw his sidearm.

And as if I'd planned it, as if I were a part of the whole thing but without thinking on it at all, I put my hand to the switch on the dome light, turned it off, and I leaned over to Tabitha, pulled her down from the window, out of the line of fire.

She took in a gasp, me leaning hard over her now, and I let myself look just above the dash.

Now the bartender had broken free, too, was running right behind her and toward us, and I saw past the two of them the cop with his gun out but pointed up, and starting after them.

Just to the left of this all stood Five, his hands in his pockets and half turned to the whole surprise, the cop he was talking to still with his arms crossed, the two of them watching all this happening just now, just now, too quick for anyone other than those involved to react.

The woman and the bartender, him just behind her and both with their hands cuffed, were across the second driveway now, onto the grass just ten yards or so off the hood of the Range Rover, and here was a sharp "Freeze!" from the cop behind them.

The bartender came even with the woman now, and bumped her hard with a shoulder, made her fall to the ground and slide a couple feet facedown in the grass. He dropped to his knees beside her, and in the blue pulse and shadowed jumble of the two of them collapsing, and of the cop coming up fast behind them, and now the cop Five had been talking to running for the whole thing, too, I saw the bartender lean in close to the woman's face, and talk at her, words out of him stiff and sharp, though I heard nothing.

I was still leaned over Tabitha, her beneath me but holding still for what she couldn't see or hear, while the bartender spoke fast at the woman, his head jerking toward her with his words, arms behind his back, him kneeling right beside her. She turned her face away from him just then, and I saw her shoulders heave there on the ground, her hands behind her, the twin tails of her plastic Zip Cuffs poking up in the air.

The cop made it to them and, his right hand holding the gun pointed up, straddled the bartender full speed, rode him down into the grass, the cop's free hand on the bartender's neck and pressing down hard, as though the bartender were the one trying to get away.

Which he wasn't. He'd been the one to stop the woman. Easy as anything to see.

The other cop rushed up, and I heard them through the glass giving hurried words, saw Five jog up, too, stand off to one side as the cop with the gun out holstered it. He pulled the bartender up onto his knees, then stood him up altogether, while the other cop helped up the woman, her shoulders still heaving.

All of this just ten yards off the hood of the Range Rover, drenched in blue.

The cop holding on to the bartender pulled him in close, yanked him toward him, and said something in his ear. The bartender was taller than the cop, so that the cop had to incline his chin, and the bartender leaned over an inch or so, and listened.

It was strange, that moment, what bordered on a kind of intimacy between them in the midst of everything going on right here, right here.

Then the bartender stood up straight, that moment between them gone, replaced just as quick with the cop yanking his upper arm, giving it a shake to show who was in charge, and now that same blue pulse as ever shot across everything, and with the way the cop was turned, his profile to me, and that quick whip of brighter blue suddenly across everything in the world, I recognized him.

The cop: Stanhope.

The master-at-*ahms* out back of the Dupont place, his sidearm drawn on me when I'd stooped to hand them the book bag with the goggles in it last night, him and Harmon there in their blue and gray digital camo BDUs, placing Unc and me under arrest for an imaginary trespass.

I sat straight up, startled into place, my hands on the steering wheel.

It was him, right here, holding tight the arm of the bartender. Stanhope. His jaw was set, I'd seen in that brighter flash, his teeth clenched, his eyes sharp on the bartender.

It was him.

I took in a breath, felt the blood to my face in an instant, my hands tight on the steering wheel, tighter, because there was nothing other I knew to do, or could.

I was aware now of Tabitha moving beside me, sitting up, but nothing more, my eyes on Stanhope. He turned away from us, the bartender's arm in his grip, the two of them with their backs to me.

CBP across the back of Stanhope's jacket, too.

I didn't know what that stood for. I didn't even know, and felt my jaw go tight, my teeth clench just the same as I'd seen Stanhope's, but even harder, and I gripped the steering wheel even tighter, tighter, started rocking now forward and back the smallest way but without any control over it, just rocking there in my seat, and I thought for a second, an instant, that I might explode, might actually feel my heart inside me burst.

Because I knew what was happening. I knew it.

Prendergast had Unc. That was Stanhope right there walking away from us with the bartender, and now the cop who'd been talking to Five and who had hold of the chip-cage woman handed her off to Stanhope too. He grabbed hold of her arm, jolted her a little, all of it with their backs to me, and I saw the woman's head disappear for her leaning forward. I saw her shoulders heaving again, and again. She was crying.

They had Unc. And now I knew the cop in the CBP jacket who'd walked Prendergast and Unc off across the front yard and away from us had to be Harmon, had to be. They weren't headed for the paddy wagon. But somewhere else.

I thought of that black Suburban before any of this had gone down, trolling in front of the house, tapping its brakes. Same as the one that'd been parked inside that clot of vehicles out front of Dupont's. The big black Suburban I'd marked off as being the one the sailors must've arrived in.

They had Unc. They had him.

But what for? They had the book bag, and the goggles. They had what they wanted.

No. They didn't. No one out of the house yet—not any of the cops, or the perps, and definitely not Unc, or Prendergast, or Stanhope or Harmon, if that was him who'd peeled off with Unc and Prendergast—had had a book bag on them, and the goggles themselves, that Borg contraption, were too bulky just to jam in your pocket and walk away with. Even in a windbreaker pocket.

CBP. CBP.

I gripped the wheel so hard now it seemed ready to dissolve in my hands, and I heard myself breathing hard in the silence, in and out and in and out.

Stanhope walked the two of them back to the driveway, the other cop stopping right where he'd been when Five walked up to talk to him, and I watched Stanhope with his CBP jacket move across the driveway, and onto the grass out front of the Whaley place, and away from us.

Tabitha touched my arm, signed something in the dark of the car, something I might have been able to see for the blue that made its way inside here. But what she was doing with her hands meant nothing. Nothing at all. Just her hands, moving.

Now the dome light cut on, and here sliding into the backseat was Five. He closed the door, the light gone.

"Did you see that?" he said, his voice full of wonder and a kind of delight. "Did you see that little piece of action right there? Never a dull moment at Dad's," he said.

Tabitha still looked at me, and now Five said, "Why's the light off in here?"

I looked away from Tabitha. I held the steering wheel.

"Whatever," Five said behind us, and leaned forward just as he'd done before he'd taken off. Him right here with us.

"I heard Tammy give out this little squeal right when she tore off. Sort of scared the shit out of me for a second. She's worked for Dad for like eight years. Almost since he started. Then Coburn takes off, too, the bartender. I think he's her cousin, and then—"

"I saw it," I said, my voice tight, too sharp: a piece of glass coughed up.

But he didn't hear, lost in the adventure. "—when that Border Patrol guy hit him, man. Shit! Did you see that? I couldn't believe that. That dude with his pistolero out. Unbelievable."

I looked at him. "Border Patrol," I said, the words still just as tight, just as sharp.

"Yeah," Five said, and turned to me. "That's what that guy was. When the cop I was talking to and I ran up, you could hear Coburn speaking Spanish at her. At Tammy. I think it was Spanish. At least it sounded like it. But when the one I was talking to got right in there with them the CBP guy tells him the two of them are illegals. Tammy and Coburn. That he and his partner'd coordinated with the Mount Pleasant PD to get these two."

CBP.

Customs and Border Protection.

They had a headquarters here. An academy right down at the old Naval Shipyard, a whole training facility.

But no. They were Navy. Stanhope, Harmon. Prendergast. They weren't Border Patrol, or Customs, or anything else.

"Get out," I said then.

It came out buried, I heard. Clouded over with whatever I was already planning to do next, though I had no genuine idea of what that was. Other than first to get them out of here. Tabitha and Five both.

I looked at Tabitha. Her hands were down in her lap. It was dark in here but for that blue streaking through us. But I could see her, and her eyes, looking at me.

Five said from behind us, "But they won't let me in the house to get the money. Or let me have my car. That's what the cop was telling me when that all happened. Can't get into the house until they're done with it. And every car unattended on this street is impounded.

Nobody gets his car until bail has been made. You're the only one won't get impounded, so when this starts to clear up you'll—".

"Get out," I said again, but this time louder, certain.

Still Tabitha looked at me, and I turned the key in the ignition, the spray of dials and numbers on the dashboard suddenly here, and I tore my eyes from hers on mine to see the last glimpse of Stanhope pushing ahead of him a squat woman named Tammy and a big bartender named Coburn, all three of them at the far end of the Whaleys' yard, about to disappear in the same direction Unc and Prendergast and Harmon had already gone.

Somewhere up the street was a Suburban. I had to get out of here. I had to follow them.

I had to leave. Now.

"Leave," I said, and turned back to Tabitha, certain she knew what I was saying, whether or not it was too dark to read lips.

She didn't move.

"Shit," Five said, and reached forward, tapped Tabitha's shoulder. "Let's get out of here. Selfish son of a bitch." He looked at me, said, "You're not going anywhere for a while anyway, my friend. You're wedged in here tight as anyone else on the block, even if your vehicle isn't in the process of being impounded. It might be tomorrow morning before this whole thing gets cleared out, but we're all ending up in the same place one way or the other. At the Mount Pleasant jail."

He pulled his hand back from Tabitha's shoulder, and I heard the door open—that light again—and him start to climb back out.

Still Tabitha hadn't moved.

I put my foot on the brake, put the Range Rover in reverse, still no clue in me of what I was going to do, and heard Five say from behind us and still with the door open, "Quit joking around. You know you're not going anywhere."

I looked up at the house. Stanhope was gone. The perp walk was over too, Unc and Prendergast and this Tammy and Coburn the last ones out.

Then I looked up the street for the Suburban. I looked up there for something I could see, something I could glimpse and know what to do about. Even if I were stuck here, and it might be hours before I could get out.

You know you're not going anywhere, Five'd said. No truer words.

It was just goggles. It was just a set of God damned goggles, Prendergast an asshole from start to finish for having wagered them at all, and to have gotten us to this point, now, when for nothing but a pair of contraband goggles Unc was being hauled off for who knew where. I felt my eyes start to go hot again, felt the wet in them, and I squeezed them shut hard, opened them again, saw only a wavering sea of vehicles in front of me, and no Unc.

Then the fingers on my right hand at the steering wheel began to peel out of their grip, and I felt the warmth of another hand—Tabitha's, Tabitha's—taking hold of that hand, and I turned to her, looked at her, took in a shimmering breath.

She was shaking her head: *No.*

"Go," I whispered. I nodded, looked out the windshield again, tried to see something, anything, of what might happen next.

And saw in a shard of space between the paddy wagon and a cruiser and way up past them both, maybe a hundred yards away, the flash of a taillight. Only a sliver of bright red, and though I couldn't be certain it was a Suburban, it was enough.

Then came a sudden hard jostle of movement from the backseat, the surprised word "Uhh" out of Five, and the door pulled closed, the light now off. For just that moment I thought Five'd left, and I turned, looked behind us.

Jessup.

He was sitting in tight next to Five, who was turned to him but leaning away, looking at him as surprised as that word out of him had been, and now Tabitha turned, too, let out a sharp sound for taking in a breath.

He had on a black windbreaker, jeans, no ball cap, and leaned forward same as Five'd done what seemed all night long now, wedged himself right up with us. Tabitha leaned away, and pressed against the door.

Here he was, right here. Like all of us, doused in blue and blue and blue.

He said, "Horry. In," two distinct words, quiet and even, then, a second later, "Copy," and I saw the earphone he was wearing, hooked over his ear on this side, a thin cord snaking down his neck.

He turned to me, nodded, and I had no choice but to nod back.

"Huger," he said.

I swallowed, said, "Jessup."

He looked away, peered out the windshield. "You don't get this vehicle out of here in the next couple seconds," he said, "we're going to lose them."

It was Jessup. Jessup.

I blinked one more time, looked out the windshield, saw up there the brake light dim to just a taillight, that piece of red seeming even farther away now.

I looked at the silver Mercedes in front of me, glanced in my rearview at whatever that car was back there. I didn't have much room. And there were these cruisers beside me, out in the street, right out my door.

"Be resourceful," Jessup said. "You were planning to leave anyway."

I glanced at him, saw him still looking ahead of us.

Just past him sat Tabitha, eyebrows up, mouth open, still pressed against the door. Her eyes went from me to Jessup to me again.

I swallowed again. I nodded at her, mouthed *Okay.*

"Who is—" Five started behind us, but before he could finish I'd let off the brake, eased the Range Rover back until the hard touch of it against the bumper of the car behind me.

I cut the wheel all the way to the right, far as I could turn it, and put it in drive, rough-bumped the Range Rover up the curb and into the lawn of this nice raised home in Hamlet Square, its blue-pulsing clapboard and front porch and joggling board all swinging across the windshield, until out front of us lay a grass runway interrupted by a series of concrete drives: everyone's lawns straight down the street, out at the curb all the cars of all those players and all the cruisers of all those cops.

I pressed the pedal down, felt the tires search for a grip on this grass, felt the rear end wag, then grab hold hard, and we were gone.

"Shit," Five whispered, Tabitha breathing hard in and out.

"Watch for residents," Jessup said beside me, calm and cool, almost as though this were some driver's ed film, "and as soon as you get back out on the street, take the first right. Sand Marsh Lane." He paused, said, "Might still have a chance to keep sight of them."

I took in a deep breath, held the steering wheel as tight as when I'd thought it would dissolve.

And with that breath in I smelled something, small and far away. But not as far away as when I'd taken it in this afternoon, when Mom came home.

I smelled it: a match strike. A burnt-out sparkler.

Out the corner of my eye I could see Jessup look down, saw him touch his ear.

"Copy," he said.

Now we're going somewhere, I thought, and punched the gas hard, stomped the shit out of the pedal.

13

"Don't go all the way to the stop sign," Jessup said beside me. "Pull over a few houses before, and cut your lights. Just wait. There." He pointed ahead of us to an SUV parked a few yards from where Sand Marsh Lane ended in a T with another street. "Behind that one."

We'd pulled out a driveway five or six houses down from where I'd done my lawn carving and past where the cruisers ended, then flown to the end of that street, turned right onto Sand Marsh, all four of us silent, and now I pulled over, closed in on the bumper of the red Chevy TrailBlazer Jessup'd pointed out. I turned off the lights, put it in park.

· A streetlamp stood at the corner up there, filled the Range Rover with hard shadows and what seemed bright light after all that blue, and I glanced in the side- and rearview mirrors for any cruisers roaring up behind us. Of course they'd seen me pull out across someone's yard, haul off away from them.

But cops following us, it came to me right then, wasn't something I had to think on. They had their hands full, and I didn't even need to waste a brain cell worrying over them.

Because right now Jessup was beside me, in the Range Rover with Tabitha, and with Five. Right now Unc was in a Suburban with Prendergast and Stanhope and Harmon. Two possible illegals named Tammy and Coburn.

Right now we were in the middle of something.

That was when the questions exploded.

"What in the fuck is going on?" Five said too loud from the back-seat, and Tabitha leaned forward, eyes on me, started hammering away with her hands, words so quick I could only pick out *Who* and *law* and *safe* before Five let out "Who is this dude? Why did you just fucking rip up Mr. Walpole's yard? Who is this dude?" while still Tabitha hammered away: *Quick* and *start* and *light*.

"I know Jessup," I shouted then, way too loud. But that's how the words came out: the big answer to everything it seemed the two of them were asking, sharp enough to silence them both. "He works Security at Landgrave Hall. Where we live. He's a friend."

Though as soon as I'd said that last word, I knew the real truth was that he had been a friend a long time ago, when we were both kids in school and sitting with our pals on the tracks at the end of Marie in North Charleston, sharing Colt 45s and doing nothing. Back before 9/11, when Jessup split for the Army, and before Unc sold a chunk of land. Before we were what we are now: a Landgrave Hall resident, and a Landgrave Hall security guard.

But there was another truth, one I had no clue to, and that I needed an answer for as well: why he was here, now. The same person who'd been in the shadows just off the end of my driveway last night, tailing Harmon tailing me. Right to where Prendergast had been.

He wasn't here about Landgrave Hall. He wasn't tagging along just in case, here to check in on how I was doing. He was here for something else.

I felt my hands still just as tight on the steering wheel. I heard Five breathing behind me, saw Tabitha looking at me, hands touching the dash, waiting.

And Jessup right there between us, the center of us all, watching out the windshield. An earphone on, a cord snaking down his neck.

"Jessup," I said, "what are you doing here?"

"And why'd you just make him drive through someone's yard?" Five shot out, then said, "I'm out of here."

I heard the pop open of a door, and Jessup disappeared from between us. But then the dome light went out as soon as it went on: Jessup had pulled closed the door Five had opened.

"No," he said to Five, his voice solid and cold. "No one driving past here's going to see a pedestrian out on the street." Then, to me, "Watch. There's no outlet for him other than here. They're coming."

I heard him move again back there, the thin scratch of the windbreaker material, and a snap. "You want to know who I am, then here," he said to Five, and I heard some small movement back there, a couple seconds of silence, then Jessup again: "I'm authorized to show that to you. That's it. And nobody's getting out the vehicle."

A moment later he leaned forward between Tabitha and me, her still with her hands just touching the dash, and handed her what looked in the dark like a thin wallet.

"Watch, Huger," he said to me, and I quick turned to the intersection, there beyond this TrailBlazer in front of me.

"You're an agent," Five whispered behind me. "Okay."

Out the corner of my eye I could see Tabitha slowly take what Jessup held out to her, lean to the window. She held it open to the light from the lamp out there, and I went ahead and looked.

It was a badge, and ID card.

"If this is about Tammy and Coburn, I can tell you my dad didn't know they were illegals," Five said, his voice thin, edged up: contrite. "Those two are just—"

"Wouldn't have needed the vehicle," Jessup cut in, and Five shut up, "if someone hadn't called in a report on an illegal poker game going on. I was doing fine until D-Day. Happened to park for observation beside a brick mailbox stand big as an outdoor barbecue. Then the Mount Pleasant force descended, blocked me in. That was that. Somebody's big idea of community service."

He touched his ear again, seemed to lean even farther between us, looking to the right out the windshield, and I knew in his moves—no glance at me or shake of his head—that he didn't know Unc was the one to call it in. And I wasn't going to tell him.

Tabitha turned, Jessup's head and shoulders between us. She leaned forward, looked at me, and held out to me the wallet, lying open.

But before I could take it, Jessup whispered, "There he is," and I looked up, saw a black Suburban cruise past.

We sat there, watched it for just that second or so it took to pass through our field of vision, and then the dome light came back on: Five's door again.

"Now you get out. Everybody," Jessup said. He was gone from between us, Tabitha still with her hand out holding his badge and ID, and I looked behind me.

Jessup had opened Five's door this time, and I saw Five looking at him, hands up and against his chest. His mouth was open, eyes squinted. He didn't move.

Jessup leaned forward, took the badge from Tabitha, then held it open to me only a couple inches from my nose. Here it was, bright gold even in the dim light. And the ID card: a black-and-white photo of Jessup up close, his mouth a tight line, beside it a round logo with an eagle, the words *Special Agent Jessup Roderick Horry, Federal Protective Service, Department of Homeland Security.*

He slapped it closed. "This vehicle is being appropriated by the Federal Protective Service," he said. He stuffed the badge into his windbreaker pocket, then looked at Tabitha, at me again. He nodded. "Two lines of egress from this development, and if I don't see which one they take, they might be gone. Now. Out."

I heard Five turn from him, heard the scuff of a foot on the pavement out his door.

I looked at Tabitha, nodded. She reached for the handle on her door. Then she stopped, turned to me.

"Go," I said to her, then over my shoulder, "You too, Five," but I could see he was already out, the door standing open. Only Jessup back there now.

I looked at him, said, "I'm staying."

He shook his head. "No way. This is FPS business. You have no choice. This isn't TV. This isn't Xbox." Here he was between us, reaching across Tabitha now and for her door, trying to open it to boost her out.

But then he stopped, touched his ear, sat back fast. "Copy," he said. "Ten seconds. Subject headed east on Old Marsh Drive," then, to me, "If you do not get out now, we will lose them." He put a hand on my shoulder, held it hard. "We have no intel on where they're going. Do you understand?"

"If you know anything at all about me," I said, "you know I'm not leaving Unc."

I looked again at Tabitha, mouthed *Go*, nodded at her door.

She didn't move.

So I let go the steering wheel, lifted my hands from the vise grip I'd held them in all this time, and turned to her. I pointed both index fingers above and then straight at her, then pinched the fingers and thumb of my right hand together, touched the corner of my mouth and then my cheek. Same as she'd given me on a sidewalk in Palo Alto at the end of a fifty-two-hour drive.

Go home.

"Tabitha," Five shouted from behind me and just outside the open door, "let's go!" As though she'd hear him.

She tapped her chest, pointed at me.

"We have to go now," Jessup said.

"Okay," I said, and nodded at Tabitha.

She touched a hand to the dash, looked out the windshield, and I put the Range Rover in drive, even if the dome light was on for the door open back there.

Then I heard Five grunt out, "Shit, this is a bad idea," as he rolled into the backseat, and the door slammed shut, the dome light off.

Jessup, his voice sharp steel, whispered, "This is out of regs. This is so out of regs," then, the words suddenly clipped and cool, "Copy. Yessir. Situation as determined." He paused. "Now in pursuit."

They were gone. No sign of them in front of me on this winding stretch of homes I'd turned left onto. The street was wider here, a main drag through the development that led back to the entrance off of Rifle Range Road, maybe a mile away. One of the two lines of egress Jessup'd meant, though it was the only one I knew of, the only way Unc and I had ever taken in here.

"No visual," Jessup said beside me, leaning in again, that finger to his ear. Then, "No sir. Yessir." He pointed ahead, said, "Turn right up here. On Sound View. He'll be taking Porchers Bluff Road. The other way out. Trying to avoid any more officers arriving on scene."

Here came a corner, the lot a large spread of lawn with a big clapboard house same as all the others, and I swung to the right, realized as I did my headlights were still off, nothing any clearer out the windshield as I pulled onto this next street. I reached down, turned on the headlights, but saw spread before us only better-lit pretty houses and lawns, a better-lit asphalt path between them.

"My dad really didn't know they were illegals. Really," Five tried to offer again. "He just hired them to work for him. We don't really need to go all nuclear with this."

"Then he'll have all their W-2s in order, I'm sure," Jessup said. "For Thursday night poker."

I drove, and felt suddenly that this wasn't actually real, Five's concern about his dad and who he'd hired to make drinks and cash out chips, Jessup's quick and snarky answer back to him. I felt for a second we were four friends in a vehicle driving too fast in a neighborhood at night, late maybe to the house of another friend. I could feel the adrenaline up in me, higher even than when Jessup'd climbed into the car, and felt still my neck on fire, my mouth dry. But I was only driving a vehicle, in a neighborhood.

And no Suburban in front of us, no cars on the street at all other than the ones parked now and again along the curbs, this mission we were on hollow and dumb for this fact. The houses we drove along were so clean, and sharp, and ready-made for families that it seemed there was nothing could go wrong here, nothing worthy or even in the offing that involved whatever we were rolling toward.

But Unc was out there, and I hoped we hadn't already lost him.

"You never answered my question," I said then. "Why are you here?"

"Sound View hits a traffic circle up here at Treadwell," Jessup said right back, "then he'll have peeled off one of two ways. Only three streets lead out of the circle, the one we're on one of them. But they're not going to come back this way for the cops they might run into." He paused, nodded ahead of us, and I glanced at Tabitha, saw she had a hand touching the dash still, but her head turned toward him so she could try and read his lips. "The only way out without coming back here," Jessup went on, "is onto Porchers Bluff, through the other side of this part of the development. So we just have to chance it, take one or the other of these feeders off the circle, make our way back through the streets and hope we see him before he sees us. And before he makes it to Porchers Bluff."

Fifty yards ahead was the traffic circle, a lamppost at the corner up there, in the circle a clutch of palmettos, a ONE WAY sign pointing to the right. Out my window and Tabitha's both the big yards and houses had stopped of a sudden, beside us now only black: woods.

This was a separate part of Hamlet Square, a part Unc and I had never been before.

"How do you know all this shit?" Five said. His voice was quiet, but seemed somehow more gathered to itself. More like the Five I knew, the smart-ass one. "I mean, how exactly do you know the lay-out of this whole place? Where I live?"

Jessup didn't answer him, only leaned forward, peered out the windshield, said, "Copy."

And he still hadn't answered my question, either: *What are you doing here?*

"Are you even talking to anyone on that thing?" Five said.

We were almost to the circle now. "Which street?" I said.

"One or the other," Jessup said. "It's a kind of maze of streets back here, but they all—"

Tabitha tapped hard at her window then, and I turned, saw through the edge of woods we were coming out of into the circle a sharp chip of bright red light, and then the taillight itself.

We cleared the trees, and I could see a vehicle on the first street off the circle, maybe a hundred yards away, and then the taillight disap-peared, gone for the houses between us, that street curving away to the left.

"Take the second right," Jessup said.

"But they're going that way," I said, and pulled into the circle. "They took—"

"Second right." He didn't look at me. "We don't want to sit on their butts. We don't want them to see us. And these streets lead out only one way."

I pulled into the circle, for a second eased off the gas as though I might very well follow after Unc—he was down there, he was right down there—but then I gave it the gas again, passed that street and its houses.

Tabitha quick turned to me, tapped hard at the glass again, shook her head: *That way. That way.*

But I went on around the circle, in my headlights the landscaped common areas around it, with their azaleas and vinca and more palmettos. And I took that next right, the only one other than the street we'd driven in on and the one Unc and Prendergast had taken, and we peeled off into more houses, and more lawns.

"What the fuck are we *doing*?" Five whispered hard, and I heard him move back there, then Jessup shoot out "No," and a jostle, a tug, then Jessup between the front seats again, and a quick chink of sound at the console. I looked down.

A BlackBerry, there with Unc's cellphone and his wallet, the bag of golf balls.

"We are not calling in anyone," Jessup said. "No nine one one, no texting BFFs, no nothing."

I could see Tabitha look down at the cellphone, then up at me, out her window again.

I sped up now, because I wasn't going to let wherever they were in this part of the development be lost to me. I wasn't going to lose Unc, and I thought again of Stanhope and his gun drawn on those two illegals, the one running away, the other stopping her, tackling her in the yard.

But losing him for what?

What was it a pair of goggles could hold over Prendergast that he'd risk kidnapping Unc?

And I thought of Jessup climbing into the back of the Range Rover, his calm words—*Be resourceful*—as I'd sat there knowing already but without any guts for it that the only way out to follow the Suburban would be to pull into that yard, and to get away fast.

He had his ID and badge. He'd tried to kick us out of the vehicle so's he could take over, follow them wherever no intel could figure.

What would a special agent be doing at a stupid Mount Pleasant poker game? And why take over the Range Rover to follow someone military, no matter what a shit Prendergast was?

Jessup'd been in the Army all those years I'd been wallowing in the lucky shit of my own life. He'd left the day after 9/11, like it'd been something he was waiting for, some sign to him he could just stand up from his desk in homeroom and give his life meaning, because he could serve the country.

He'd been to Iraq twice, and to Afghanistan. And though I'd thought he was done with that, done serving the country, now here he was: a special agent with Homeland Security. Something called Federal Protective Service. Nothing I'd ever heard of.

"Bryden Lane," he said in his microphone voice as we moved past a street on the right. He looked out Tabitha's window, and though Jessup only leaned a few inches toward her, I could see she was pushing herself as deep into her seat and away from him as she could, as though he meant to touch her by peering out that window. Then we were past the street—no headlights coming at us, no taillights—and Jessup eased back, looked out the windshield.

I said, "Talk to me, Jessup." I gripped the wheel, pressed a little harder on the gas. "Why are you here?"

"Listen," he said, and I could hear him breathe a little easier suddenly, as though he were relieved, "I'm authorized to show you my ID. Authorized to appropriate this vehicle." He paused, said, "Clancy Road," as we passed the next empty street, then said, "Official statement: The mission of the Federal Protective Service is to render federal properties safe and secure for federal employees, officials, and visitors in a professional and cost-effective manner by deploying a highly trained and multidisciplined police force."

"What does that have to do with a poker game?" Five said behind us, his voice lower, unimpressed. "All's we're doing is playing Texas hold 'em, and if my dad has two illegal aliens making drinks and cashing chips, what in the hell does that have to do with Homeland Security and some half-assed car chase in my own stupid neighborhood?"

Jessup said nothing, only looked ahead of us. Tabitha leaned forward in her seat, waved to get my attention, then shook her head, pointed at her eyes: she couldn't see his lips to read them.

I said, "Federal Protective Service. Security for federal property and people," and looked out the windshield: houses, and houses. The street started to curve off to the right, and it seemed this was a kind of loop, the rim of a half wheel that had the traffic circle as its hub. If we weren't careful, I thought, this street would lead us head-on into Unc and Prendergast and company, coming straight at us after having peeled off in what had looked the opposite direction.

"I said, what does all this have to do with a poker game?" Five said again, and I heard him move in his seat, pictured him with his arms crossed and waiting: a kid.

"It doesn't," Jessup said, though his voice was so low and quiet beside me it seemed it was more for me than any answer to Five. "It's about Landgrave Hall."

"What?" I said quick, but as soon as he'd said it, I'd known. I'd known.

Landgrave. I was wrong. This *was* about it. This was about a body. That woman. Jessup had been there when Unc and I found it. And he'd followed Harmon, right to my house.

"You don't think the federal government," Jessup nearly whispered, "is going to let a piece of marshy real estate wedged between the Naval Weapons Station and the 841st Transportation Battalion sit unattended all these years, no matter it looks like nothing other than a bunch of rich folks whacking at golf balls for fun, do you?" He paused. "Present company excluded."

I swallowed. I glanced to my right, saw Tabitha leaning forward, shaking her head for being left out altogether from what was being said. But I only looked at her, then out the windshield again.

"Especially with the fact battalion command's just the window dressing over there. SPAWAR's only three hundred yards inside the fence from the sixteenth green." He stopped then, took in a breath.

"The United States Naval Consolidated Brig," he said, even quieter but as solid as rock, "with all those nasty terrorists holed up in there, is only eleven hundred and seventeen yards in. Not to be too precise."

He paused. "You don't know how valuable the land you live on is. Agents of the Federal Protective Service have been parked at Landgrave since the Navy jumped the creek and bought the weapons tract. Nineteen forty-one. So you may think Tyrone and Segundo and I are glorified rent-a-cops. But you'd be wrong. We're standing watch. And because of the high-value target this place is, and how important it is to keep it secure, we take this very seriously."

"So what are you, some kind of spy?" Five said, and I couldn't quite tell if he was being a smart-ass now, or if he meant it. But I knew I wanted him to shut up.

Here came another street, and we all looked down it to nothing, though there might have been in this moment the sense this was of course what we'd see. Nothing.

Where were Unc and the Suburban?

"Zinser Lane," he reported, then, quieter, "No. No spy." He turned toward me the smallest way again, said over his shoulder to Five, "But I do know, from fact sheets passed around regarding known affiliates of soon-to-be visiting dignitaries, that you graduated Duke with a 1.78 GPA, you been through six jobs as a glorified bank teller in five years, and the only reason you can afford that loft condo on Hill Street up in Charlotte on your punk-ass thirty-two grand a year is because Warchester Four made the down payment and splits the monthly with you." He paused, shook his head. "And I know if I turn more than ninety degrees away from Dorcas Lydia Galliard, better known as Tabitha, she can't read my lips and hear all this data about said affiliates, all of which she knows nothing about."

Five was silent, didn't even move.

Jessup faced front, and I looked at him. He nodded, said, "Eyes on the road."

I turned, but glanced at Tabitha again, hands palms up in front of her: *What is happening?*

I shook my head, my hands to the wheel.

See my mom, Tabitha'd said was why she was here, but then Five'd put in *She's here for an interview,* and made the lame joke she'd have to kill me if she told me.

She was here for SPAWAR. To become a computer somebody at Space and Naval Warfare Systems Command.

Ahead of me was a street, only knowable as far as the reach of my headlights. Around me were homes of people I didn't know, and most likely never would. Somewhere someone was taking street names from Jessup, and giving him orders. And somewhere between this moment of asphalt beneath my tires and whatever back way that led out to another street called Porchers Bluff Road was Unc, held hostage.

Somewhere someone had a fact sheet on Tabitha and all known affiliates, prepping to lead her into a life inside the fence at the bottom edge of Landgrave Hall, and I gave myself the luxury inside the middle of this all to wonder what facts there might be lined up about me.

Driver, I saw. Follower. Errand runner.

Thursday night Maps app monitor. Golf ball retriever.

Viewer of a dead body.

I blinked, blinked again, felt this idiot adrenaline in me rushing up again, felt my breaths coming quicker at the vision one more time of that woman bathed in green, a crab picking delicately at her jaw.

And now the neighborhood around us was changing: next to the landscaped house out my window stood an unfinished one, wrapped in torn and faded Tyvek, same as the condos out to Hungry Neck since the developers gave up and went home. Out Tabitha's side sat a house only framed up, the dirt yard littered with trash, pieces of wood.

We'd come to the far end of the development world now, us moving through unfinished homes in various forms of decay, the live ones suddenly behind us. Some of these houses were framed, some just foundations, some with clapboard halfway up the walls. But all of them dead. The place where life at Hamlet Square cut off, us just this quick inside the handbasket the whole real estate world had gone to hell in.

And the place where at any second we ought to see a black Suburban coming at us.

"Yep. Everyone over at SPAWAR knows Tabitha's the one," Jessup said, and now my stomach was starting to tighten. I looked over at Tabitha, Jessup leaning in between us, and saw she was reading his lips now. It was darker in the car, those streetlamps and lit-up houses gone. But there was still the dull glow of the dashboard lights, and I could see by them her mouth was shut tight, her eyes open wide.

I looked ahead. Houses were disappearing altogether now, just empty lots on either side up there. "She's here for an interview, but there's no interview to do," Jessup said, still looking straight ahead. He touched his ear, said, "Copy. As determined," then to us, "The postdoc she's doing fits like a shell in a chamber for SPAWAR. Data Visualization and Probabilistic Function in Aggregate Encryption." He paused. "Now *she's* a spy," he said. "Or sure looks like she'll be one soon."

Tabitha tapped hard the dash, and I looked at her, saw her shake her head, then three times in a row put her hand to her mouth and sweep that hand down and away. Tough little moves, and fast.

Bad bad bad.

I quick looked at the street, thought to gun it, to do something fast, because I understood her, and knew this was bad, whatever we were in.

But there, up ahead and at the outermost edge of where the headlights reached, I could see a row of trees, the strip of asphalt we were on heading straight at them. Trees up there, like a line of men on horseback, waiting.

"But that's not even the real story," Jessup whispered. "That's gravy, sure, having her with us. But that's not why I'm here," and I heard again that thin scratch of windbreaker material, heard that snap of a button. "That's not why *we're* here," he said.

"Wait a minute," Five said from nowhere, his voice a quiet shock. I'd forgotten him, and heard him move now. "I know where we are. I know where this goes." He paused. "This is a dead end."

"Like I told you, the real story," Jessup said, "is Landgrave."

He disappeared from between us again, and I heard in the same moment a solid thump of sound from behind us, a dull groan of air out of Five, and the slow slide down of him against the backseat.

And next a cold jab at the side of my neck: a pistol barrel, the instant of its fact coming at the same moment I saw the end of the street in the headlights, the cul-de-sac I'd driven us straight into. Trees all around. No homes anywhere, dead or alive.

Tabitha screamed, a high and dark shock of strangled noise, the sound maybe the only surprise to come at Jessup this whole night long, and I felt the barrel quiver an instant at his turning to her, heard the word "No" solid and cold.

Here in the rearview came a pair of headlights.

"No heroics," Jessup whispered.

I could give it the gas hard, circle back around them coming up from behind us, just drive like hell away from here.

But Jessup would still be here in the Range Rover with a gun on me, Tabitha and Five with us and ready to be shot. And Unc would still be in the Suburban.

I pulled to a stop in the middle of the cul-de-sac, put it in park. Dull green pines stood in the headlights, in front of them pavement edged with a concrete curb, poured at the direction of some developer who'd counted on houses going up forever. Like everything we knew would never end.

Tabitha breathed fast beside us, and I cut my eyes to her, barely shook my head for the pressure of the barrel against my throat.

"Good," Jessup said. "Tell her to keep quiet." I could feel him turn to look behind us then, and saw in the rearview the headlights disappear beneath the rear window. In my side-view, the Suburban's door opened, someone climbed out, the door closed.

Prendergast, I could see, their headlights banging off the back of the Range Rover.

Tabitha took in thin snatches of air, her back pressed hard against her door, each breath the brink of a scream.

Then I said it, because I wanted to know. Because knowing would seem to give some reason to this whole thing. There needed to be a reason.

I said, "Who killed her?"

"Not me," he said, and gave a small laugh. "Oh no. Not me."

I heard another car door close, saw in the side-view Prendergast look across the hood of the Suburban, nod.

I said, "Do you know about the goggles?"

The barrel against my neck, I could feel the way Jessup was moving, looking out his window, then out Tabitha's side, waiting. But he stopped, pressed the barrel even tighter into me. "Know about what?" he said.

Then came a sharp knock at Tabitha's window. She jumped, seemed to scatter to pieces for what she'd felt, turned and pushed away from the door with both hands, legs stiff against the floorboard until her back was to us and against the console, and Jessup took the gun from my throat, hit the side of her head, a quick pop of his hand, the gun right back at my neck just as quick.

"No!" I shouted, and reached a hand out, even with the barrel jammed as far against my throat as it could go.

She slumped forward, her legs folding beneath her so that she seemed to pour down the seat until she filled the leg well, her in a kind of ball on the floorboard.

"Now here's our man," Jessup said.

I tried to breathe, looking there at Tabitha. I tried to get air into me, but only felt a kind of quiver in my chest, a shallow nothing in and out.

Then I looked up.

There stood the bartender in his white shirt and black vest, bent to the window for how big he was. Coburn, who'd tackled the chip-cage girl, then'd spat words in her ear.

He was smiling, nodding.

"Unlock the door," Jessup said, and I reached to the dash, pressed the button.

Because I wasn't here. I wasn't here.

The dome light came on, and Coburn leaned in, still smiling.

He looked at Jessup, and spoke, friendly words out of him. It wasn't anything long, these words from him, just a handful of syllables that flowed out of him as calm as any of us would say hello to a friend.

I didn't understand them.

They sounded familiar, sounded for a moment like Spanish. But not. These were sounds that came from back in his throat, hashed up and shimmed in. But still only a handful of syllables, and I thought in this moment I'd heard wrong, that it was me with the problem.

Because I wasn't here.

I could feel Jessup nod, then words from him right here beside me, words in that same calm tone, and with those same hashed sounds.

Wallay koom sallem, it seemed he said, though I had no idea. They were sounds, syllables, a friendly greeting. That's all I knew.

Coburn looked at me, the smile gone.

"Situation as determined," he said, and in the instant I saw him raise his fist and reach across the seat toward me, inside just that moment before the world went black, it seemed a remarkable thing, how suddenly I understood what he'd said, how these words were as clear and available to me as some kid speaking them to me on the tracks at the end of Marie as he handed me the communal Colt 45.

These words were English, it came to me at the same moment as his fist, and those others were Arabic.

14

Water moved against the hull. Wind touched at my face and in my hair, only enough to let me know we were moving, that we were going somewhere. An outboard motor droned, just easing us along.

I felt the slow nod of it all, of everything. I felt the boat, and the water, and the air, and the calm.

I was home: in a boat, out on water.

"Might've broken his cheekbone," a voice in close said loud, and slammed through me, exploded in my head.

My left eye hurt. But more than that, more than pain. It was a kind of white light blossoming in me, filling me, and then it wasn't only my eye, but my ear, and down to my jaw, the laser white pain of it suddenly down into my lungs too and pulling even deeper. I tried at a breath, a good one, but felt my mouth taped closed, the air in through my nose another shallow nothing of a breath.

My hands were together and behind me, my wrists bound tight. I knew I was sitting up, my legs straight out in front of me, my shoulders against the hull. I knew these things.

But my hands wouldn't move, or my legs. Nothing, and I tried at another breath in, felt the tape pull at my lips and jaw and below my ears and at my hair, all the way around my head.

And then, like it was some ragged curtain rising, my right eye opened.

A shadow squatted a couple feet away from me, haloed by the night sky: Prendergast.

I was in the bow of a boat, nothing more than a good-sized bass boat with the platforms stripped out. Just beyond Prendergast I could see two others sitting across from me, black shadows huddled against the hull on that side, legs drawn to their chests. Just lumps, dark masses against the lighter gray of the hull.

"Wish I'd hit him harder, killed him outright," another voice said, away and to my right. "Save us the trouble."

I worked to turn my head, to see who'd said this, because I hadn't yet recalled it had been a big tanned bartender who'd hit me. Because a part of me, even inside the white sear of pain and the hard jolt of words, even inside seeing this shadow squatting beside me and knowing who it was, and knowing too that the shadows across from me were Tabitha, and Five—even inside all of that, a part of me was still out in a boat on water. A part of me was still home, and I wanted to know what this interruption was, the scope and breadth of it, and how I might banish it. I wanted to know how I could get back to that calm, that nod through water in the someplace else I'd been.

I turned my head a couple inches toward that second voice, the shock of pain at my eye suddenly sharper for it, then gave in to the move altogether, let my head loll that way.

There stood another shadow against the night sky, this one behind the console only a few feet away, the wheel in his hands. I could see the white arms of his shirt, the rest of him black for that vest.

Oh yes. Him: Coburn.

Prendergast's shadow clicked on a flashlight, and light stabbed into me, a dagger deep in my head. I squeezed my eye shut, the pain in me ten times bigger in just that move.

"He's awake," Prendergast said, and the flashlight clicked off.

And then I kicked at him, swept my leg low along the deck with everything I had toward that voice. I swung my leg at him, the move without plan or measure, simply what I knew I had to do, because here was the sudden recollection in me of Jessup hitting Tabitha, and of Coburn's fist fast at me, and of the groan of air out of Five in the seat behind me, and of Unc being hauled away by Harmon.

Here was the bright memory of Unc telling me what Prendergast had done to my mom.

My leg hit him hard, and I felt contact just above my ankle, felt his leg bend in, his own ankle folding away. I opened my eye, saw he'd stood up after he turned off the flashlight, but now that shadow was twisting, falling backward.

He let out a sharp piece of sound, tried to gain his balance, and I drew my legs up fast, out of the way as he sort of hung there in mid-collapse. Something fell out of his hand and hit the hull—the flashlight—and then he was full on his way down, his legs giving out beneath him, and he slammed to the deck.

But he was up on his elbows soon as he hit, whispered loud, "Son of a bitch!" through gritted teeth.

I heard a squeal of sound from the shadow on the right across from me: Tabitha. I saw the other shadow push away with his feet, try to jam himself into the hull as far from Prendergast as he could: Five.

I heard a dark and heavy grunt from somewhere to my right, back at the stern.

Unc.

And I wondered: Why hadn't I listened to him, when he'd told me to stay put?

Had he known Jessup was in on anything?

And what was the all of this, anyway?

204 | Bret Lott

If I'd stayed, it would only be Unc here, and not Five, and most important not Tabitha.

But Jessup had jumped in, and I'd listened to him instead.

Jessup.

I tried again to turn that way, toward the console and Coburn, to see if I could somehow spot Unc back there, but the move made the pain in my eye blast everything to pieces, a knife prying open an oyster jammed just under my skin, so that I lost my breath for it, felt my stomach spasm and go tight, the air in me out hard through my nose, the tape around my head a sudden band of metal cinched tight.

Here was Coburn, stepping around the console, and moving toward me, and here now was his foot, and I closed my eye just as he kicked me in the stomach.

I came around, still on a boat, still with an outboard droning, still with water coursing beneath me across a hull.

But there was nothing about this that was anything like home. Not now.

I was on my side, my knees drawn up near to my chest, the deck cold beneath my right cheek. My stomach felt hard somehow, like it was made of concrete, but with none of the strength of concrete. Just dull and thick and pointless, buried somewhere inside it another pain I didn't even care to think on, a pain different from that of my eye and jaw and ear. My stomach felt hard, felt over and done with.

I tried to breathe in again, but the air was even shallower now.

"Should've killed *all* of them on the spot," Coburn said.

"We've got the plan," Prendergast said, and it sounded as though they were both back at the console. But Prendergast's words came out squeezed and tight, his teeth still clenched. "We stay on the plan."

I opened my eye, saw from where I lay Coburn still at the console. To the left of him sat Prendergast on the gunwale, a hand down at his ankle and rubbing it, and I wondered where Jessup was, and what had happened to Stanhope and Harmon, too. And the chip-cage girl,

Tammy, who for a second seemed maybe not to have anything to do with any of this.

But then I remembered it was Coburn who'd knocked her down, nearly tackled her once she'd tried to run away, then whispered hard those words in her ear, Five climbing back into the Range Rover to tell us it sounded like Spanish, what Coburn'd been saying to her. And Stanhope hauling her away right alongside Coburn.

She was one of them too.

But who were they?

And where were we going?

I could see Prendergast now, that dark silk shirt he had on, and khaki pants. I could see the barest features on his face, a grimace, that haircut, and I could see too Coburn, both hands on the wheel right over there, right over there, his eyes straight ahead.

Because here was light again, its sudden presence the same kind of surprise as when those cruisers had pulled up out front of the Whaley place, and I'd been able to see Tabitha's face in the dark, her smile, her eyes, the way her chin curved just so.

I looked at Tabitha across from me, maybe four feet away and still sitting up against the hull. Her hands were behind her, too, her eyes closed, her chin high, around her head at the jaw a gray band of duct tape. Leaned hard against her was Five, his head on her shoulder, his face down so that his chin touched his chest, his shoulders shaking. He was crying.

I could see all this, the light nothing bright but here all the same, seeped-in and artificial, and I heard a quick double-click of sound from above us, heavy and hollow, here and gone.

And now from behind me and arcing across the sky, moving slow and filling for a moment everything I could see above us, was the underside of a bridge, and here was another hollow double-click: a car across the joints. It was a low bridge, maybe fifteen feet above us, and now as we passed beneath it I could see the metal cage of girders above the roadway, and knew it was the Cainhoy Bridge over the

Wando River, and that the light had to be from Detyens Shipyard just ahead, the small commercial yard where there were always a couple trawlers being worked on. Light had to be coming in off that, and from the Kangaroo mini-mart that sat at the top of the boat ramp beside the foot of the bridge.

The Wando here was maybe three hundred yards wide, the bridge low and hugging it all the way across. A peaceful place, a bridge that marked in my mind where the development in Mount Pleasant stopped, across it Highway 41 launching a straight shot out into the Francis Marion Forest, the all of Mount P and poker parties and Towne Centre and fabulous houses nothing but somebody else's dream. Once you crossed the Cainhoy Bridge and were headed north out on 41, there was nothing but woods for thirty-five miles, all the way to the Santee River. A stretch of the world I'd be happy to spend the rest of my life driving down, if it meant I didn't have to be here.

The bridge disappeared behind us, and I knew we were heading toward the Cooper, the Wando and Cooper meeting at the bottom edge of Daniel Island maybe a half hour away. Whatever boat we were on, I figured they'd had to put in at Paradise public landing, not but two or three miles from Hamlet Square and the closest one to the development. And though I couldn't figure why we were in a boat and not in one or the other of the vehicles that bogus chase had involved, I let myself imagine the route we'd take home from here, how we'd round the thin beach at that bottom edge of Daniel Island, then turn to the right and head up the Cooper past the Naval Shipyard, then under the Don Holt Bridge, that same beam-and-girder skeleton we'd driven over on our way to poker. Then past all the lights of the paper mill, and finally to the mouth of Goose Creek, and on in to our house, where our dock butted up against that silver arc of water.

An idea that seemed stupid, certainly: we weren't going home. We were going somewhere to die.

I tried at a breath again, made myself take in what I could slowly, carefully. My stomach still felt hard, that ache still buried deep and waiting to spring from where it hid.

"You may have a plan," Coburn said then. "But I have obedience. The plan we share is from Allah almighty, and you are only a tool within it, while *ibada* gives me purpose. You are doing nothing Allah almighty hasn't designed to his glory. But I am glorifying him. I am—"

"Would you just shut the fuck up?" Prendergast shot out, still with his teeth clenched. He sat up straight, both hands to the gunwale now, and looked at Coburn. "We have the plan, you know what the plan is, you'll comply with the plan."

"The only reason I work with you is because the plan serves the greater good," Coburn said. "Surah eight twelve, I am with you: Give firmness to the Believers. I will cast terror into the hearts of those who disbelieve. Therefore strike off their heads and strike off every fingertip of them." He looked at Prendergast, a quick glance, then faced forward. "This is my plan. But I should have killed them all on the spot. It wouldn't have mattered. We're as close as we are. This time tomorrow—"

"This time tomorrow I'm still going to be a Navy commander," Prendergast cut in, "and every military investigator in the country's going to be descending on the whole complex, top to bottom, sniffing every butt they can find to figure out how it all happened. So dispatching five collaterals who have no strings attached to any part of the objective requires a little bit of thinking. This whole thing's come to be a clusterfuck beyond measure only me and my men will be left to clean up, and all you want to do is give me chapter and verse of Allah be praised."

He looked away from Coburn, back toward the stern, and now the light was fading on us, the bridge and boat ramp and shipyard all behind us. "This time tomorrow you and Jessup'll be squeezing the titties of seventy-two dark-eyed virgins apiece," Prendergast said, quieter, as though the words were only to himself, "and I'm going to be standing around trying my damndest to melt into the wallpaper."

Before I could understand what I was seeing, before I could take it in, Coburn was away from the wheel and had one hand to Prendergast's throat, the other holding tight the back of his head, him still sitting there on the gunwale. And I could see Coburn had a knife in the hand at Prendergast's throat, a dull gray glint in whatever last light was on us.

"Do it," Prendergast croaked out, the words ice. "Fuck this enemy of my enemy shit. Do it. See how close you can get to the target by yourself."

Coburn took in a quick breath, let it out slow. Then he was silent, held the knife without moving. A moment later he let go, stepped back to the wheel.

A target. Collaterals. Jessup, and Coburn, and seventy-two virgins apiece.

No.

No they weren't.

Prendergast and Coburn were quiet a few seconds, and I thought I could see Prendergast reach to his throat, rub at it. Then he stood, a hand out to the console, and seemed to hop closer to Coburn on one foot for whatever damage I'd done when I'd swept his leg out.

But Jessup, and Coburn. Those words between them, that friendly greeting I couldn't understand, that language. Arabic.

They were Muslim?

They were martyrs? They were *terrorists*?

No.

Prendergast stood next to Coburn at the console now. We were full in the dark, above us the stars out here on the river, us only a boat on the Wando in the middle of the night, headed toward Charleston Harbor.

Prendergast said, "The only thing going to save me is the fact how low under the radar you people are. All six of you." He paused. "Even Ellen and Robert."

His voice was no longer the ice of a moment ago, but now had a kind of ugly glee to it, the words dark and happy at once. "You guys are so far under the radar your knuckles are dragging ground. Which I have to hand to you is the genius of you people. You hear it a million times: The West has clocks, but you people have time. Guess this'll prove the point entirely."

Coburn said nothing.

Jessup and Coburn were terrorists. Martyrs.

I closed my eye, opened it again, tried at another breath, and another.

No.

I looked at Tabitha. I could feel my blood bolting through me, felt these next breaths in and out quicker and quicker, and even though the pain in my eye and ear and jaw and that pain still hiding out deep in my stomach had all turned now to nothing for how loud blood banged through me, crashed through me, I looked at Tabitha, because I thought seeing her might somehow change this.

I thought that if I could see her face, and the curve of her chin and her eyes, her eyes, that somehow my heart might slow down and I would be able to throw away this idea of terrorism, of people I knew—someone I'd called a friend—being terrorists.

A terrorist. A fucking *terrorist*.

I thought if I saw her, even only a nod from her, that I could walk away from what any of this meant—A target? Who were Ellen and Robert? And where were we going? What was the *target*?—and begin to live.

A terrorist was a word. It was a word, loaded into it a million tons of the shit of the world, a million tons of the ugly and bloody and heartless stupidity of the world.

A word that had always been only on TV. Always only a word on the Internet, a description of unknown assholes to get pissed off at and to bitch about and to punch your fist in your hand over, like I'd done when I'd watched again and again and again the World Trade Center collapse, and when late one night when no one else was up I'd gone to the Web and found the filthy rush of watching Daniel Pearl get his head cut off, a rush that left me wanting to kill, to *kill* the men doing it, the same rush in me when I'd seen a double-decker bus in London torn to pieces, and the rip of fire out the windows of that hotel in Mumbai, while terrorists held a gun to the neck of the city for days.

I thought if I could only see Tabitha, then this stupid word, the unbelievability of it suddenly here with me and suddenly real, might disappear, and I might find myself only in a boat on water. That I might be home.

But I couldn't see her. We were in dark now, and she was only a shape against the hull across from where I lay, another shape leaned up against her. Just shapes.

"We're not under the radar," Coburn said, his voice flat but sure, nowhere on it anything other than purpose. "The radar can't see us because we *are* the radar." He paused. "Freedom is the greatest disguise ever invented. We came here, we were raised here, we were given purpose by the words of the great Prophet, peace be upon him, and no one anywhere even sees it, because freedom hides everything from everyone."

"There's not going to be any hiding once you push the button on that Haji tux," Prendergast said, and I could hear him give a sort of laugh. "But you got that right about freedom hiding what it does. Poker night case in point." He'd raised his voice a little now, said the last words louder, and it sounded like he was looking behind him. At Unc.

"If only some dipshit had just handed over the goggles instead of calling in a battalion of cops," he went on, "we would've had the *free-dom* to just get those damn Gen 4s back and let you walk away from it all. But no. Leland Fucking Dillard has to phone in the whole Third Army to make some idiot point about a commander playing poker, wreck the *freedom* of playing poker for half of Mount Pleasant, and in the process win him and his son and chums the *freedom* to end up a do-it-yourself project on YouTube that—"

He stopped, and I waited for some reason he'd cut himself off. Maybe he saw something out on the river, or maybe he figured Coburn would say something.

Or maybe he'd heard his own words, and what they meant: a You-Tube do-it-yourself.

Still I looked for Tabitha's face, and still I couldn't see her.

"Freedom is worse than a disguise," Coburn finally said. "Freedom is a whore. Freedom is who let us into the country. Twenty years ago, the first Gulf War ends, and Freedom opens her legs for all refugees from Iraq. But our three families aren't refugees."

His voice had gone different altogether, him somewhere else. Not out on a river, not in a boat headed toward strapping on a suicide vest and reaching a target only Prendergast could get him close to. He was somewhere else.

I waited for Prendergast to tell him to shut up again. But he didn't.

"We are three families on the one true path," Coburn said, "sent here because even twenty years ago we knew Charleston was ready to be plucked. A nuclear submarine base, the Weapons Station with its storehouses of missiles. Fuel storage tanks a hundred feet past a chain-link fence that Freedom thinks will keep the tanks safe, because they are here in America. Our fathers know all this before we ever get here, and because the whore Freedom sells herself so cheap, all our fathers had to do to get us here was to say we are Shi'a, we hate Saddam Hussein, and Freedom winks at our parents and we children and says *Come right in*."

He paused, and I felt that water still coursing beneath me, saw night stars out here on the river, heard my own blood still pounding through me.

"Save it for the video," Prendergast said, but there was nothing in it. They were only words out of him.

"And the whore Freedom doesn't look behind the doors of our homes," Coburn went on, "because Freedom says in America we must respect the lives of everyone. We three families have Christmas trees, we have Christian names, we go to Sunday school, we get good grades and play baseball and have no accents. But behind our doors our parents teach us our whole lives we live in *ibada* to Allah Almighty, that we live in obedience to him and the one moment when our duty will be made known to us, praise be to Allah. And when that sign finally comes after all those years, Freedom doesn't even know us anymore, because we're now only six young Americans from three American families. Coburn and Tammy, Jessup and Nina, Robert and Ellen. We have kept our eyes on Allah and on each other through all those years."

Jessup, the kid I'd thought I'd known my whole life. A kid three or four rows in front of me on a hot and sweaty school bus, sitting inside the havoc of a busload of kids on a field trip to Hampton Plantation. A kid behaving, while paper airplanes and pencils sailed through the air around him.

A kid sitting on the tracks down at the end of Marie Street, passing me a forty-ounce Colt 45.

An empty desk in homeroom the morning of 9/12, when we all stumbled into school.

And a man leaning out the gatehouse the first time we pulled into Landgrave Hall after we'd closed on the sale of the land down to Hungry Neck. A man I thought I might recognize, leaning out the gatehouse while the gate swung open.

Jessup Horry. Hidden from me, from everyone, all his life.

"And then the glorious day of jihad arrives right here," Coburn said, "where we have been waiting. September eleventh is the signal we have waited for. Jessup joins the Army, I join the Navy, and Robert goes to Georgia Tech to study chemical engineering, because why do you want to risk learning anything at some training camp in Pakistan, when you can stay right here, and learn with the best equipment and training and teachers in the world? Ellen and Tammy work housekeeping for officers on base, because the whore Freedom subcontracts everything it can, and because we're the right color—we're all the right color—and because we do not know what we will find inside the officers' lives that will help us. Nina becomes an LPN and works home health care, because one day we will need a home from which we can work, just the right one, one no one will suspect is anything but the home of an old and respectable and private person. She will find a home in which that person lives alone, and has no family left, and then she will let him die, and we will use this place as our base for whatever imminent measure we are led to take."

"I said save it," Prendergast said, but this time the words had an edge to them, that ice he'd had coming back. "Save all this shit for you and Jessup's fucking video."

"Allah leads Nina to Landgrave Hall," Coburn said, no difference at all to his voice, "and to the home of Judge Dupont."

Nina. The screaming Guatemalan nurse of Dupont's, a Guatemalan without any accent. A nurse it had been Jessup to tell me was Guatemalan to start with.

Jessup'd disappeared into the judge's house with her once she'd started that screaming last night, stayed in there with her so long I'd forgotten about him until he walked into my line of sight, me parked in a wrought-iron chair on Judge Dupont's patio while Unc and Stanhope had their bitchfest, Jessup walking down the yard to stand next to Harmon, and Stanhope.

Nina: his sister.

And Harmon, his hand on the stock of his M4 and scanning the growing Landgrave crowd, had nodded at Jessup once he'd made it out to them from inside the house. Like they knew each other.

"Allah's almighty glory brings us," Coburn said, "to the piece of land at the center of every opportunity our cell can hope for. And Allah leads the whore Freedom to give the Army hero Jessup his job with its own Federal Protective Service to oversee the land, and Allah leads you, Navy Commander, to a strip club off base to watch whores at work, and to tell me behind the bar, a Navy vet and so a comrade already, about a poker club in Mount Pleasant, and to help me get the job pouring drinks there, and a job for my sister Tammy cashing chips. A poker club where Allah reveals to me you are a gambler who needs more money than you make in ten years to pay off your debts."

He paused, took in a slow breath. "A gift from Allah, because you are on security for the Weapons Station, and you know exactly who of our brothers is in the United States Naval Consolidated Brig, and now you are one of the few who will be told exactly when tonight the confessing traitor Muhammad al-Qahtani will be transported back to Guantanamo from here, so that we can kill him for the dog he—"

"Shut. The fuck. Up," Prendergast said, cold and low.

They were both quiet now, and I thought of that name: al-Qahtani.

The twentieth hijacker. He was here, at the brig.

The target, to be killed by his own Muslim brothers. A statement to the world: We can strike again in the United States, and we will kill even our own who are so weak as to betray us.

"This whole thing is compromised because of you," Prendergast said, still just as cold. "You're the reason this whole thing has turned into as big a shitstorm as it has. You're the asshole who goes apeshit over Ellen and Stanhope. You're the fucker goes and kills her because he smiled at her a couple times, and because she smiled back. You're the motherfucker—not Robert, like you told us all—who goes and throws acid in her face, then strangles her, then has the audacity to call us up to help dispatch her body in the fucking pluff mud out back of the place."

He took in a breath, said quieter, slower, "There's no honor in that no matter how you look at it."

Coburn said nothing.

My eye was open as wide as it would ever be, and searching.

I wanted to see the stars above us. I wanted to see the wide band of stars behind stars, the Milky Way up there, and the black that held them all, cupped them like velvet.

I wanted to see Tabitha's face, her eyes. I wanted to see her.

I wanted to see Unc's eyes, too, him back at the stern of this boat and listening just like I was, just like we all were. I wanted to see the white marbles of his eyes I could only see with his sunglasses off, wanted even to see those scars across his cheeks and eyebrows. To touch them.

I wanted to see anything, everything—even a row of three pens tight in a shirt pocket, even a floorboard strewn with Red Bull empties and fast-food wrappers—because all I could see just then, and what seemed might be forever, was her face.

A woman named Ellen, now. A person. A human.

Her face was green, and bright. It was a grimace of bare teeth, a ragged pull of flesh away from them. It was a nose and chin the same ragged matter, a burl of loose flesh down to the cheekbones, the bones two green shards beneath where her eyes should have been. Her face was a swirl of flesh at her jaw, picked at by a blue crab.

A woman named Ellen, who'd smiled at an infidel.

An honor killing.

"Don't think I don't know it's you killed her, you towelhead son of a bitch," Prendergast went on. "Don't think I don't know it's your self-righteous *ibada* shit you're always talking about made you have to kill her for the dishonor of it, of her doing nothing but fucking *smile* at Stanhope. Robert wouldn't even do it, her own flesh and blood wouldn't kill her for honor, so you decide to do it yourself, then decide to kill Robert because he'd turn you in to me, and to Jessup, and to Stanhope and Harmon, and we'd deal with you."

He stopped, took in a breath, let it out hard. "But not for killing her. We'd deal with you because of the compromised situation you've brought into the whole thing. Because if you hadn't killed her, then none of this would have happened. None of this Leland and son turning up a dead body, because there's no fucking dead body to turn up!"

He slapped something hard then—the console, maybe—and took in another breath. Still Coburn hadn't said a further word. "If there's no dead body, there's no *you* trying to tell Stanhope and Harmon and me it's Robert did it. No need for you to kill Robert too, because he

wouldn't kill his own sister. Then there's no need for you to get rid of
his body while we try to get rid of Ellen's, and you don't end up doing
the shittiest job of it ever by dumping a body in the trunk of a car not
ten feet from the fucking bridge at Wambaw Creek so's it'll show up
on the evening news the night of the operation. *Shit!*"

"You've got your money," Coburn nearly whispered. "You have
your way out."

"Fuck you!" Prendergast nearly shouted. "You better pray to Allah
the one thing actually works in this whole thing is that that convoy
with al-Qahtani in it comes down Perimeter Road on its way to the
heliport tonight, and the fact a body showed up at Landgrave last
night hasn't shut everything down. You better pray *two* of you can
blow up that son of a bitch instead of the *three* it would have been if
Robert were here. Because we don't know which of the fucking three
vehicles he's going to be in. Do you understand that?"

Coburn said nothing.

And I thought of the Chinook helicopter I'd seen making a night
landing while Unc and I'd been on our way to poker tonight.

I thought of Perimeter Road, and the way it cut so close to Landgrave Hall you could see it in winter from the green on sixteen or the
tee at seventeen.

I thought of Judge Dupont, dead for who knew how long, his
house empty but for a set of homegrown terrorists, waiting their
whole lives—the ones left alive—for this night. Now.

And I thought of Major Alton Tyler out on Wambaw Creek
at the Echaw Bridge, and a body in a trunk, and I prayed that
somebody—Tyler, SLED, any of the crew-cut crowd of investigators who'd come to our house and interviewed us about the whole
thing—would piece together something that would lead them to
know what had happened. That the man in the trunk was related to
the body at Landgrave, never mind they were found fifty miles apart.

I prayed to the God I knew—the good one, the one who had a
wrath all His own but who loved us, it was reported, enough to save

us all from ourselves—that somebody'd save Tabitha and Unc and Five and me, and do it now.

But in the middle of that prayer there came to me another thought, a digging pain rising up into me, same as the pain in my eye and jaw was coming back, that oyster pried open under the skin, and same as the pain in my stomach from being kicked was rising in me, a hidden and spring-loaded pain about to let go any moment: Tabitha and Unc and Five and I made only four people.

We were only four collaterals, when Prendergast had said five. He'd have to dispatch five collaterals.

Here was the pain: I knew now where Jessup was.

I saw him knocking on the door of a 4200-square-foot cottage at Landgrave Hall, and saw my mom all smiles as she opened it to him, someone she'd known a long long time. She'd known him since her son, Huger, was a boy, known him from all the way back when they all lived in the same neighborhood in the shadow of the Mark Clark Expressway.

Jessup Horry. Someone she could trust.

Mom'd talked to Prendergast last night. Once some suicide ambush had taken place, she'd be asked questions same as every single person on Landgrave would be asked, and she'd mention him.

And she knew him for what he was, had known since all the way back to high school: Prendergast was an evil man.

She might talk about that time to an investigator, tell someone, finally, what had happened, and one extra word about Prendergast might make all the difference in whether he could melt into any wallpaper at all.

And then I knew, too, exactly where we were going: straight back to Landgrave Hall, the place I'd figured we'd never end up. Landgrave, where we'd be the subject of a video in the empty house Judge Dupont had left when they let him die.

We five collaterals.

15

I'm a kid, and have on my yellow nylon Jurassic Park backpack, the padded shoulder straps cinched down tight. In the backpack is a huge and bright blue lidless cookie jar.

It's supposed to be an apple. I'd painted it with something that seemed red when I'd put it on. But now, stepping down out of the school bus at the corner of Attaway and Sumner, all I'm carrying in my backpack is something bright blue, and heavy.

It's not what I'd thought I was making.

I'll lie to her. I'll tell Mom it's a giant blueberry, and she'll believe me. Because she's my mom, and she loves me.

The bus pulls away, and I and the rest of my friends—Matt and Jessup and Rafael, LaKeisha and Polly and Deevonne—all split up, each of us headed for home.

I know the way to mine. First I have to walk along Sumner away from the C & S Grocerette and McTV Repair, the afternoon sun behind me, then pass houses just like ours: short concrete driveways, concrete steps up to front doors. Oil stains in the driveways, room air conditioners in the windows.

At the corner where Marie hits Sumner, I'll turn right, and see at the far dead end of the street the Mark Clark Expressway high up on huge concrete pilings. The train tracks are down there, too, though Mom warns me to stay off them, that they're dangerous, kids have gotten killed messing around on train tracks.

But we play down there anyway, put pennies on the rails and watch the trains lumber past, then go get the thin disks, medals from some kid war. We throw rocks from the tracks hard as we can up at the Mark Clark, hoping one day one of us will land something up there, but no one ever does.

Cars rush by up there, horns honk, sometimes brakes squeal. Everyone up there moving, heading somewhere, doing something.

From that corner where Marie hits Sumner, my house will be the seventh one on the left, and I'll have only that far to walk.

That's where my mom will be, waiting for me, and where I'll be able to unload this backpack, and tell her the lie that what I'd made is what I'd intended, that this heavy blue thing is a lidless blueberry cookie jar.

I'll be home.

I look around. Everyone is gone, all my friends already headed toward where they have to go, and I put a hand up to my forehead, look back toward that afternoon sun.

It's still a couple fists above the trees out here, and I know I'm only looking back at it because I don't want to turn, start that walk home. Because my backpack pulls at my shoulders, weighs me down, and because this thing I'm hauling home isn't what I'd thought it would be. It isn't what I'd hoped it would be. It's just a giant blue ceramic thing without a lid. And the sad thing is it's the best I could do.

I turn back, toward the way I have to go, and now I can see my shadow, long and thin out in front of me. Pointing straight down the street.

And I go, finally, because I know the way home. I know the path I have to walk, and I know too I'm the only one can carry this thing in my backpack.

I start for home, but only two or three steps in, the pavement rises up in front of me, a tarred carpet pulled up in a wave in front of me, and my next step is a stumble, and I'm starting to fall backward for the way this path rises too quick, too quick in front of me, and I woke to the boat speeding up, the outboard gone loud, the hull rising with how it cut quicker through water.

Here was my eye, and that pain. Here was my stomach, and that pain still hiding.

I felt something coarse across my face, felt it even through the pain there. Something lay across me, over me, covered me, and I knew from the smell what it was, and from how coarse it was on my cheek and forehead and chin, but I couldn't name it. It was something I knew well enough, a word just over there, in a place I couldn't grab hold of or see.

Fish smell, and coarse.

A croker sack. They'd thrown a burlap croker sack over me, and must've done the same with Tabitha, and with Five and Unc too. Because, I realized, the boat speeding up like this meant we were out in the open on the Cooper River, headed back up it toward the mouth of Goose Creek.

We were gunning it up the river right past the wharves where the 841st Transportation Battalion complex butted up against the Cooper, right where the Army loaded ships with sand-colored MRAPs and tanks and transport vehicles. If anyone was watching us from over there, even with night-vision goggles on, they'd see only two men motoring up the river, and not four people tied up and sitting in the hull of a boat.

And figure, too, that the boat we were on was most likely registered to Judge Dupont. If someone watching zeroed in on the numbers on the hull and did any kind of check, they'd find they saw a boat from some local just passing through, some moneyed dude from over to Landgrave Hall out doing a little night fishing. Just a local: let him go.

So why not just hide your hostages with croker sacks? Why not motor into Goose Creek at whatever time of night this was, the Naval Weapons Station on your right, SPAWAR and the transportation battalion and the United States Naval Consolidated Brig on your left, and act like you were just headed home with whatever fish you'd caught in these burlap bags?

Why not keep staying so low under the radar your knuckles drag ground? It'd worked so far for all parties involved.

A few minutes later the engine cut way back, and I could feel the roll stern to bow as we slowed, the hull dropping. We were in Goose Creek.

And of course I thought of what I could do. I thought of how I could try and save our lives. Because, and I mean this true, my own didn't matter anymore.

I was someone whose life had come to retrieving golf balls in the middle of the night. I was someone whose life had come to sitting out in a vehicle and waiting for my father to finish gambling. I was someone who'd banked somehow on a girl—a woman, a person—named Tabitha, who seemed somehow still to like me, maybe even still to love me, but who was a part of the trouble we were in, and so someone who deserved to get out of it somehow, to be delivered of it, and if not by me, then by who?

And there was Unc, too, in this same trouble, in this same dead end we were headed toward. He deserved better, I knew, than to end in what was about to come: some video to be broadcast on the Internet, a video to accompany the destruction of the twentieth hijacker, a Muslim terrorist who'd turned evidence against his brothers.

Unc deserved better than to be a part of the shit this knuckle-dragging terror had already brought into the country. He deserved to live, as did Tabitha. And Five.

And my mom.

I could stand right now, right now, here where Goose Creek began to narrow in toward Landgrave on the left, the Weapons Station still on the right. Even with my hands Zip-Cuffed behind me, I could roll onto my knees, stand up, this cloak of burlap falling away from me as I did, and launch myself at the two of them standing at the console, try to knock them both down, maybe luck out and get them both. And maybe then Unc would hear what was going on, get himself up and have at it, too, and then maybe Five would join in. Maybe we could all of us, even Tabitha, tackle them, take them out.

All four of us with our hands cuffed behind us, duct tape around our heads.

And Coburn most likely with a gun, Prendergast too, and this would be the end, right here, for all of us.

Mom would be the only one left for any video to be made. Mom, alone.

Or maybe I could just pitch myself overboard, try to stay on my back with my hands behind me, swim to whatever side of the creek was closest, and make it away.

Through pluff mud, with my hands still behind me, unable to get a good breath, my ribs kicked in, my eye broken, to some unknown place or person. All if they didn't shoot me first.

But would they shoot? Would they risk that, a pistol shot in the dark on the creek, right here between the Weapons Station and Landgrave?

And even then, even if I got to that pluff mud by swimming on my back with my hands behind me and with duct tape across my mouth, even then Tabitha and Unc and Five would still be onboard. And Mom still held by Jessup at Judge Dupont's.

But what if when they heard me jump in, they all jumped in, Unc and Tabitha and Five getting to their knees and standing and pitching into the water on the creek to get away? What if we all right then—

The engine cut off now altogether, silence around me but for the thin whisper of water just moving along the hull, and then I felt a nudge against the hull where my back was pressed against it, the smallest touch on land but a touch enough to push us away from it, and then came an answering nudge against the other side of the hull: more land, the boat nosing into the head of a finger creek.

And then we hit ground for certain. A pitiful bit of momentum that jostled me same as last night, when I'd dropped that cinder block.

But nobody'd hear anything this night. There was only the touch of a hull against pluff mud. There was only this quiet around us, not even the odd and cold whir of cicadas I'd heard after I'd seen the body, a strange sound that had come to me in the same moment I felt the surprise shock of my own pulse through me.

After I'd seen a woman named Ellen. A member of the cell, killed for honor, but mutilated first. For honor.

"I see Jessup," Prendergast whispered then, and the words broke whatever spell it seemed lay over us for this quiet, this no-sound of a world about to end for all of us. His voice sounded like he was looking away, maybe somewhere ahead of us, but then, right here, he whispered, "Fifty-seven minutes before al-Qahtani's on his way. You get these fucks off this boat and I wipe it down and I'm gone." He paused. "You and Jessup do what you're going to do with them. But you be ready for my signal it's a go. Because I'm not making it twice."

Coburn said nothing, and I heard movement, felt Prendergast hop again, the boat rock a little for it. I heard a push of some kind, another low and heavy grunt from the stern: Unc.

I saw him on the dock out back of our house, him in a folding chair he'd pulled from the marine storage locker and sitting in light from a sun a couple fists still above the trees, a ghost of smoke off his cigar. Beyond him lay the marsh on the other side of the creek, the grasses all mid-spring colors, the brown of winter hustled out by the sharp green of new growth, a hard push of colors one against the other out there.

And in this silence I saw Mom, too, saw her beside me in our old tan Corolla, us driving away from the closing on the chunk of land at

Hungry Neck and on our way to Landgrave for the very first time. I saw her black leather purse in her lap, the black suit and purple silk blouse she'd worn. I saw her smiling, her eyes straight ahead, and saw she was still pretty, her eyes still that same sharp green, her red hair still in its soft curls, a spray of freckles across the top of her nose what somebody'd think was cute.

"Stand up, you blind fuck," Prendergast whispered hard, and I felt the boat give a quick totter, heard again movement, Unc's grunts, then two stiff thuds, and Unc groaning.

"Stand," Coburn said.

There was movement again, slow this time, and then I felt the croker sack whipped from off me, the rush of cool air behind it, and saw above me a shadow, what looked like Prendergast.

A thin wash of stars behind him.

"The easier you make this the quicker we'll be done," he whispered, and reached down to me, took hold one arm and pulled me to standing, but the pain in my eye and in my gut staggered me, swayed me to one side and another, no matter I tried to focus, tried to focus.

And still I figured if I pushed against him in some way I could topple him, his ankle like it was. I could butt him and push him and push him, and turn as I pushed him to where he'd be at the gunwale, and his ankle would give, and I could get him over the edge and into the creek and pluff mud, and Unc could butt Coburn somehow, and Five would see, and Tabitha could—

But as I stood there all I could do was snatch at a breath through my nose, tear at a breath, and try to stand firm.

I was nothing.

I swung my head toward the bow of the boat, blinked once, twice.

Five stood there, hunched over not two feet from me, only a shadow, and weeping.

And here beside him was Tabitha, just forward of him. She too was a shadow, but I could make out the sweep of her hair back into a ponytail.

Tabitha. Here.

I'd driven all the way to Palo Alto for her, met her one late afternoon out front of her Spanish fortress of an apartment complex, leaf shadows moving at our feet. She'd had on an old pair of jeans, a gray sweatshirt, her hair back in a white headband, and had never been more beautiful.

Go home go home go home go home go home, she'd shouted at me with her hands, each point of her fingers two shots into my chest, each touch to mouth and cheek a fist to my face.

But then she'd softened, looked at me with her perfect brown eyes, and slowly, carefully signed, *You have a purpose. Get through the past. Then be Huger.*

And just beyond her, just off the bow of this boat, just out there and far enough away so that it seemed a dream I might have had, some place I'd known only in sleep—I tried at another hard breath through my nose, and another—stood a white stucco house twenty yards in, beside it a waist-high brick fence almost down to this creek.

No light on in an upstairs room this time.

"You first," Prendergast whispered, and I felt him push me from behind toward the bow, and knew the jab beneath my shoulder blade was a gun. A pistol barrel, same as Jessup'd held to my neck.

The push made me bump hard into Five, who nearly fell, and then here I was beside Tabitha, and I looked at her, looked at her, tried to see her eyes what might be this one last time.

But there was nothing. Only the shadow of her face.

"Go," Prendergast said again, and I turned, looked toward the house. But past it, too, to the Cuthberts' place fifty yards farther back and to the right through the trees, where last night I'd seen their coach lamp on, that dime-sized halo it cast on the brick wall it was mounted to.

Maybe they were up. Maybe they'd see a boat sneaking into the Dupont place, and call it in.

But even that light was gone. Nothing. Only black.

Prendergast shoved me, a spike twisted in my ribs, and I lurched past Tabitha, then turned and sat on the bow.

I was facing away now, and saw them all, a jumble of shadowed ghosts, waiting for some purpose, waiting for the next move.

Here was Tabitha just to my right, behind her Five. Here was Prendergast to the left, past them all and beside the console Unc, and Coburn.

Behind them all the whole of the marsh, the uneven spread of blacks and grays and silvers out here. Across it all, a good half mile away, the low jagged tree line: a long line of men on horseback, watching, waiting.

"Now, Huger," Prendergast whispered, "you're going to walk on up to the house, and you won't make a single move otherwise. I've got a gun, and Coburn here has one too. And what you're going to see soon as you get close enough is Jessup standing up there and waiting on you. And you're going to see he's got his very own gun too. One he's holding on your momma." He paused, and I heard him cock the pistol in his hand, a thick metal chunk of sound. "Believe me," he whispered, "you make one move to bolt and I'll pop the girl here, Coburn will do dear Leland, and Jessup'll have his own fun with Eugenie." He paused, gave a little laugh, said, "We'll bat cleanup with baby Warchester the Fifth here," and Five whimpered loud.

But I was already turned to the house, because Mom was there. She was there, just like I'd thought she'd be, and I knew she was scared, and so I closed my eye, eased down off the bow a little sideways, my arms still behind me and sore for it, the wrists, I felt now, raw for the cuffs, my shoulders a solid band of ache. I slipped down from the bow, ready for the sink into pluff mud, the same mud that'd turned my arms into stumps only last night. The same mud that'd served the purpose to hide a body, until Unc had touched it with a pole.

But it was hard ground I hit, the bow of this boat far enough in, the tide not yet at dead low. I was on ground.

I opened my eye.

The world hadn't changed. I hadn't been delivered, nor none of us. No one'd saved us, no answer to prayer here. But I was standing on hard ground.

I took in a breath, stepped out and away from the boat, toward the house, and toward my mom.

And saw the path.

The same one we always used when we came in here to golf. Even to call it a path was to give it more credit than it was due: just the simple parting of cordgrass to left and to right, only a break a few inches wide. But clear to me, even in this dark.

A path. The way we always walked in, and the way we always left.

I stepped onto it, and looked ahead of me, saw the white stucco house, gray in the dark, and saw up there, those twenty yards away, a set of French doors, where Nina had stood and screamed at the knowledge suddenly in her of what Coburn had done: the honor he'd bestowed upon Ellen.

And now I was through the cordgrass, out on the grass. I heard from behind me Prendergast whisper loud, "Move, Warchester!" and then what I knew was Five's crying, a shredded squeal that sounded full of air somehow, and now I could make out, standing there to the right of the doors, two people.

My mom, there in a white top that'd nearly blended in with the side of the house. Beside her a shadow: Jessup. He stood a couple feet from her, had an arm out perpendicular from him, his hand, I could see, to her neck.

Five still cried behind me, and I heard steps through the cord-grass, quiet snaps of it as he walked through them, and now I heard too a heavy thump, and another: Unc and Coburn, or Tabitha and Prendergast.

But it didn't matter, because now, now, the dark of this world was fading around me, and all I could see ahead of me was the end of the path I'd walked, the one I'd been on my whole life long.

I saw the purpose, the why of my being here, right now. Here.

This was the end of my life, I knew. This was the end.

Inside the house was a video camera. Inside, too, had to be a woman named Nina, another named Tammy, the both of them afraid, I knew, for their lives, and I saw again Nina scream last night, and saw Tammy tackled by Coburn, her shoulders heaving for the way she sobbed.

I moved closer, saw clearly now Mom, her arms behind her, duct tape around her head as well, and I saw Jessup beside her, saw the gun in his hand, while the rest of the world around me disintegrated into ash, into wind and nothing and night, and now I ran at him, because none of it mattered, and all I knew to do was to try to arrive at the end of this path, the one that was only mine and that would end only with my stopping the man in front of me from harming my mother, whom I loved and would love and had all my life.

The man was Jessup. He had been a friend. But he was a terrorist. He was death.

This is enough, I thought. This is enough, and all I will bear. I will give up my life, I will give it up.

And I ran the last few feet at him, across the patio, staggered and lurched and tried to breathe inside this pain beyond pain in me, and still ran at him, because I knew this was the end.

"Shoot him," came Prendergast's voice from far far away, and I heard a strangled cry from back there too, and knew it was Unc, my father, and that he was crying out to me, and for me.

"Not yet," Jessup said, his voice cold, sure, and I saw his arm with the gun in it swing from my mother's neck to me, heard now Coburn's voice behind me say, "Then I will," the words no whisper at all, and closer than Prendergast: It'd been him and Unc to climb off the boat after Five.

And Jessup fired, two times in a row.

I saw the flash off the muzzle two feet in front of me, twin explosions of light, and I fell forward, pitched toward him, and hit the side of the wrought-iron table, crashed to the ground.

But I was here.

I felt pain, but the same pain I'd known the whole ride here: there in my ribs, and in my eye.

Here now was Mom, the duct tape pulled down from her mouth. Mom, pushing at me, touching my shoulders, my chin, my forehead. "Huger!" she cried, her face crumpled up.

And standing there behind her, still with his arm out and holding his gun back toward the boat, was Jessup.

Then here were lights down on us, a blast of them from all around us, a flood of them from what seemed inside the trees and beside the house. Lights, and lights, as though midday'd burst down upon us, as though I were suddenly inside a different dream than the one I'd been in only a moment before, the one in which I'd been shot through and still felt only the pain of a fist to the eye, boots to my stomach.

Mom's face was lit up now, and she squinted for it, and I saw her glance up and away from me, toward where Jessup was pointed.

"That's it, Commander," Jessup said loud, and stepped away from us.

Mom peeled down the tape at my mouth, and I breathed in as far as I could, breathed in relief beyond relief, though my ribs wouldn't allow much in at all.

And now I heard sounds: movement in the trees and bushes around us, just beyond the light smashing down on us, and I rolled over, sat up with all the strength I had left in me, and saw.

Unc was on his knees ten yards away in the grass, breathing hard. Beside him, on his back, lay Coburn.

Jessup'd shot him. Jessup.

He'd saved me, shot Coburn just as he was about to shoot me.

To the left and a few feet from Coburn stood Five. He was trembling, his hands still behind his back, mouth still taped over. He was looking down at Coburn, his eyebrows sharp together, in his eyes the wild look of fear.

And past them, his back to us and maybe ten yards out from

the end of that cordgrass path, stood Jessup, his gun still out and pointed.

At Prendergast, who stood in the bow of the boat, lit just as clear as the rest of Dupont's backyard, with Tabitha's head in a choke hold, his gun at her temple.

"No!" I shouted, and rolled to my knees, tried to stand.

Mom, kneeling beside me, pressed down on my shoulders, held me in place, and Jessup called out, "Please put your weapon down, sir." He took another step toward them, called out, "We're all here. You're zeroed in, sir. It's over. Sir."

Even from here, twenty yards away, I could see the charged look in Prendergast's eyes, his mouth open, the gun tight to Tabitha's head. And I could see Tabitha's eyes too, squinted down near to shut, her forehead furrowed sharp, the quick shiver of breaths in and out of her.

I tried to stand. I tried.

But it was Mom who stood, right here beside me, and I watched her walk away from me, and toward Jessup.

Her back was to me, and she moved past Five, still trembling, then past Coburn's body without a moment's pause. She didn't even look at Unc still on his knees as she walked down the lawn, and now she was almost to Jessup, still with his gun out and pointed at Prendergast and Tabitha.

And now I saw her reach behind her and up into the bottom of the white blouse she had on, saw her hand work a second, and pull from there her gun.

A Beretta subcompact.

"Say it," she said loud. "Say what you did," she said, and moved past Jessup a few feet, then stopped.

She squared up to the boat, the gun in both hands: perfect form.

"You got to be kidding me," Prendergast said, and shot out a laugh. "You got to be fucking kidding me," and he cinched down tighter in just that moment on Tabitha, whose eyes closed altogether. Prendergast shook his head hard once, blinked, tried at a smile. "Is this a joke?"

"Mrs. Dillard, you need to—" Jessup started, but then a voice cut in from somewhere in the trees to my left, heavy and dark and no one I'd ever heard before: "Put down your weapon, Commander."

Prendergast looked up quick, squinted at the light as though he could see through it to whoever this was.

"There's others I know of," Prendergast said loud. "There's others out there. Other cells." He paused, swallowed, scanned the trees. "You make me some guarantees and we can talk."

"Say it!" Mom nearly shouted now, the gun out and right on him. "You tell them all who you are! You tell them!"

"What in the fuck?" Prendergast said, and looked down at Mom, shook his head once more, like he couldn't believe she was really there. Like this wasn't a piece of what was happening right here, this moment.

Like what he'd done so very long ago could ever matter to anyone involved. Least of all him.

He yanked Tabitha up off her feet a moment, nestled his head right down next to hers. His eyebrows were together, mouth open in disbelief at this woman, there with a gun.

"What do you want?" he said. "You want me to kill this bitch over what happened forty years ago?" He paused, shook his head again, then looked up, scanned the trees. "You going to dare me to kill a prize Space and Naval Warfare Systems Command recruit," he yelled, then looked back at Mom, "because Gloria Deedham couldn't take someone shitting on her porch and kills herself?"

"Commander," the voice called out, and I heard Jessup, still with his gun out and pointed at Prendergast, say, "Mrs. Dillard."

"*Say it!*" Mom screamed, and it seemed her arms were out even stiffer now.

"Fuck you and your peashooter," he said. "You're a piece of trash and always will be." He leaned toward Mom, his head away from the crook at Tabitha's neck, and for an instant Tabitha leaned away from him, the barrel of his gun no longer at her temple. "So I fucked you when you were passed out in a trailer a hundred years ago. So I—"

"Now," Jessup said, and I saw Prendergast's forehead burst, the shot from somewhere else.

The world was silent a moment. Nothing moved.

Mom stood with the gun out, as did Jessup.

Tabitha still leaned away, her eyes still squinted shut above the band of duct tape at her mouth.

Five still trembled, and Unc, not ten feet from me and still on his knees, took in a breath.

And Prendergast, his eyes open and mouth open too, hung in the air a moment, before him a mist of red mixed with bits of matter like a cold breath out in the frozen depths of hell. In this same instant his arms fell limp from Tabitha, and he collapsed into the hull.

Mom dropped the gun in the next moment, and I saw her look at her arms, the spray of blood on her, and then she screamed, Jessup beside her and holding her, and now here was a sailor kneeling beside me in blue and black and gray digital camo, Kevlar and helmet, an M4 on his shoulder.

Harmon.

He nodded at me, and I saw in his gloved hands what looked like nothing more than pruning shears. He reached behind me, cut off in a second the Zip Cuffs, then snipped the duct tape at the back of my neck.

Then he stood, went to Unc, did the same thing, but helped him peel the tape away from his mouth. He patted Unc's back once, said something to him, then went to Five and did it again.

And now here were more sailors, a swarm of them in from the dark beyond the trees and into this light they'd brought in themselves, lights off the back of four or five MRAPs backed up on either side of the house and hidden behind bushes and trees, all these sailors in BDUs and helmets and Kevlar and carrying M4s, and I watched while Unc finally stood, and while Five turned from Coburn's body, around it now a cordon of sailors, and dropped to his knees, touched his face to the grass. Still he wept.

"Huger?" Unc called. He'd lost his Braves cap in all this, a suspender down off one shoulder. Somewhere, too, was his walking stick, but not anywhere here.

Beyond him, down at the boat, I could see sailors standing with Mom, a blanket already across her shoulders. And sailors were up in the boat, helping Tabitha out of it now, the tape away from her mouth and cuffs off, and sobbing as she stepped down off the hull, sailors helping her the whole way.

And I saw come out of the trees, there to my right down at the waterline of the yard, yet one more sailor, and saw at the same moment he emerged Jessup peel away from the sailors surrounding Mom and Tabitha, start toward him.

The sailor had a rifle, different than the others. A sniper rifle: long barrel, thick scope.

The two met, nodded at each other, and the sailor reached up, slipped off his helmet.

Master-at-*Ahms* Stanhope.

I closed my eye, and saw a woman named Ellen smiling at him, her murdered for such a dishonorable act.

"Right here," I finally answered Unc, "I'm right here," though the words didn't sound like me. They sounded like someone older, like someone sick and frail had said them.

I could open my eyes later, I knew. I could see things then.

But for now I kept the one that worked closed, and I tried to breathe, and tried. Unc stood next to me now, I could feel, and said, "You all right?"

Though I couldn't see him, I knew his hand was out and looking for me. He didn't know I was sitting, and I reached out in my own blindness to find his hand, squeezed it hard as I could. "I'm fine," I said: that same pitiable voice.

Then Unc was on the ground beside me, and put an arm to my shoulder.

"We made it," he said.

I thought to answer him, if there were any answer to give. I thought to try and put one word with another one, to speak them, to expend the air those words would end up needing. But the work seemed too much at this particular moment, and suddenly two other people—they were medics, identified themselves as such—were here with me, and now they were easing me to my back, talking to me, asking questions, and all of it seemed just fine with me.

Because we made it.

Epilogue

We finish dinner a little early, before us the picked-over carcass of a roasted chicken and remains of a bag salad Mom picked up at the Super Bi-Lo over on North Rhett.

A Thursday evening, Unc and Mom and me at the glass table off the kitchen, out the window a summer marsh, too many greens to name.

A Thursday evening. But we're not headed for any poker game.

Warchester Four's still fighting the raid on his house, and hasn't reconvened anything yet. We see him in the paper and on the news now and again, ranting about the archaic laws of South Carolina, the provincial state of mind we have going on here, the cracker mentality that just keeps holding back this state.

But there's still no poker. And far as we can tell he still doesn't know it was Unc to call it in.

Mom leans forward, pinches up a piece of white meat from down near the wishbone, pops it in her mouth.

"You sure you're ready?" she says to me, and smiles. "The doctor says it's up to you, but that doesn't mean you should."

"Leave the boy alone, Eugenie," Unc says, and now he reaches to the chicken too, peels off a last bit of dark meat down where the thigh's been pulled off. "He's fine. He needs this."

He sets the piece of chicken, no bigger than a postage stamp, on his plate, then reaches for the salt where we always keep it, there at the empty fourth spot at the table, and tips the shaker, sprinkles what he deems is enough.

But he's missed the chicken entirely, sprinkled instead the empty space where his salad had been.

He picks up the piece, puts it in his mouth, chews it. "Perfect," he says, and Mom and I just look at each other, shake our heads yet one more time.

Then: "You buy the airplane tickets to the blind duffers' golf tournament out to Palm Springs today, like I asked you to do?"

And me: "Not yet. Because we're not going until you try to golf in daylight."

And Unc, like always: "One day."

Three months gone already. I had four broken ribs, and a fractured eye socket. The best treatment for which was to just lay low. Just stay home. Just do nothing.

That had sounded all right, until three or so weeks in, and I wanted nothing more than to be out to Hungry Neck on a boat, or driving an ATV out there, or even just taking a long walk somewhere, anywhere.

Tabitha's come by a couple times. She had to take a leave of absence from her postdoc in order to try and sort out everything that went down. It wasn't like she could just jump on a plane and fly home to Frisco, start Aggregating Encryptions and Probabilistically Functioning.

At least that's what she told me when I asked her the second month why she was still here in town.

Actually, it's been more than a few times she's been over. And one night two weeks ago, the night before she headed back, we went out together. I took her to Cypress in downtown Charleston. A very nice place. And now things seem closer to possible between us. Or at least the possibility for possibility seems possible.

Because things changed after that night. After all of what happened.

Five went back to Charlotte and that job he has not but a couple days after what happened, for one thing. It's like he was running away, tucked his tail and took off. Which no one can blame, because we all deal with what we're dealt in our own way. He hasn't posted on Facebook once since then, either. And Tabitha turned her status back to single.

Jessup is gone. And somewhere are Tammy and Nina. Maybe in the brig itself.

And though we were debriefed in the days that followed, though we were brought over to the Weapons Station offices across Goose Creek and sat in windowless rooms being asked question and question and question from people in suits who identified themselves as being representatives of, in turn, Space and Naval Warfare Systems Command, the United States Naval Consolidated Brig, the Naval Weapons Station, Homeland Security itself, and, finally, Federal Protective Service; after all those questions and all those hours and all those suits, the only thing we received was a verbal thanks—and a warning not to tell—from a man with two stars on his shoulder. Not even someone in the Navy, but someone in the Army.

But I had a question myself, for the man in the suit across the table from me who'd told me he was from the Federal Protective Service: "Will you tell Jessup I said thank you?"

He only smiled, one side of his mouth going up, and let his eyes meet mine a moment. "I'll see what I can do," he said, and nodded.

The news reported it all as a domestic disturbance that erupted at Judge Dupont's house when Coburn Graham, a boyfriend of the judge's in-home caregiver, Nina Sanchez, motored in on the judge's stolen boat to the property at Landgrave Hall, only to find her there with another boyfriend, Commander Jamison Prendergast. They killed each other. She fled the state when it was discovered that Judge Dupont had in fact passed away seven months before.

These are the ways that things have changed for us all: we know something.

But the most important thing that's different is that there's something I want to do now. There's a path I think I can see. A way I think I want to go. From here.

And now that Tabitha's back at Palo Alto, she's not even sure she wants to be out at SPAWAR because of what happened, the profile of events too high. She's got her eye on NSA now, she says. Maybe that's where she ought to land, she says, though I've told her it can get cold in D.C. in the winter.

These are some of the changes. There are others. But this most important one begins tonight. The thing the doctor says I'm ready to do.

Once we've cleaned up the kitchen, me washing, Unc drying, we step out onto the deck. Mom is upstairs, touching up, I know, though I've told her I don't want this to be something she thinks she has to primp for.

And as soon as we're out the door onto the deck, there it is, like always, like every time I ever come out here. Right in the center of our own wrought-iron table: the planter, bright blue. A sprig of rosemary growing out of it.

I haven't told anyone of what I dreamt just before everything happened. I haven't told anyone about that whole thing with seeing a path, with me being a kid and knowing what I had to do. No one.

Not even Tabitha.

Because I wouldn't know what to say about it. Only that it gave me what I needed, though what I needed I cannot name.

I saw what I had to do. This time I saved no lives. I killed no one. But it was that moment, when all else fell away except what that path before me called me to do—to follow it—that has made all the difference.

Here I am. Starting.

I think of Jessup a lot. I think of what he might be doing right now—think of him serving somewhere for counterintelligence. What he'd done right here among us. I think of him working to save lives somewhere else, or maybe still right here, though he hasn't been here since that night. But I think of him serving the country somewhere right now, somewhere.

I think of him raised within a secret, and him seeing enough of the evil in that secret to shut it down.

And I think too of a quiet kid I knew, riding in a hot bus on field trip day. I think of a kid I knew who threw right along with us all rocks as high as he could toward the Mark Clark, hoping to land something up there.

I think of that empty desk in homeroom that first day after, when the whole world changed.

I miss him.

Mom steps out the door behind us onto the deck. The sun is down, the sky a pale violet stretching back into a slate blue in the east. But before we start down the dock toward the creek, that silver arc of water, I lean to this hideous planter, smell the rosemary in it, and say, "Mom, did I ever tell you this is the best blueberry planter I ever made?"

Because what I'd intended no longer matters.

"No," she says, and gives a small laugh.

"Here he comes," Unc says, and starts out onto the dock, his stick—it was in the poker room at the Whaleys', left there when Harmon and Stanhope hauled him and Prendergast away—tapping before him.

And the goggles never even made it into the Range Rover that night. They're out in the garage right now, hidden in the piles of military and security gadgets Unc has out there, Unc having put them there while I'd slept that day. He'd only wanted Prendergast to think he'd brought the goggles in to poker night, knowing full well the cops were on their way to arrest them all. No need to give Prendergast what he demanded if he was going to get busted.

Or at least that had been Unc's plan. What he'd intended, but not where the path led him.

I turn from the table, and this planter, and from Mom across the table from me, to see the boat Unc'd heard and headed out for. It's a Boston Whaler, curving in on the arc Goose Creek makes to Landgrave Hall right here. A Boston Whaler, trolling in low, standing at the wheel—I can make him out now—Major Alton Tyler.

I look at Mom, see her smiling out to the water, her eyes on the boat, and I reach to her arm, loop it in mine, and we walk down the dock, Unc already almost there to the end.

"You got you a bottle of Cutter?" Mom asks. "Because you're going to get eaten alive out there."

"Already in my book bag, sitting out there on the storage locker."

We take a few more steps, Major Tyler's boat almost here, and now he cuts the engine altogether, steps from the console, and throws the bow line out to Unc, waiting.

The rope lands precisely in his outstretched hand, and Unc kneels, cleats it off, and now Tyler is out of the boat and on the dock himself, cleats off the stern line. Unc stands, holds out a hand, and Tyler, there in his olive green ball cap and DNR uniform, the gold badge above his right shirt pocket visible even from here, grabs hold Unc's hand hard, and shakes it, slaps Unc on the back.

But now Mom stops, and I have no choice but to turn to her, because her arm is looped in mine, and I look at her, see her eyebrows together, her mouth a thin line.

"Is this what you want to do? Be an agent with DNR?"

I swallow, look past her to the marsh, the myriad greens out there dimming down with the evening light. Then I look at her again.

Tyler and I have been setting this up the last six weeks or so. I've signed the papers for me to ride along. We've talked about everything from salaries to shrimp balls, from baited dove fields to drug busts. From water rescues to water recoveries.

We've talked.

I look down at the planks of the dock, give a quick nod, then look back at her.

"It's what I want to do," I say. "Yes."

"You know you'll have to finish college. You know you have to go back and do that, right?"

"Yes, ma'am," I say. "I do."

She looks at me again, holds my eyes on hers a long moment. Then she nods, and turns, starts the last few feet we have to the boat.

"Here he is," Unc says, maybe too loud, and sidesteps a little toward me, his hand finding my shoulder. He pats it, says, "Taught this young man everything he knows."

"We can cook that out," Tyler says, and smiles. He takes off his hat—that forehead tan line again—and says, "Eugenie, we'll be taking good care of this boy tonight. Heading out to Clouter Creek to start with, follow up on a report about somebody stealing crab pots."

Mom smiles, nods. "Put him through the wringer," she says, then Unc says, "Give him hell. Only way to teach him."

Tyler puts his cap back on, and it's then he puts out his hand, and I shake it.

"Let's go," he says.

And we're gone.

Acknowledgments

This book could not have been written without the help of Gregg Anderson, Kevin Kalman, Brian Stanton, Jeff Deal, and Zebulun Holmes Lott, whom I thank especially for his advice, insight, and service to our country.

About the Author

BRET LOTT is the bestselling author of twelve books, most recently the novel *Ancient Highway*. He has been a Fulbright Senior American Scholar and writer-in-residence at Bar-Ilan University in Tel Aviv, has spoken on Flannery O'Connor at the White House, and is a member of the National Council on the Arts. He teaches at the College of Charleston, and lives with his wife, Melanie, in Hanahan, South Carolina.

About the Type

This book was set in Minion, a 1990 Adobe Originals typeface by Robert Slimbach. Minion is inspired by classical, old style typefaces of the late Renaissance, a period of elegant, beautiful, and highly readable type designs. Created primarily for text setting, Minion combines the aesthetic and functional qualities that make text type highly readable with the versatility of digital technology.